MRS. PEABODY'S PARTY LINE

Previously published Worldwide Mystery titles by
MARIANNA HEUSLER

MURDER AT ST. POLYCARP
CAPPUCCINO AT THE CRYPT
NO END TO TROUBLE
TROUBLE PURSE SUED

MRS. PEABODY'S PARTY LINE

MARIANNA HEUSLER

W❂RLDWIDE

TORONTO • NEW YORK • LONDON
AMSTERDAM • PARIS • SYDNEY • HAMBURG
STOCKHOLM • ATHENS • TOKYO • MILAN
MADRID • WARSAW • BUDAPEST • AUCKLAND

If you purchased this book without a cover you should be aware that this book is stolen property. It was reported as "unsold and destroyed" to the publisher, and neither the author nor the publisher has received any payment for this "stripped book."

WORLDWIDE™

ISBN-13: 978-1-335-40545-6

Mrs. Peabody's Party Line

First published in 2019 by Hilliard & Harris.
This edition published in 2021.

Copyright © 2019 by Marianna Heusler

Recycling programs for this product may not exist in your area.

All rights reserved. No part of this book may be reproduced or transmitted in any form or by any means, electronic or mechanical, including photocopying, recording or by any information storage and retrieval system, without permission in writing from the publisher.

This is a work of fiction. Names, characters, places and incidents are either the product of the author's imagination or are used fictitiously. Any resemblance to actual persons, living or dead, businesses, companies, events or locales is entirely coincidental.

This edition published by arrangement with Harlequin Books S.A.

For questions and comments about the quality of this book, please contact us at CustomerService@Harlequin.com

Harlequin Enterprises ULC
22 Adelaide St. West, 40th Floor
Toronto, Ontario M5H 4E3, Canada
www.ReaderService.com

Printed in U.S.A.

Dedicated to my dear cousin, Marilyn Grace Monahan,
my first reader, with much love.

ONE

IN THE LITTLE town of Honeyspoon, overlooking the Taconic Mountains, sits a one hundred year old nunnery.

At seven thirty-seven—after the five-fifteen bell rings, after Mass and Holy Communion in the chapel, after breakfast of either oatmeal and fruit, toast and eggs, waffles and bacon—all eleven sisters cram into their mini bus and are driven into the town of Honeyspoon to teach at *St. Hedwig's School*.

The school is located on Tulip Street, flanked by *Betsy's Bakery* on one side—known to have the best Pineapple Crunch and Butter Cream Cake in the state—and *Danny's Diner* on the other—no one can refuse their crispy French fries.

Honeyspoon Library is across the street, not too far from *Honeyspoon City Hall* and the *Honeyspoon Police Station*. Young children flock to *Casey's Candy Store* after school and beg their mothers for penny candy—*Red Hots*, *Boston Baked Beans*, jelly candies, jawbreakers, *Necco Wafers*, *Mallo Cups*, candy cigarettes, *Bubble Gum Cigars* and *Fireballs*.

And then there is *Nick's Nest*, where the hot dogs are steamed in butter, the root beers ice cold, the baked beans piping hot and the corn is freshly popped.

The teenagers hang out at the corner drug store, *Philpots*, jockeying for a stool to drink egg creams, malted milk shakes, cherry lime rickeys, vanilla cokes as Elvis Presley and Jerry Lee Lewis blast from the juke box.

The streets are dotted with small five and dime stores, like *Neisers*, where breaking a balloon might mean you can get a hot fudge sundae for a penny, where hurried office workers enjoy a cup of coffee and a tuna down, or a BLT, hold the mayo. There are two hat stores in town, so ladies can purchase a pillbox or a veiled Juliette Cap, displaying them at Sunday Mass.

In the very center of town the old *Finster Mansion* stands like a sentinel. Mr. Finster owned the largest paper mill in town and had built a twenty-seven room house for himself, his wife, and their seven cats. But Mr. Finster had long ago died and the mansion is now an art gallery, a music hall, a town museum and a lecture platform for would-be politicians. Unfortunately, the mansion has fallen into disrepair, the structure built on wet lands is coming undone. Last year two bricks fell off and hit Mr. Portela in the head as he was raking leaves. For two weeks Mr. Portela did not recognize his wife—for which Mrs. Portela was grateful—and, when he got his memory back, he stopped caring for the mansion and became a short order cook for Neisers.

About a mile from the center of town the *Morning Glory Projects* had been built in the late 40s. Peppered with young couples and a few elderly women, the neighborhood is ripe with gossip, especially for the people who share a party line.

For the most part though, Honeyspoon is a quiet town, where nothing much happens.

Of course, there are the usual worries, the cold war is waging and children practice crouching under their desks, their heads buried in their arms, as they prepare for missiles from the Russians to come raining down.

Men argue about Joe McCarthy and women talk animatedly about the latest drama on *The Guiding Light* and *Search for Tomorrow* while everyone is busy searching for flying saucers.

Yet within the borders of the small town of Honeyspoon in 1957, it's always seventy and sunny, at least in the minds of most of its residents.

But all of that peace and quiet came to an abrupt and bloody end in late October.

TWO

Mrs. Nancy Peabody lived at 15 Lily Lane in the Morning Glory Projects. She had lived there the moment the buildings had gone up, which was on May 4th, 1947. That meant for ten years, Mrs. Peabody more or less ruled the neighborhood.

Or so she thought.

She liked living in the project, where there was always a lot going on. The homes were occupied with young couples, with various degrees of troubles—and Mrs. Peabody was a woman who loved trouble.

Mrs. Peabody knew all the neighbors, Connie and Bill Maloney resided at 9 Lily Lane with three bratty boys, Andrew, Adam and Arthur. Bill worked in a funeral parlor and made caskets for dead people. Occasionally, he gambled and Mrs. Peabody had listened to some very scary phone calls.

Joanne Kennedy's husband had taken off with a woman, a telephone operator named Helen. Bruce had met her through his job—selling sweet rolls and pies and cakes, out of his station wagon. In spite of the fact that Helen had a bald strip on the very top of her scalp—the hazards of wearing heavy ear phones day after day—Bruce had fallen madly in love with Helen. Now Joanne had to go back to work, as a secretary at the *Finster Mansion* and the two love birds had headed somewhere far away to avoid the scandal.

Next door to Joanne was Kate Tringali. Kate worked at *Honeyspoon Public Library*. She had grown up in Honeyspoon but, after attending high school, she packed her bags and she left to go to New York. She once told Mrs. Peabody that she envisioned herself living in a high rise building with a terrace overlooking the city, eating food from the automat, hoping to meet a man, who would give her a glamorous and posh life. She lasted two years, when she suddenly returned. Evidently something terrible had happened to her in that crime ridden city and Mrs. Peabody would like to know what it was. Mrs. Peabody had heard that it was Kate's dream that someday she was going to return to New York.

Mrs. Peabody didn't think that Kate was going to do that anytime in the near future.

Kate didn't get along with the Maloneys. She had called Bill on several occasions, complaining about Andrew's behavior in the library. Andrew wanted to take home publications that were not allowed to be checked out. But Bill had defended his son, claiming that as a tax payer, everything in the library belonged to him.

Next door to Kate were Rita and Lawrence Eastman, who had one son, Terrence. Lawrence worked down at the paper factory. Rita Eastman had been picked up several times at *Steigers Department Store* for shoplifting. The police said that if it happened one more time, they were going to put her in jail. Rita cried and asked who would take care of her son, because she doubted that Lawrence could do it all by himself. So Wayne Grenier, the chief of police, told her if she was truly concerned about her son, she should stay out of the stores. Mrs. Peabody didn't think that was possible. She had read up on shoplifters and it was some sort of disease. After all, Rita hadn't stolen a pint of milk, or a loaf of bread, but a powder compact, a pair of nylon stockings, and a gaudy pair of orange clip on earrings.

And from where did Mrs. Peabody get her information about the various degrees of trouble? She shared a party line, which simply meant that three tenants were on the same telephone wire, enabling her to listen to her neighbors' conversations. Of course, you were not supposed to do such a thing. When the phone rang one ring, it was for the Maloneys, two rings for Kate and three rings meant that the call was for Mrs. Peabody. But no one ever called Mrs. Peabody, so she often raced to the other calls.

Yes, Mrs. Peabody loved trouble and she was about to have plenty of her own.

THREE

Sister Regina Rachel had a hard time getting out of bed, on a rainy Monday. She had drifted into an uneasy sleep at two in the morning and the bell peeled at five-fifteen, giving her a mere ten minutes to dress in her habit and go down to chapel. It was the middle of October, but Indian summer was just a dream. The convent was cold and damp, and although she didn't have a window in her small cell, she could hear the rain pounding on the other side of the wall.

Monday was the worst day of the week. She went straight through, religion, math, English grammar, history, lunch duty, recess duty, geography and penmanship. After school, there was detention duty, which usually consisted of her fifth grade boys. And today because of the rain, recess would be inside. What a ruckus!

The bell rang again, five minutes until prayer time. After a half an hour of Mass and a quick breakfast of oatmeal and toast, her day would begin.

A day not unlike a day twenty-five years ago.

A day not unlike a day, which would happen twenty years from now.

Students grew up. They went on to high school— usually Sacred Heart—then the brighter ones would go on to college, eventually they would get married and have children and sometimes you would read about them in the *Honeyspoon Herald*.

And sometimes you would teach their children when they reached fifth grade.

Students moved on. While Sister Regina Rachel was stuck—almost frozen in time. Her body concealed by a black habit, she probably didn't look very different as the years whizzed by. Not on the outside.

Only on the inside.

She hurried out of her room, down the convent steps and prepared for the hellish day ahead.

FOUR

KATE TRINGALI REACHED inside her handbag and fished until she found her keys to the *Honeyspoon Public Library*. The door was locked and bolted, telling Kate that she was the first to arrive.

No doubt Margaret Shelby, the head librarian, would come later. A woman in her sixties, she claimed that she had never been an early riser, and now it was just too hard to wake with the sound of the alarm clock—especially after she had watched the late movie. So it was up to Kate to flip on the lights, go down to the staff room, put on the percolator for coffee, and lay out whatever sweets had been stored in the small ice box.

The key stuck, which wasn't unusual. Kate had been asking Margaret to change the lock for the longest time but Margaret was reluctant to make any changes to the library. For some reason she thought change was always followed by bad luck.

The door creaked open and Kate stepped inside the vestibule—a small hallway with a staircase at each end—one staircase descended up, and one staircase descended down. The staircase that went up would take Kate to the main library. The down staircase led to the staff room and the children's library—which didn't open until three o'clock, at which time Kate would descend and take on duties, which involved scolding rambunctious children.

The moment Kate walked in the door; she knew that something was wrong. For one thing, a strange odor filled the air, not the usual tobacco—Margaret was a chain smoker—or the rich scent of old books bound in leather, the smell of lemon wax and bleach—on Thursdays when Violet Rose, the cleaning woman had been there. No, this was the scent of carnations and something else, something earthy and unpleasant.

It seemed to be stronger towards the children's room.

Kate was tempted to go straight up to the main library, throw the light on, and unpack the drawer, placing the stamp and the cards and the tin money box on the desk, with the Rolodex. She'd go to the back door and grab the morning papers—which Timmy, the paper boy, always carelessly threw on the ground—place them on the newspaper sticks, so they'd be ready for the old folks—and some young mothers who just needed to get out.

Except.

Except she first had to go to the staff room, to deposit her roast beef sandwich, her potato salad, and her *Yoo Hoo* in the ice box. And Margaret would expect the coffee to be percolating and the left over banana bread to be neatly cut into squares and placed on the small card table.

The staff room was right off the children's library.

She could always wait for Margaret, who, after all was said and done, was a formidable woman or at least a very plump one. But when Kate looked at her Timex watch, she realized that it was only a few minutes past nine. Margaret might not be in for another half an hour.

Kate told herself that she was just being silly. Just because the library had a different odor—and it wasn't even a bad smell, well, not really—didn't mean that something sinister had happened.

All those Agatha Christie mysteries were playing with her head. Everyone knew that Honeyspoon was the safest place on earth.

She drew a deep breath and descended down the stairs.

The door to the children's library was closed—funny—Margaret always left it open.

Kate put her hand on the door knob, touching it cautiously as though it might be on fire, opening it inch by inch.

The first thing she saw was the large framed poster of the quote *Make One Person Happy Each Day* on the floor, the frame broken, the glass shattered.

The Honeyspoon Children's Library had been ransacked. The cookie jar shaped like *Little Miss Muffet* lay smashed, sending shards and slivers of glass all over the alphabet rug. The two yellow parakeets, Lucy and Desi, were flying around aimlessly, shrieking as they bumped into the orange walls, their cages overturned, bird seed covering the floor. Books had been removed from the shelves, their spines open, and some of the encyclopedias were crushed. An electric train set had been stomped on and the tracks thrown in the trash. The ants had been let loose from their farm and they scrambled on the floor, disappearing into the walls, carrying some of the bird seed.

But Kate really didn't see any of that.

Instead her eyes rested on a body in the middle of the floor. It was Violet Rose Shaw, the cleaning woman, dressed in her usual purple pedal pushers, her gray hair tied back with a purple ribbon and one purple earring in the shape of a lilac dangling from her ear.

Kate had never seen a dead body before, at least not a body, which hadn't been preened by an undertaker. But it was obvious from the deep marks around Violet's throat, that she had been strangled.

But it was Monday, not even Violet Rose's day—what was she doing here? Had Margaret changed her schedule and someone came to rob the library? Violet Rose was probably in the back room, taking out the cleaning supplies, had interrupted the thief, getting killed for no good reason, except she was in the wrong place at the wrong time.

But what was there to rob in the library? Except for ten dollars in loose change—for those who brought back books late and had been charged a nickel a day—there was no money, no antiques, no jewelry, no nothing. But someone had done this and why?

Kate's first impulse was to run into the street, but first she had to call the police. But not on the phone in the staff room—someone had cut the wires—had Violet Rose tried to call for help and that's what got her killed?

After screaming at the top of her lungs, Kate turned around, took the stairs, two at a time, and raced up to the main library, leaving her lunch behind. She turned on the lights, reached for the telephone, which slipped out of her hand and landed with a soft thud. Kate bent down, her heart racing.

"Hello, who is there? Who is listening?"

Oh my God, the party line thing again, which the library shared with Betsy, the owner of the town's bakery.

"So I'm going to need more flour," Betsy's demanded in that very nasal voice of hers.

"How many more pounds?"

"Well, at least…"

"Excuse me," Kate said.

"Excuse me!" Betsy snapped, "But you can plainly hear that we're talking."

"I know and I'm sorry to interrupt you…"

"This is very important," Betsy insisted. "The Millers are having a big party for their daughter's sixteenth birthday and I'm supplying all of the pastries. I'm in a bit of a hurry…"

"So am I," the man at the other end said. "I got a lot of deliveries."

"The library has been broken into." Kate was aware of her own panicked voice.

"What's in the library that's worth stealing?" Betsy sounded deeply suspicious.

"It's not just a robbery." Kate's heart was hammering so rapidly and she was having trouble breathing. She hoped that she wasn't having a heart attack, like her poor father, dead at 46, ten years from her current age.

"What did they take?" Betsy asked.

"Look, I really need to call the police. It's about murder." The moment she said it, Kate realized that she had made a mistake.

"Murder!" Betsy and the man at the other end yelled simultaneously.

"Who has been murdered?" Betsy shrieked. "Not poor Margaret!"

"No, not Margaret. Please, I'm begging you. Hang up so I can call the police!"

"All right, all right," Betsy finally said. "We will hang up as soon as you tell us who was murdered."

"The cleaning woman, Violet Rose Shaw."

Kate heard two gasps and then, thankfully, a dial tone. She quickly dialed the operator, as she heard another click. Betsy was listening in.

"I need to speak to the police." Kate's voice trembled. "It's an emergency."

"Hold on," Ethel Thompson, the police's secretary, ordered in a bored voice.

And Kate did, as she heard Betsy breathing on the other line.

"Honeyspoon Police. Gary speaking."

Gary, a young cop, was known to be lazy and ineffective. This was one time when it would matter.

"I need someone to come right away." Kate was trying not to sound hysterical.

"Who is this?"

"Kate Tringali. I'm at the Honeyspoon Library. There has been a murder."

"What?!"

"There's a dead body, lying in the middle of the floor of the children's library. It's the poor cleaning woman, Violet Rose Shaw."

"How do you know she was murdered? Maybe she just fell on her head or had a stroke."

"She has red marks around her neck."

"Maybe she's fainted from the measles."

"She's dead! The place has been ransacked. I think it's a robbery gone wrong."

"Where's Margaret Shelby?"

"She hasn't come in yet. Please stop asking me all these questions and just come."

"Don't touch anything. We're coming over right now."

Kate had no intention of touching anything. She put the phone back in its cradle, and sank on the stool.

And she waited.

FIVE

Mrs. Peabody caught the mailman on the way out. Steven Shea was barely a teenager with his side burns and his slick back hair and yet here he was with the very important task of delivering for the post office. Mark Kitchenmaster, the old mailman, had been put on disability, after the McAndrews' German Shepherd bit him on his left hamstring and his right shoulder. But Mr. Kitchenmaster was not nosy, and Mrs. Peabody suspected that Steven was. She didn't like Steven one bit and she frowned as he handed her a catalog from Sears and Roebucks—featuring a girl wearing a horrible bright blue poodle skirt on the cover—and three envelopes, all of them marked in red ink—*Overdue*.

Mrs. Peabody saw Steven smirk and she wanted to slap him right then and there. Instead she grabbed the mail, put it in her tote bag and made her way to the bus stop, where she waited with a bunch of unruly teenagers to catch a ride downtown.

While she sat alone on the bus, she dared to open her mail. One letter was from the electric company. If she didn't pay the $13.82 cents she owed—she was three months behind—they were going to turn off her electricity in five days. In small print there was a notice which said that if she was old—she was—and poor—she was—she could

go down to City Hall and they might give her more time—
after they humiliated her.

One was from the department store *Steigers*. They had lent her credit to buy a black cardigan and a pair of brown hose. She agreed to pay on the first of the month when her social security check came in—two months ago.

The last one was for some vitamins she had ordered a year ago—they promised vitality but since they lied, she felt no guilt. They said that the bill had gone into collection and they were going to sue her. Well, good luck with that.

Mrs. Peabody wasn't sure how her life had gotten so out of hand. Well, maybe she did. It was all her husband Louie's fault. He had gone and died, leaving her with no savings and no life insurance. And not of an awful illness—that she could have forgiven—but really, by his own hand on the roller coaster at *Bear Paw Amusement Park*. He fell off the ride and broke his neck, dying instantly. She got a lawyer and they tried to hold the park responsible, but since several people had seen him standing—clearly against the rules— the judge—young and arrogant—deemed them not responsible. She still owed the lawyer, but he lost the case so, again—she felt no guilt.

She looked inside her pocketbook, thirty dollars for groceries for the next three weeks. Her change purse contained thirty-three cents. And she had to eat. Besides, one more row of *S&H* stamps and she would qualify for a free percolator. The one she had now had a broken light, so she could never tell when her coffee was ready.

Of course, what good would the percolator be with no electricity?

What she was going to do right now was take herself to the library, sit in the nice airy room and read the morning papers—if Mr. Stringer hadn't gotten there first.

THE DOOR TO the main library was ajar but, strangely enough, the door to the adult room was closed. However, it seemed that someone had opened the children's library, which meant that something peculiar was happening. She glanced down at her watch and saw that it was after nine. Kate was usually very reliable, so none of this made sense.

As Mrs. Peabody was trying to decide what to do—should she stand in the vestibule, should she venture downstairs hoping to find the librarian, should she sit in the park and wait?—it was rather nippy fall weather. Slowly she descended down the stairs, feeling as though cold needles were sticking in her ribs.

Then she heard a loud, blood curdling scream. "Don't go in there," Kate screamed at the top of the staircase to the main library. "There's a dead body."

Mrs. Peabody stopped and gazed up at Kate, open mouthed.

"Someone murdered Violet Rose Shaw and ransacked the library."

Mrs. Peabody didn't have to be told twice. She turned around and scurried back up the stairs to the vestibule—the best she could with her arthritis.

"Do you think the murderer is still there?" Kate asked suddenly.

"I doubt it. You certainly made enough noise."

"I can't imagine what the killer was looking for. There's no money and the books are hardly worth stealing. And to think that Violet Rose got killed! I don't understand any of this. It wasn't even her day…she usually comes on Thursday."

Mrs. Peabody hesitated. After all, why should she get involved in a dangerous situation? She wasn't young and she wasn't brave but, in the end, as it often did, her curiosity overrode her caution.

The entrance door sprang open suddenly and Mr. Stringer came in followed by Mrs. Vogt. She was carrying a stack of library books.

"Don't worry," Mrs. Peabody said. "I'll take care of them."

Kate stood still, as Mrs. Peabody said, "I'm sorry but the library is closed today."

"Is someone sick?" Mr. Stringer asked.

"Has something happened? Was there a flood?" Mrs. Vogt guessed, slightly taken back.

"Trouble with the roof?" Mr. Stringer looked up at the ceiling.

"I'm afraid I can't give out that information." Mrs. Peabody looked up at Kate, whose face was blank as she turned around and re-entered the main room.

"Who are you to have information?" Mr. Stringer said as he cast a suspicious look her way. He pushed his way up the stairs. "Just because you were here first, just because you wanted to beat me to the morning papers…"

Mrs. Vogt followed him and dropped her library books on the counter, two Agatha Christie novels, one copy of *My Cousin Rachel* and one book promising how changing your attitude could make you a millionaire. Mrs. Vogt was a woman in her sixties and had recently retired from housekeeping at *St. Hedwig's* rectory. Mrs. Peabody doubted that at Mrs. Vogt's age she could change her attitude, much less become a millionaire. But then again, Mrs. Peabody supposed, anything was possible.

"I hope you don't expect me to pay for overdue charges because...let it go into the record that I'm bringing my books back today, when they're due. It's hardly my fault if the library is closed."

She stomped out as the sirens blared.

Mr. Stringer had no intention of moving.

WAYNE GRENIER—the chief of police—and Gary Bennis—his assistant—marched into the library. Mrs. Peabody followed them downstairs, Kate and Mr. Stringer trailing behind.

Mrs. Peabody tried hard not to look at Violet Rose, who was lying still and pale on the library floor, her neck swollen and scarlet, her blue eyes open wide and a shocked expression on her white face.

Everyone glanced around without saying a word, although Mr. Stringer did gasp.

"Kate was right. This looks like a robbery gone bad," Wayne concluded. He turned towards Kate. "Do you know what the thief was after?"

"No, I don't. Obviously I haven't had a chance to take inventory."

Gary looked at Mrs. Peabody and asked what she was doing there.

"I came into the library and Kate started screaming. I thought it best to stay until you arrived." She half expected Gary to say that she could go, but he didn't.

Instead he asked, "So this was exactly how you found her?"

Kate nodded glumly.

"Kate, do you have any idea of who might be responsible?" Wayne took out a little pad and a broken pencil. "Someone hanging around the children's library?"

"No, I can't imagine."

"You have anything here worth stealing?" Gary asked the obvious question.

"I don't think so."

"Could something have been hidden in one of the books?"

"I guess it's possible, but these are children's books. They are not big or heavy."

"I don't understand..." She picked up a copy of Grimm's Fairy Tales.

"Don't!" Gary yelled and Kate dropped it with a loud bang— it landed on top of the broken ant farm. "Not until the crime lab is finished."

The crime lab consisted of one person, Marvin Kaufman, who taught chemistry over at *Honeyspoon High School*. Sometimes the police had to wait for hours until he arrived because they couldn't find a substitute for his class.

"Where is Margaret?" Wayne asked, as though the thought had just occurred to him.

"She should be here any minute. I doubt if she knows anything."

"Well, of course, we'll have to question her," Gary said.

"Bad business," Wayne shook his head as he stood over Violet's body. "We haven't had a murder here since 1951. And that was a domestic situation."

Kate leaned against the wall when Bruce Johnson entered. The crime photographer—he was usually busy shooting weddings, birthdays, and first communions.

"This is very puzzling," Kate said, "because Violet Rose should not have been here. It wasn't her day to clean. She's usually at the *Finster Mansion* on Mondays and she comes to us on Thursday."

"Well, that explains some of it," Wayne said. "The thief didn't expect the cleaning lady and she surprised him. And he killed her. You have no idea what he took, Kate?"

"None. I need to get something to eat," Kate said suddenly. "I feel sick. Is it all right if we go over to *Danny's Diner*? I mean, I'm not a suspect, am I?"

Wayne shook his head.

"We'll let you know if we need you," Gary said and he directed his gaze towards Kate.

Mrs. Peabody couldn't help but smile when Kate said *we*. That meant Kate was inviting her to go along. Mrs. Peabody could only hope that Kate would be picking up the check.

"I CAN'T BELIEVE that this is happening," Kate said in a low, worried tone as she sat down in the booth at *Danny's Diner*. "I've been a librarian for fifteen years and something like this, well, it's unheard of. I get the willies just thinking about it. It will be hard for me to go to the children's library again. The staff room is right down there near the hall, so I was on my way to prepare the coffee but what if...what if...the murderer didn't find what he was looking for and what if...what if...he comes back? I suppose I will have to call Margaret, although the police will probably reach her first.

Why, we could both be in danger. I can't believe that this is happening," she repeated.

"Why don't you take a deep breath," Mrs. Peabody suggested because that's what people always advised when others were upset—although it had never really helped her. "And order a nice cup of tea with maybe a blueberry muffin and some homemade marmalade?" Which was what Mrs. Peabody had in mind.

"So what will you have?" Danny came over and slapped two menus down. "I heard what happened at the library. What is this town coming to? Murdering a poor cleaning lady. I know Violet Rose. My wife plays bingo with her every Friday night. Such a nice person. Just her bad luck, I suppose. Being at the wrong place at the wrong time. Of course, it's scary. A murderer on the loose. Those darn Communists!"

Mrs. Peabody thought that from here on there was going to be a lot of theories. And she just hoped that one of them didn't involve her. It was a well-known fact that she and Violet Rose did not get along. Mrs. Peabody didn't want to say it—because it was bad luck to speak ill of the dead—and she didn't even want to think it but Violet Rose happened to be a very pushy person—although now that she was dead, killed in cold blood, everyone was going to speak about her in glowing terms. But the truth was that she wasn't a nice person at all. Several times she had cut in front of Mrs. Peabody at the deli counter and once when Mrs. Peabody asked her to move over in the pew at Sunday Mass at *St. Hedwig's*, Violet Rose claimed that there was no room and Mrs. Peabody should go to the back of the church and stand, knowing that Mrs. Peabody had arthritis, making standing in place very painful. And at bingo on Friday night she once sneezed on Mrs. Peabody's board, when she just needed one more number to win. And then Violet Rose won the steam iron.

"The police are investigating," Kate said quickly. "I'll have two eggs over easy, buttered white toast, French fries crisp, bacon well done and a cup of coffee with cream on the side."

Danny looked at Mrs. Peabody, who quickly decided it had been a long time since she had a substantial breakfast and it probably would be a long time before she had the chance again. "I'll have the same thing."

"Yep." Danny said, "Like I said, I don't know what is happening in this poor town. First that kid, what was his name?" He looked at both women, but neither one responded because Mrs. Peabody had no idea what he was talking about, and apparently neither did Kate. "You know the one, Chester, somebody or other, who jumped out the window of the top floor of the *Finster Mansion*, for no reason at all."

"Suicide," Kate said.

"Yeah, that was the verdict," Danny scooped up the menus, "but no one ever commits suicide, here in Honeyspoon. I mean a young man, like that, what's he got to be sad about?"

"Drugs?" Mrs. Peabody guessed and then she saw something that made her stomach sink ever so slightly.

The door of the diner opened and Joanne Kennedy walked in, bumping into Danny, without apologizing. Mrs. Peabody knew that Kate and Joanne were best friends—she had listened to their phone conversations on more than one occasion—and she knew that the quiet breakfast was about to be interrupted. Besides, she never liked Joanne, mostly because she thought

Joanne didn't like her. In fact Mrs. Peabody once overheard Joanne refer to her on the phone as a "busybody" which, of course, she very much might be, although Mrs. Peabody liked to think of herself as someone who had an innate curiosity about people, which wasn't a bad thing at all.

"Oh my God!" Joanne flew down to the booth, her swing coat, hitting Mrs. Peabody in the face. Joanne gave a little gasp of surprise and then covered her red painted mouth with her fingertips. "Oh my God! I just heard what happened at the library. And this is all my fault."

"How do you mean?" Kate asked.

"We have a big meeting at the *Finster Mansion* on Friday and, of course, I wanted it to be clean. So I asked Violet Rose if she would switch and come on Thursday and do the library on Monday. I told her to ask you but Violet Rose said you wouldn't mind." Joanne hesitated. "Would you have minded?"

Kate shook her head. "No, of course, I wouldn't have minded then. But now it's different. Because if she hadn't..." Kate let her voice trail off.

Joanne went on, without once looking at Mrs. Peabody. "If I hadn't asked Violet Rose to change, Violet Rose wouldn't have been at the library and Violet Rose wouldn't have gotten murdered. How?"

"How what?" Mrs. Peabody asked.

Joanne then looked at her, like a queen would look at a cockroach. Then she turned to Kate. "How did the poor woman die?"

"I think she was strangled. The police are still at the library, looking for clues."

"Someone was obviously there to steal something. But what?"

Kate shrugged. "No one knows."

Joanne shivered. "This is bad, really bad. Are you all right?" She patted Kate gingerly on the arm.

"It's okay. I'm doing fine." Kate turned towards Mrs. Peabody. "Mrs. Peabody was helpful."

"Oh really," Joanne said in a disinterested voice. "Well, I'm here now." Joanne sank down, her garnish green coat sprayed under her as she pushed Mrs. Peabody to the side. "Do you think it's possible that something was hidden in one of the books, a code perhaps, or even a great deal of money, and the killer went back to claim it and Violet Rose saw him?"

"You've been watching those British murder mysteries again at the Victory Theater," Kate said as Danny dropped two cups and a pot of coffee in front of them.

"Oh well. At least it wasn't you." Joanne patted down her bouffant hair do, which was stiff and dry from hair spray. "Here's the thing," Joanne said in a muffled voice as she leaned forward and began to whisper, as though she didn't want Mrs. Peabody to hear what she had to say. But her motion didn't deter Mrs. Peabody in the least. She just craned her neck forward also. "If the killer did not find what he wanted, he's bound to be back. After all, he's already murdered once for it. He's liable to do it again! I would not be alone in that library. I would demand police protection."

"From one of the two policemen in town?" Mrs. Peabody put two sugars in her coffee.

Joanne threw her a dirty look. "Kate, I want to talk to you about something else," Joanne said, "but it's rather private." She eyed Mrs. Peabody, as though she expected her to move, but Mrs. Peabody had no intention of doing that, at least not until she had finished eating her breakfast—which she was very much looking forward to. "Well, I guess I could call you tonight."

That was fine with Mrs. Peabody. She could listen in on that conversation as easily as she could listen in the booth.

"Anyway, I want to tell you what's been happening at work. That stupid mayor, honestly, I don't know how he got elected, everyone suspects him of taking bribes from the contractors, who are going to build the playground. He lives way above his means. That's why he wants to tear down the mansion. Danny," she called, "could I have an English muffin dry, not burnt please, a piece of cantaloupe and some hot water with lemon. The committee is going to have to vote, of course, the three of you. The mayor will vote in favor of tearing the mansion down. I know you'll do the right thing and keep the mansion open. After, all it's my job and I put so much effort into the renovation of the attic, turning it into a writing room. You really should come and look at it sometime. So it's going to come down to Rita Eastman. I have no idea how she will vote." Joanne continued to talk about the mayor and the committee—which was so boring.

But that was all right. Because Kate picked up the tab.

SIX

SISTER REGINA RACHEL was in the middle of teaching the objective case when she heard the sirens. She put the chalk down and made the sign of the cross and thirty-one fifth graders followed her in a Hail Mary. Whenever they heard sirens—which weren't too frequently—they always said a prayer for the poor soul who was being put in an ambulance.

Or burning to death.

She wondered what had happened. Sirens weren't usual at Honeyspoon. Except for an occasional shoplifter at *Neisers* or someone trying to pocket costume jewelry at *Steigers*, crime was unheard of.

"All right, children," she tried to get them back to the task at hand, "We are going to identify the objective case, that is to say the object of the verb. By now you should know what a verb is and, if you don't, then of course, you're going to have a huge problem diagramming. Take out your notebook and your rulers. Everyone should have a pencil." She turned around to continue writing on the board and, from the small mirror which she had glued on the wall—some of the slower students still thought she had eyes in the back of her head—she saw Andrew Maloney slip Terrence Eastman a note. Her first impulse was to ignore it because sometimes that was just easier. Scolding and punishing a child took energy and also took time away from class. The truth was she just didn't care but the students were beginning to realize that and it was only October. The principal, Sister Hilda Anthony, had already spoken to her about her classroom management skills but all Sister Regina Rachel could hope for is that somehow she could be fired. Maybe become the school nurse—although she had no nursing skills—or the convent's cook—no cooking skill either. But the smirk on Andrew's fat face changed her mind.

"Andrew Maloney," she called out, "would you please give me the note you attempted to sneak to Terrence?"

Andrew's ruddy face turned even redder as he stood up and slowly walked down the aisle. The other students watched him with a smirk—glad that someone else was in trouble and glad that someone else was Andrew. Because no one liked Andrew.

In a way, Sister felt sorry for him, although he was simply not an endearing child. He was big and beefy looking, not peculiarly smart, he wasn't at all generous with his belongings—particularly with his food, in fact, he was downright greedy, especially when sweets were doled out, he bragged frequently about his rich and titled relatives. Sister suspected that they were all lies in attempt to be liked and Andrew hadn't learned what most people missed—in order to be liked, you have to show genuine interest in other people. Still—elementary school was a difficult period and Sister knew from her own experience how lonely you could be, and—as a bride of God—she should make an effort to love all of her students, or—at the very least—like them.

Andrew handed her the note. Usually she would read it aloud but instead she looked at it herself. *When ya wanna make the trade?*

Andrew wasn't a good speller either.

"May I see you and Terrence in the hall, please?" Sister didn't miss the disappointment on the other students' faces—they were, no doubt, hoping for drama.

Terrence rose, following her out of earshot. A stellar student, with big blue eyes and two dimples, he wasn't used to being in trouble.

She closed the door quietly after threatening the class they better be quiet or there would be no recess—a punishment for her more than them.

"You know I disapprove of trading," she told both boys. "It never works out well. Someone always gets the worse of the deal."

Terrence's eyes were downcast but Andrew stared at her with a sour look.

"What is being traded?"

The boys eyed each other.

"Well?" Sister insisted.

"I'm giving him my *Red Ryder BB Gun*," Terrence said, "Because my mother won't let me use it, anyway."

"Your mother is a wise woman. And what are you giving, Andrew?"

"Some books. Good ones."

Sister shook her head. "Don't make this trade on school grounds and under no condition are you ever to bring that BB gun to school, Andrew. Do you understand?"

Andrew nodded rather weakly.

"You wouldn't want me to call your father."

That was the reaction Sister had hoped for. A wave of fear washed over Andrew's face and this time he shook his head vigorously.

"You may go inside now." She retrieved her watch

from under her white starched bib. English Grammar time was over. It was time for American History where the students would take turns reading in dull, monotone voices while Sister would struggle to stay awake.

SEVEN

KATE WAS UP the entire night. Every time she closed her eyes visions of Violet Rose flashed by. And, as the night grew darker, and the hours grew later, her imagination grew wildly. What if—what if she had seen something sinister when she walked in? What if—what if the murderer was hiding—maybe even in the staff room and the moment she left to call the police, he removed the incriminating evidence. But she didn't know what she saw, nor did she know the significance of whatever it was she might have seen. But the murderer didn't know that—and he might think she could put two and two together and he was in danger from Kate. Only, of course, he wasn't. But he didn't know that.

She wasn't quite sure why her future hadn't turned out as planned. Ever since she could remember she wanted to escape Honeyspoon and live in New York City, a place of glamour, of excitement, a place of endless possibilities. She worked two jobs in high school and saved her money, kissed her mother good-bye—she died in a car accident a few months later, but Kate had no way of knowing that good-bye was a final one—and got on a Greyhound Bus, headed for the bright lights. She could work for a fashion magazine, maybe in time become the editor of *Harper's Bazaar*. But she flunked the typing test and by the time she taught herself how to type, well, it was all too late.

She didn't count on things being so expensive or the competition so fierce. She was a pretty girl, but New York was full of pretty girls. She was a smart girl, but she was up against girls who had graduated from college with degrees in English and journalism. She had a little bit of money, but she was surrounded by girls whose parents paid their rent in places like the famous *Barbizon Hotel* on the Upper East Side, while all Kate could afford was a dark, dank studio on 7th Street and Avenue B.

Until the unthinkable happened and she came running home.

The worst part about it about was the doubt—maybe she had given up too soon. Maybe she should have stayed in New York longer. And the thought that she couldn't quite escape—the idea that was always buried deep in her mind—was the best of her life already behind her?

SHE JERKED AWAKE at six thirty just as the local news was being televised. A grim looking man, wearing a grim looking suit, talked about the murder of Violet Rose Shaw at the *Honeyspoon Library*. According to the newscaster, the police had no motive for the apparent robbery, no suspects and no clues. They had cornered Margaret at her home, while she was raking leaves, and Margaret spoke glowingly of Violet Rose, what a nice person she was, how reliable, what a great job she did cleaning the library. All which Kate found rather ironic since Margaret had frequently complained what a lousy job Violet Rose did and how she was going to look for someone to take her place.

Kate turned off the television, put on the percolator and, and toasted two pieces of *Sunbeam Batter Whipped Bread*.

"EVERY SINGLE BOOK has to be accounted for," Margaret said. "We'll start with the shelves and check off each book on the master list. Then we'll do the same for the books on the floor. It's really important that we know which books are missing."

"And what if there aren't any books missing?" Kate was feeling very discouraged and already very tired.

"Well, we won't know that, will we?" Margaret snapped. "Until we take inventory. This may take us a few days, but, as you know, I'm a great believer in doing what needs to be done."

It wasn't that Kate minded the job so much, she minded that Margaret talked non-stop, while she puffed on her cigarettes, dropping ashes on the floor, which Kate was going to have to sweep up with the bird seed and the dead ants. Margaret talked mostly about her grandchildren, Susie Lee, who was nine years old and was going to enter the pageant world, because with her golden curls and bright blue eyes, she was bound to be a great beauty. She'd be Junior Miss, then Miss Massachusetts and eventually win the title of Miss America. She could try out for Miss USA but Miss America was a more refined beauty contest. And then there were her twin grandsons, Michael and Maurice, Michael was a genius, six years old, and he was reading third grade books. Maurice was the athlete in the family. He could run like the wind, and hit a ball over the fence. Scouts would be after him for a national team right after he graduated from *Honeyspoon High School*. They were watching him now!

And all Kate could think of was—why should I care?

Margaret never asked Kate anything about herself, which was probably just as well because Margaret was not the sort of person Kate wanted to share secrets with.

"Do you want me to do the magazines too?" Kate asked with a heavy heart as she looked down at *Jack and Jill* and *Humpty Dumpty*.

"Of course, just check them off."

Well, Kate wasn't going to check off every issue but as she looked at the shelf, she said, "The comic books are missing."

"What?" Margaret dropped a copy of the Hardy Boys Mystery on the floor, which created a cloud of dust, causing bird seed to fly in the air, while Lucy and Desi squawked loudly.

"I don't see them anywhere." Kate shrugged. "Of course, it's possible that some kid took them before the robbery and I never noticed."

"Well, you should have noticed!" Margaret's tone was harsh. "Those weren't just any comic books. For one thing, they were encased in plastic. There were five of them, *Action Comics*, *Detective Comics*, *Superman*, *Marvel Comics*, *Batman*. Those books are vintage, at least a hundred dollars each. They're valuable!"

"No one told me that," Kate said. "I would have watched them more carefully."

Margaret frowned. "You should have been watching everything carefully. We have to report this to the police. It's possible that they were missing before and you never noticed, but it's also possible, that they were the reason for the robbery."

"I'm sorry about that," Kate said.

"So am I," Margaret said angrily.

EIGHT

"I DO TOO," Andrew said. "My father doesn't know but I found them buried in the basement under another pile of magazines—not so nice magazines."

"What does that mean?" Terrence asked. "Not so nice magazines?"

Andrew merely shrugged. He was too embarrassed to go into detail about the scantily dressed women, placed in not so lady like positions.

"Still don't believe you," Terrence said, "because you lie. Everyone knows that."

Andrew felt his face flush. It was true, he did lie. But that was only because he wanted the other kids to like him. In the fifth grade class at *St. Hedwig's School*, he was known as the fat boy. What was even worse was that he was known as the dumb fat boy. Even Sister Regina Rachel called him that when she knocked his head against the blackboard, because he didn't know his nine times tables.

And Andrew did the unforgivable thing.

He cried.

A lot.

He cried when they had to hide beneath their desks, preparing for nuclear destruction, because one of these days it wouldn't be a practice and the entire world was going to burn to a crisp. Didn't the Lady of Fatima predict something like that? He cried when his mother forgot to put two *Little Debbie Cakes* in his lunch box because he couldn't go through the long morning without some sort of snack.

Andrew cried in school because he didn't dare cry in front of his father. His father was far scarier than any of the Frankenstein or Dracula movies he saw, far more terrible than *The Monster Who Ate Minnesota*, far more threatening than King Kong.

"They're Marvel comics and I saw them myself," Andrew insisted. "Five of them."

Terrence shook his head in disbelief.

"And it doesn't matter whether or not you believe me. They're there and I'm even willing to trade them." And indeed he was. Andrew wanted that BB gun that Terrence's grandfather had given him for Christmas. Terrence's mother wouldn't let him play with it anyway, unless Terrence was deep in the words somewhere, but Terrence wasn't allowed to go deep into the woods without his father and his father was never home, so really Terrence had no use for the gun. While Andrew—Andrew could make good use out of it.

"I know you want my *Red Ryder BB Gun*," Terrence said, causing Andrew's heart to soar. "But just so know, that gun cost a lot of money."

"So did these comics. I mean, they're really old, like ten years."

Terrence was losing interest. "What good are ten year old comic books?"

"They got good stories in them. I swear."

"All right. But if your dad finds out, won't he be mad, and want them back? I don't want any trouble."

"Nah. He probably won't even know they're missing, hidden like that in the cellar. So want to make the trade on tomorrow morning? I'll meet you by the railroad tracks."

Andrew nodded. He had a feeling that his luck was about to change.

NINE

Mrs. Peabody was in a good mood. In spite of the fact that Joanne had invaded what might have been an intimate breakfast with Kate, Mrs. Peabody had an ample meal, and, when she was well fed, she felt good. And grateful because at least she wasn't Violet Rose Shaw. At seven o'clock, she turned on the television, hoping to catch the movie *Storm Warning* with Doris Day, after a half an hour of *Ozzie & Harriet*.

But when the phone rang and she heard that it was for Kate, she was overjoyed. This was better than television, learning just what Joanne had tried to keep from her.

"Hi, Kate. What a long day yesterday must have been for you, finding a dead body! And then if that wasn't enough having to have breakfast with that horrid snoop, and imagine her thinking you should pay for her meal!"

"I didn't mind. The poor thing is probably lonely."

"The poor thing probably has more money than you and I combined. Did you hear from the police?"

"No, I guess they don't have any clues. Margaret came in and helped me to clean up. All of the books were accounted for but..."

"But?"

"The only thing missing were some comic books."

"Oh." Joanne was clearly disappointed.

Kate continued. "Not just any comic books. For one

thing, they were encased in plastic. There were five of them, *Action Comics, Detective Comics, Superman, Marvel Comics, Batman.* Those books are vintage, worth over a hundred dollars each. They're valuable and are only going to increase."

Mrs. Peabody fought the urge to cough.

"Oh. It's hard to believe that anyone would ever murder over comic books. There is something I've been meaning to tell you," Joanne said. "I've been corresponding with someone from the *Lonely Hearts Club*."

Silence.

"Please, don't say anything. Just hear me out. It's been nine years since Bruce ran off with Helen. I've been alone. You don't mind being alone."

Kate didn't answer, which made Mrs. Peabody curious.

"But I liked being married. I like having someone support me, not having to get up for work every day. Someone to dress for, to put lipstick on, to watch television with…we have been corresponding for a couple of months. Anyway, he's a very nice guy, buys and sells antiques and he does quite well. He's coming to town tomorrow and I invited him for dinner."

"I don't think you should have a strange man in your house. I mean, wouldn't it be safer to meet him in a restaurant?"

She tried but the second attempt was unsuccessful. Mrs. Peabody started to cough.

"Get off the phone, you old bat!" Joanne screamed.

"Mrs. Peabody, really!" was all Kate said.

So Mrs. Peabody had to hang up. But not before she looked out the window and saw something very interesting.

IT WAS TRASH night and Mrs. Peabody loved trash night. People threw away the most interesting things. The problem was she had to wait until eleven o'clock, when the neighborhood was quiet and no one could see her poking through the garbage. So at precisely that time, she took her own trash, which was neatly bagged and tied, and sashayed out of the door.

Although this particular heap was not especially interesting. Someone had thrown away a baby carriage, several trunks—she wondered if there was anything inside and she tried to open them but apparently they were locked, which was peculiar—a pile of dirty linens—disgusting bed sheets—a broken rocking chair, a few *Reader's Digests* and *Car and Driver* magazines and then some other sort of publications. Mrs. Peabody could see that they were shameful magazines. She looked down and saw Bill Maloney's name on them. How awful for Connie to be married to a man, who looked at such smut!

There was also a broken bicycle, a picture of ice skates—which someone had taken a knife to and sliced down the middle—no doubt a person with a vicious temper—and then a black pocketbook, which looked rather new. She was betting that someone had left some forgotten money inside and even if they didn't, it was still a nice handbag and Mrs. Peabody could use a nice handbag. The one she was carrying had a ripped lining and a strap, which was about to break.

Quickly she took the pocketbook and went inside.

She found three pennies in the bottom of the bag and then something else, which really excited her. It was a half written letter to a Malcolm. A love letter.

My dear Malcolm,

I cannot tell you how excited I am about your impending visit. I've been dreaming about it for weeks. I feel as if I already know you. We have become so close through our letters. I know that connection will only be firmer when we finally meet.

It's taken me a long time to trust. You know more than anyone how devastated I was when Bruce left me for that harlot. But because of you, my heart has been open.

I know you've had it rough too. But that is our bond.

The letter ended here and Mrs. Peabody had a good idea why. For one thing, the purse obviously belonged to Joanne and she had written the letter to this stranger she met through the *Lonely Hearts Club*. But, in Mrs. Peabody's estimation and probably in Joanne's as well—which is why the letter wasn't finished—it was too much too soon. A letter like this might very well scare Malcolm away.

And he would be plenty scared when he finally met Joanne, such a thin, nervous lady.

Mrs. Peabody was tempted to throw the letter away. Instead she folded it and put it in her large tin box.

TEN

SHE WAS ALONE in her room, the favorite part of Sister Regina Rachel's day. She could be downstairs with the rest of the chattering nuns, who were mildly debating whether it was better to use Crisco or butter in the chocolate chip cookies for the bake sale. She wasn't in the mood to watch *What's My Line*. Somehow all the sisters sitting in the parlor, a bowl of burnt popcorn between them depressed her. So instead she sat on the bed, rereading her favorite novel, *Rebecca*.

When Sister took her vows, she promised to give up all worldly goods, and that included her books. But years later, she managed to sneak in a copy and hide it under her bed. She loved the premise of the book, a young, shy girl meets a millionaire, lives in a glorious mansion, but is tormented by the memory of his first wife, a beautiful—Sister wondered what it was like to be beautiful, which Sister wasn't and never had been, which had limited her future options quite a bit—charismatic, brilliant woman by the name of Rebecca. If Sister had a daughter, she would have named her Rebecca. Of course, Rebecca doesn't turn out to be such a nice person, but she was strong lady, a determined lady and no one could take advantage of her.

The thought that Sister could admire such a woman, what did that say about Sister? Maybe Sister wasn't such a good person at all.

She would go to confession on Saturday morning, a confession to Father Preston, who was the most understanding of the three priests. But she wouldn't be confessing the reading of her book. Because who was to say that was a sin? Disobedience? Maybe.

But Sister was in more trouble than simply the reading of a book. Something was lying heavy on her mind, something she hadn't shared with anyone at all. Not even with Father Preston.

She had been sneaking out of the convent every morning.

Of course, that was against the rules. The nuns were never allowed to go anywhere alone, or even with another Sister, without the permission of Mother Superior. But she had a good reason for doing what she was doing. She was trying to persuade Thelma Lou, the homeless woman who lived under the bridge, to get help.

They wanted to lock Thelma Lou up in a mental institution and Sister knew that Thelma Lou was not insane, just down on her luck. If she only turned herself in and stopped running away from the police, they might be able to help her.

Sister had to go out in the early morning because once the dawn struck, she had to be in the chapel for morning mass.

And when all was said and done, it was a good deed, wasn't it?

Sister had been doing that for a few days and then on that gray day, she was passing the library when she saw someone in the park. It looked as if this person had just emerged from the children's library. But maybe not— maybe this person was just enjoying a little morning air. Yet, no doubt, it was puzzling.

Then there was that murder in the library.

Sister was conflicted. She couldn't go to the police and report what she had seen, because she would then have to admit that she had broken the rules. Mother Superior would be furious and Sister would be punished. The punishment usually consisted of doing some horrible chores, like hand washing the nuns' underwear, or going down on your hands and knees and scrubbing the tile in the bathroom, cleaning the oven, defrosting the ice box. But it wasn't even the chores that bothered her—it was the reaction of the other nuns. When someone broke the rules, the other nuns seemed to shun the sinner, even though they weren't supposed to, all while gossiping merrily away.

Sister Regina Rachel was lonely enough, already feeling like an outcast.

Besides, the person she saw running, well, that wasn't possible.

She would keep mum and hope for the best.

And say an extra rosary.

Except when she got back to the convent, she noticed that her rosary beads were missing.

ELEVEN

MRS. PEABODY BOLTED upright when she heard the shrill ring of the phone. This was not an unusual occurrence—the Maloneys frequently got early calls, usually from teachers about their unruly sons—but eight-thirteen was early even for them.

Except the phone didn't ring once or twice, but three times, indicating that the call was for Mrs. Peabody herself. At this hour, who could be calling her? It was going to be bad news, she just knew.

But maybe not. Maybe it was the police with questions about Violet Rose Shaw's death. Maybe they wanted to ask her advice, maybe they suspected Kate. After all—she did discover the body.

Mrs. Peabody leaped from her bed, which left her slightly dizzy as she dashed into the living room and grabbed the phone.

"Mrs. Peabody?"

A woman.

"Yes, that's me. What do you want?"

"My name is Maureen Hines. I'm calling from the *Egan Electric Company*."

Mrs. Peabody should not have answered the phone.

"I'm calling about your bill. You are three months behind, owing us the sum of $13.83."

"It says right at the bottom of my bill, that if you're elderly, exceptions can be made." Mrs. Peabody thought she heard someone pick up the phone, but before she could say anything, Miss Hines spoke.

"That's true. And we will certainly make provisions for the elderly. We can work out a payment plan, for instance. But the bottom line is that you have to pay the bill."

"Okay," Mrs. Peabody said hurriedly, hoping to get her off the line.

"Well, when can we expect at least partial payment?"

"Soon."

"If we don't get partial payment very soon, I'm afraid we're going to have to turn off your electricity."

No electricity? That meant no dim light in the bathroom, so it would be totally dark in the middle of the night. That meant no television, no *Homemaker's Movie*, no *Wagon Train*, no *As The World Turns* or *Edge of Night*. That meant no coffee in the morning with her broken percolator.

"Perhaps you should consider getting a job," Miss Hines said rather cheerfully. "You live on Lily Lane. There are a lot of children there and I'm sure there are mothers who could use a babysitter."

"I don't like children. They're noisy and dirty."

"Well, I happen to know that *Steigers* is looking for sales clerks…"

"I can't be on my feet. I have an irregular heartbeat and arthritis."

"My doctor is actually looking for a receptionist…"

"I can't be around sick people. I just told you I'm not well."

"Is there someone you could borrow the money from? Perhaps a sibling or a child?"

"I only have one sister, Mildred, and she lives in

Iowa. I haven't had a letter from her for months. I have no children, only my husband, who caused his own death by being stupid and falling off a roller coaster. I have to live off his social security, which isn't much."

"I am very sorry for your troubles, Mrs. Peabody. But there is not much I can do. I don't own the electric company and if you don't come up with at least a fourth of that amount which would be," there was a pause, "let's say $3.25, they will turn off your electricity at five o'clock in the evening on Monday. You have a good day."

Mrs. Peabody, who was now furious, was left with a dial tone. Shaking, she was just about to hang up when she heard another voice. "Mrs. Peabody?"

"Who is this?"

"This is Connie Maloney. I'm sorry for listening in. I picked up the phone to call Sister Regina Rachel because Andrew has a sore throat and I couldn't help but overhear…"

"Nosy parker!"

"I had to go back to work, because, well, people aren't dying the way they used to, except for Violet Rose Shaw, of course, so Bill hasn't been making too many coffins. Anyway, I got a job as a waitress at Howard Johnson's, and I'm going to need a babysitter, the few nights when Bill has his Elk meetings."

"If you heard my conversation, you know I don't like children."

"I understand that, but as I explained, it would be in the evenings and my boys are usually in bed by eight, so really, all you have to do is watch TV, or read magazines, or listen to the radio."

Even with a stab of annoyance, Mrs. Peabody hesitated. She had heard somewhere through the grapevine that the Maloneys got UHF, which was a premium channel, sometimes offering different game shows and some new comedies. And also that they had a color television.

"I can pay you $.85 an hour, and that's a dime more than minimum wage."

How many hours would she have to work to accumulate $3.25? Was it even worth it?

"I could call Miss Hines and tell her you have a job. Perhaps she'd give you an extension."

"Well, I guess I could try it," Mrs. Peabody said, hesitating slightly.

"Thank you! Thank you! Thank you! Can you start tonight?"

"Tonight?"

"Be at my house at 7:15."

"Well, I…"

"Thank you again!"

THE LINE WENT dead before Mrs. Peabody could respond. This was not good, not good at all. She didn't want to work. She didn't want to babysit. She wanted to stay in her nice cozy house, and drink sweet tea and eat cookies and watch *The Lawrence Welk Show* in peace and quiet.

Which she couldn't do without electricity.

But circumstances had backed Mrs. Peabody in a corner. And when she was backed in a corner, she got desperate, which wasn't a good thing at all.

THE THOUGHT THAT she might be earning money soon— even in a job she hated—gave Mrs. Peabody some cause for celebration. She decided to take the bus downtown— she could walk but it was an overcast fall day and rain was expected. One of the spokes on her umbrella was broken and there was a slight hole in her saddle shoes. She was going to treat herself to a cup of coffee at the counter of *Neisers* and a piece of their homemade orange chiffon pie.

By the time she bathed and dressed and caught the bus—she missed the ten twenty and had to wait until eleven o'clock—the counter was filling up fast with early lunchers. Mrs. Peabody didn't know them by name, but she knew all the regulars at the counter, usually women, clerks from *Steigers* or *Dorothy Dodds*, secretaries from city hall and nearby insurance companies. Sometimes the mayor himself, Mr. Poduck, would shoot over, for a hamburger with fries, a glass of *Dr. Brown Cream Soda* and a piece of apple pie topped with chocolate ice cream. Nellie, the waitress behind the counter, loved him because he was such a big tipper, even if Joanne spoke so harshly against him. It would be nice to chat with Nellie, who often gave her a second cup of coffee on the house and even a broken piece of pie or the crumbled end of the chocolate cake. And if it wasn't too busy, she would gladly gossip with Mrs. Peabody.

But it was very busy so Mrs. Peabody was on her own.

When Mrs. Peabody saw Kate come in and sit beside her, she was happy to have someone to chat with.

"Do the police have any clues," she asked Kate after Kate ordered a tuna sandwich on white bread, a side of coleslaw and a cup of coffee.

Kate shook her head. "Not that I know of."

"It's horrid." Nellie plopped down the pie in front of Mrs. Peabody. "I never thought that such awful thing could happen in this town. And in the children's library, no less." She bent down and whispered. "I heard talk that maybe Thelma Lou was involved."

"You mean that homeless lady who lives under the bridge?" Mrs. Peabody asked. "Why would she rob the library?"

"Maybe she just broke in because it was cold and she needed a warm place to stay. And maybe Violet Rose found her and there was a fight. And maybe Thelma Lou then made it seem like a robbery, just to cover her tracks."

"I don't know Thelma Lou," Kate said quietly, "but I don't think she's capable of planning all this."

"Well, you know what I also heard. I heard that Violet Rose was mixed up with the Reds."

"The Reds?" Mrs. Peabody and Kate asked in unison.

"The Communists. It was a political murder."

Kate smiled and shook her head.

Nellie shrugged and then went on to the next theory. "There's a stranger in town." She was still whispering as she pointed down the counter.

Mrs. Peabody strained her neck to have a look. The man that Nellie was pointing at was indeed a stranger and yet Mrs. Peabody thought there was something very familiar about him.

His clothes were high end, as though they were custom made. His monogrammed shirt was fastened at the sleeves with gold cuff links and decorated with a red bow tie. His brown belt looked like expensive leather and his brown hair was slicked back, his side burns perfectly cut, his beard short and pointed. Mrs. Peabody watched as Nellie approached him and slapped down a menu.

He smiled with perfect teeth and she noticed a dimple on his right side. "I'd love a cold drink. How about a black cherry? How are your hot dogs?"

"Okay." Nellie smiled widely. "You new in town?"

"Just passing through. I'm an antique dealer, always looking for a treasure." He winked.

"I know a lot of unclaimed treasures," Nellie blushed.

"Hey, Nellie," the cook, Pete screamed from the kitchen, "your chicken pot pie is ready."

Nellie smiled at the man again and batted her heavily mascara eye lashes before she waddled away.

And then Mrs. Peabody knew just like that, exactly who the man was. Joanne's beau from the *Lonely Hearts Club*, like James Dean, a bad boy. She couldn't deny that he was handsome, but there was something about him that was also dangerous.

Of course, she couldn't share any of this with Kate—because she couldn't admit overhearing the telephone call—so instead Mrs. Peabody drove her fork into the tangy orange chiffon pie and enjoyed every last bite.

AFTER SHE FINISHED with her pie and her coffee, Mrs. Peabody took herself to the grocery store. On the way she passed a dour looking woman—well, if the truth be known, Mrs. Peabody herself was looking rather dour—standing in the cold, ringing a bell, collecting for the *March of Dimes*. Mrs. Peabody didn't recognize her, which meant that she probably wasn't a local woman. Mrs. Peabody hurried by—she had no extra money for charity, although she did feel somewhat sorry for the poor woman, who had to stand outside. Mrs. Peabody stopped on the way to the supermarket to check the two phone booths. Sometimes she found dimes in the coin returns from someone who made a call, which didn't go through and they rushed out without checking for their change.

But not today. Today both phone booths were empty.

She couldn't afford to buy much and she had to be very careful not to buy treats, because she really needed to use her money for nourishment. Although she was happy to know that today was double stamp day, so she was getting closer to that brand new percolator.

Then she saw Rita Eastman.

Rita Eastman was not looking at honey dip donuts or the pecan pies. She was staring at a box of *Fanny Farmer Chocolates*. Mrs. Peabody saw Mrs. Eastman's eyes dart around as she placed the white box underneath her coat. She then walked to the snack aisle and grabbed a box of *Hostess Snowballs*, then some *Twinkies*, and finally a box of *Puffed Wheat Cereal*. All of which she hid beneath her ample beige trench coat—which was slightly stained probably from other lootings. And while she was doing this, Mrs. Peabody filled her own cart with eggs, white bread, bacon, three cans of tuna fish and a bag of sour apples to give out on Halloween evening to the ragamuffins who would end up at her doorstep.

She watched Rita make her way to the front of the store, preparing to leave. If anyone had seen her—besides Mrs. Peabody—they would have stopped her and apparently they weren't going to. So Mrs. Peabody took matters in her own hand and wheeled her cart in front of Rita, thus preventing her from exiting.

"Excuse me," Rita said with a touch of irritation in her tone, "but I'd like to leave."

"Oh, you can leave," Mrs. Peabody said, "But just so you know, I saw you shoplifting."

Rita, clearly rattled, reddened and then turned pale. "Are you going to tell on me?" she whispered.

Mrs. Peabody shook her head and said, "No, but I wish you wouldn't do that. Sooner or later you're going to get caught and they will put you in jail."

Rita ignored the warning and instead she said, "Let me show my appreciation and pay for your groceries."

Mrs. Peabody hesitated because she wondered if it was wise to take money from someone who was really a criminal. On the other hand, Mrs. Peabody was poor and every penny counted.

"That would be fine." Mrs. Peabody grabbed a *Skybar* and threw it into her cart. This was turning out to be a splendid day.

TWELVE

KATE HAD JUST arrived home when the telephone call came. Since she left New York, she always feared that the day would come when she would have to walk down that road.

She just never thought it was going to be today.

"So, baby, I'm out."

She recognized Stanley's voice right away. How could she not? It had been fifteen years and he still sounded the same, upbeat and happy. As though all those years in prison hadn't made him bitter. Or at least you couldn't tell from his tone.

"That's wonderful." She, too, tried to sound excited, but she wasn't a very good actress and even to herself, the statement sounded forced.

"You don't seem too happy to hear from me. They said I had to do twenty years but they let me out for good behavior. And I was real good in prison, baby, you would have been proud of me."

"I sure would." Kate swallowed, aware of the lump in her throat. "So how did you find me?"

"It wasn't hard. I knew after the accident you'd go back to your home town, so I just asked for information and the telephone operator was real cooperative. I am staying at the *Roger Roberts Hotel* now but it's not like I got a lot of bread. When you leave they give you your wages, what you earned working, for me, that was in the laundry room. It amounted to a couple of hundred dollars. Do you believe that? Not even minimum wage. I'm going to need directions to your house…"

"No, that's not a good idea!" Kate was insistent.

He was more insistent. "I need a place to stay."

"You can't stay with me. This isn't New York City. This is a small town, people talk."

"Who cares?"

"I have to care. I have a job, I'm a librarian. My boss is conservative. She'll fire me…" She heard a click.

"Excuse me," Kate recognized Mrs. Peabody's shrill voice, "but I need to use the phone."

"Who is this?" Stanley demanded.

"This is Mrs. Peabody. Who are you?"

Kate thought it best to nip this in the bud. "Do you need to use the phone, Mrs. Peabody?"

"Yes, I do. I need to call the electric company. They are threatening to turn off my electricity for nonpayment, which is ridiculous. I told them that I was going to pay them soon. I'm babysitting for the Maloneys tonight and the money will go right to that bill. Can you imagine if they do that? I'm an old woman…"

"I think we should talk later," Kate said, happy to have a reason to end the phone call with Stanley.

"I agree," Stanley said cheerfully. "If you give me your address…"

Before Kate could think of a reason not to do that, Mrs. Peabody snuck her nose in once again. "She lives at 13 Lily Lane."

"Fine. See you in a bit."

Thoughtfully, Kate hung up the phone. And sank to the floor.

Somehow she had been hoping—hoping what? That

Stanley had died in prison? That he wouldn't get out for years and years—well, he had been in for 15 of them—but that once he did get out, he had forgotten all about her. That maybe he had met a girl in one of those pen pal clubs and he had someone else.

And she was never going to think of him again.

Or that horrid night.

STANLEY WAS FROM Staten Island, a place that Kate had never heard of. But he had a car and, when she met him in a bar on the Upper East Side, he seemed like a gentleman, even though he worked as a car mechanic and was hardly her idea of Rock Hudson. They went on several dates. He took her to nice restaurants and never forced himself on her, never seemed to mind when she didn't invite him up to her small studio. He took her to plays and even once to the Museum of Natural History. She wasn't madly in love with him, but Kate was, if nothing else, practical.

He liked to drink and Kate didn't mind having a few herself. It made her relax. It made her feel sophisticated and happy, like a real New Yorker.

They had been dating for a few months on that fateful night in January. She was drinking highballs, three was always her limit. After that she began to feel woozy. Stanley was drinking scotch straight up and it didn't take her long to realize that he was drunk, very drunk, much drunker than she had ever seen him.

When he offered her a ride home to the Lower East Side, she refused. But it was a stormy winter night, it was after three in the morning and taking the subway was not an option. She would have hailed a taxi—even though that meant no lunch money for a few days—the only thing that broke up the monotonous job of opening mail for a group of lawyers who specialized in bankruptcies. But no taxi was roaming the streets and Kate didn't have a license and she couldn't drive, even if she wanted to.

He took the FDR drive but he missed the exit, got off on Houston and was totally lost. He never saw the homeless man, who had wandered into the street, until they felt a thud against the car, when a body flew through the windshield.

She would never forget the thunderous scream as the man came hurling towards her, propelling through the windshield, splattering blood everywhere, on her black leotards, on her camel hair coat. Closing her eyes, she crawled out of the car. Moments later, Stanley came to and hollered, "What have I done?"

Kate had once read that in those moments of crisis, when you are forced with a choice, that's when you learn just what you are made of, that's who you discover who you truly are. Well, Kate knew then that she was not a person of character, just a person who didn't want to be mixed up in an accident when someone might have been killed.

Stanley wasn't a person of character either. He immediately stepped on the gas and fled the scene. But he was driving so erratically that he had only gone a few blocks when he went up on the curb and almost hit two other people, a woman and a man, who were exiting a club. They called the police.

Kate walked the rest of the way home. When Stanley was taken in, and convicted on vehicular homicide, he never mentioned Kate. Perhaps he was so drunk, he had forgotten about her. But he had 15 years to think about it, and his memory had returned.

Now Stanley had found her. She couldn't refuse to have anything to do with him. If she made him angry, he might retaliate in some way. At the very least he would certainly ruin her reputation.

So she did the only thing she could think of. She settled down to watch *Stage Fright*.

THIRTEEN

"I WANT POTATO CHIPS!"

"I want a story!"

"Adam is hitting me!"

"You hit me first!"

"My mother said we could stay up until nine thirty."

"I want to watch *Roy Rogers.*"

"It's my turn to watch *The Lone Ranger.*"

"You're supposed to read me a book!"

Mrs. Peabody, who wanted to watch *Lawrence Welk*, screamed. "Enough! You've being very disrespectful."

"Very what?"

"I think she's means we're being bad."

"Not me. He's being bad."

"He just kicked me. Didn't you see that?"

Mrs. Peabody wanted to kick all three boys. "Listen," she growled, "and listen well. I'm a witch."

"That's what people say," Andrew gasped.

"Well, they're right. I can cast spells particularly on troublesome little boys." She stared at each one of them. "How many of you would like a pain in your head?"

"I think she's already doing it."

"My leg hurts. Did you do something to my leg?"

"Can we watch *Stage Fright?*"

"Mommy said we are not supposed to watch that. It's too scary."

"Well, your mother is right and besides I want to

watch *Lawrence Welk*. The music will be very soothing." Mrs. Peabody turned the television on but it took some fiddling with the antenna—and the oldest son, Andrew was quite helpful—before she was able to access the program. But when she did she was immediately struck by how vivid and interesting everyone looked in such bright, eye catching colors. Why you could even see just how pretty the Lennon Sisters appeared with their baby blue dresses and their yellow sashes. All three boys were quiet, although sullen, looking quite bored.

Mrs. Peabody sat down and dived into the bag of potato chips—which she had found and ripped open—and then the phone rang, one ring, which meant it was meant for the Maloneys but, after all, she was the babysitter and wasn't she supposed to take messages?

"Hello."

"Hello, Mrs. Maloney? This is Sister Regina Rachel. I'm calling about Andrew."

Mrs. Peabody eyed Andrew, who was now shoving his younger brother.

"He's not behaving in class. And there is another thing that is rather disturbing. He is always trading with the other boys. He and Terrence Eastman and David Worth. I've told them it's against class rules, even if they are trading their own things, because someone always gets the short end of the stick and they want to trade back and an argument ensues. At any rate, I wish you would speak to him."

Mrs. Peabody decided that now was the time to admit that she wasn't Mrs. Maloney—after all she had already heard the information. "I'm sorry but I'm just the babysitter. I can tell Connie, if you like."

"Oh, I see. Well, please have her call me at her earliest convenience."

As Mrs. Peabody hung up the phone she decided she wouldn't bother to relay the message. Connie looked as if she had enough troubles of her own and trading was not a bad thing. Besides Mrs. Peabody didn't like nuns. They seemed judgmental and sour—although who wouldn't be sour having to wear that awful cumbersome black habit day after day, season after season.

The phone rang again startling her. Was it Sister Regina Rachel a second time, something she forgot to say?

"Johnny here. I need to talk to Bill." Mrs. Peabody recognized the voice immediately, a voice she had heard before when listening in on the party line. A rough sounding tone that could erupt in rage at any moment.

"He's not here."

"Well, if you're his misses I have a message for him." She wasn't his misses but the man didn't give her a chance to dispute that fact—not that she would have. "Tell him if we don't get the money he owes us, well, let's just say he won't be walking too good."

"How much are we talking about?" Mrs. Peabody said, and then quickly added, "So I can tell him."

"None of your beeswax!" he said gruffly, "He knows."

She was left with a dial tone.

The three little boys were staring at her, their faces white, their brown eyes wide and round. She didn't know if they were frightened by her or the phone call.

"You can watch TV for twenty minutes more and then you all have to go to bed."

"But I get to stay up later," Andrew protested.

Mrs. Peabody stared at Andrew's legs.

He fell silent.

AFTER SHE HAD gotten the three boys settled in their beds—it was hard to figure out whose bed belonged to whom because all three boys wanted to sleep in the top bunk—after she had gotten them each a glass of water, and forced them to say their prayers, after she examined the closet and under the bed for the boogey man—which wasn't such a stretch considering that someone had threatened their father and a cleaning lady had just been murdered—Mrs. Peabody did what she did best.

She snooped.

First she examined the cabinets and found that the Maloneys were rich in junk food. There were not only the potato chips—which she and the boys had finished—but pretzels and corn chips, small chocolate bars, marshmallow cookies and orange candy. There were also several unopened bags of *Chuckles* jelly candies and little *Sugar Daddies*. Probably Connie intended to hand these treats out to the trick or treaters on Halloween. Mrs. Peabody found a plastic bag and helped herself to a small portion of everything except the unopened candy. After all, babysitters were allowed to eat at the job, and just because she chose not to eat certain items while she was physically in the house didn't mean she couldn't take the food for later. The icebox contained a more healthy array, cheese, cold cuts, some vegetables, leftover tuna casserole, fruit in a gelatin mold. The freezer had a variety of TV dinners, pork chops, Salisbury steaks, and frozen macaroni and cheese. Since she counted five macaroni and cheeses, she figured Connie wouldn't miss one. Behind the TV dinners Connie had stuffed several cartons of orange cream pick-up pops. Mrs. Peabody couldn't very well take the ice pops with her, so she grabbed one, sucking on it as she entered the Maloneys' bedroom. Next time she would bring an empty Tupperware container and take home some *Tang*, which she could mix with ice cold water for breakfast at home.

She had to admit that Connie was a good housekeeper. The bed was nicely made, even though the quilt covering it was hideous, a combination of burnt orange and mustard yellow with dabs of olive green. On top of the bureau sat loose change, seventy-two cents in all and, for one moment, Mrs. Peabody debated on taking it, but then decided not. If Connie suspected that she was a thief, then she wouldn't hire her again and really the babysitting job wasn't as bad as she had thought. She got to watch the colored television and eat plenty of treats. Besides taking food was one thing. Taking money something else entirely.

She opened the first drawer, which obviously belonged to Bill. It was crammed with unmatched socks and a piece of paper, which was sticking out under the liner. She pulled it out. Written on the paper someone—she imagined that someone was Bill—had scribbled, *Johnny, $500*.

Was that the Johnny who had called? Was that how much Bill owed? How was Bill going to pay him? Poor Connie!

She quickly closed the door. The less she knew about Bill's goings on, the better. She turned her attention to the small jewelry box on top of the bureau and opened it gently, exposing a lot of costume pieces, beads of loud, garnish colors, a rhinestone pair of clip on earrings, a ring with a stone missing and a very pretty broach. She picked up the broach, surprised at its weight—although it was only ceramic, the Scottish terrier appeared remarkably real. It would look smashing on her winter coat or just on her plain black dress, which Mrs. Peabody wore to funerals. But, of course, she would never take it. And then there was a ring, a small sapphire, but it looked as if it was set in 14 carat gold. Maybe it was expensive.

Still holding the broach in her hand, Mrs. Peabody bent down to open the bureau drawer and the broach fell out of her hand and underneath the dresser. When she bent down Mrs. Peabody saw that it was too far in for her to reach it, but really it didn't matter. Connie might think she herself had dropped it. But, as she rose, Mrs. Peabody saw a group of magazines in the corner.

Her heart quickened as she examined them, all the latest copies of *Movie Story*, *Photoplay*, and *Silver Screen*. There were even some *True Confession* magazines there, which were her favorite—her natural curiosity extended not only to the rich and the famous but also for the indigent who had bizarre stories to tell. When she went grocery shopping, she always stood in the longest line, so she could read these magazines, because she really couldn't afford to buy them—she also spotted a few *Redbook* and *McCalls*, but these housewife magazines did not interest her.

There was a stack, at least a dozen of the magazines she loved and surely if Mrs. Peabody took a few home, Connie would hardly miss them. Perhaps she had already read them and was planning to throw them away.

Mrs. Peabody took four from the bottom and buried them in her pocketbook. She took a few more to read while she watched television.

Maybe she could make this babysitting thing work for her after all.

FOURTEEN

THE CONVENT RAN like clockwork—where every sister had a duty to perform. The duties varied and were assigned on a weekly basis. They consisted of preparing meals—Sister Regina Rachel wasn't much of a chef and she was frequently assigned to chopping vegetables for the salad—setting and clearing the table, washing the dishes, drying the dishes, dusting, sweeping the halls, scrubbing the bathroom, ironing, doing the laundry and hanging it out to dry.

This morning Sister Regina Rachel's chore was to hang the laundry before school began.

This was her favorite duty, something she didn't mind doing at all. Shaking the wet garments, she held the wooden clothes pins in her mouth, securing them on the heavy rope and watching them wave in the breeze as she pretended she was an ordinary housewife, just going about her day, caring for her husband and her children.

It was early—just a little after seven and yet there were some boys playing in the yard. She recognized Andrew Maloney and David Worth. They were throwing around a ball in the small space that serviced as a recess yard.

Sister bent down to grab a large pair of white panties, hoping that the boys would not see her—she knew how boys could make fun.

She never saw it coming.

She felt a tremendous jolt at the back of her head, through her black veil, hitting her with such force that she staggered and fell to the ground, seeing nothing but darkness.

Sister Regina Rachel had never had a headache quite like this. The pain was almost unbearable. From the back of her skull to the front of her forehead, it was as though a nail was going through her brain.

They had given her morphine, which dulled the throbbing but it made her groggy and sleepy. She closed her eyes for a few minutes and then woke up to violent vomiting. At least she was in a hospital.

After she finished throwing up in the gray metal pan, the nurse cleaned her off and Sister lay back. She was closing her eyes, when Mother Superior came in, followed by a policeman.

They both asked her how she was feeling, and because nuns were not encouraged to complain, she merely mumbled, "All right," although that was a lie and she wondered if she would have to confess it.

"Sister, this is Detective Wayne Grenier," Mother Superior said, as she sat down on the one chair. "I taught Wayne in first grade and then again in seventh grade. He was an excellent speller. He wants to ask you a few questions."

"Of course." Her voice sounded hoarse and raspy. "I don't know what I can tell you. I didn't see anything."

"Well," Detective Grenier leaned against the wall and took out a small pad and a chewed up pencil, "we talked to the boys who were in the yard, playing ball. They denied throwing the rock. Said there were no stones around them and they would never do such a thing."

"Well, maybe it was an accident," Mother Superior said firmly, "and Sister Marie Patrick saw them running. She happened to be throwing away the garbage."

"They claim they ran away because they were frightened."

The only response from Mother Superior was a hiss.

"Sister, you were hanging clothes. Is that correct?"

"Yes, I was."

"And therefore you were facing south. Right?"

Sister's head start to hurt again and, for a moment, she was confused about her directions.

"In other words, you were not facing the school."

"That's right."

"Well, you see that's where we have a problem."

"What sort of a problem?" Mother Superior snapped.

"Sister Regina Rachel was hit in the back of the head but, by her own admission, she was facing the front, actually looking at the boys. Therefore they could not have thrown the rock at her since she was hit from behind."

It was silent in the hospital room, except for the low beeping of the machine beside her. No one could possibly refute this information.

"So now I am asking you, Sister," Detective Grenier paused, "is there anyone you could have offended?"

"I am offended by the question." Mother Superior snapped to her feet. "We are sisters of the Lord. We don't offend people."

But the detective held his ground. "With all due respect, Sister, we are trying to find the perpetrator of this crime. And I know that no one in the convent would purposely offend anyone. But some people can be unreasonable." He turned his attention to Sister Regina Rachel. "Perhaps someone you gave a bad mark to?"

Sister wanted to shake her head but it hurt too much. "I can't imagine a student doing this to me."

"Well, maybe someone in your past life."

"What do you mean her past life?" Mother Superior glared.

"I don't have a past life," Sister said. "I joined the convent when I was eighteen. This year I'll celebrate my twenty-fifth anniversary."

"Okay." Detective Grenier shut his little pad and stuffed it into his pocket. "Maybe it was just a random accident. Let's hope so. If you can think of anything else…"

And that was it. That was the moment when she could have spoken up, when she should have spoken up. That was the moment when she could have admitted that she had been visiting Thelma Lou and that she saw someone running from the library. That was the moment.

But she missed it.

Detective Grenier left the room and Mother Superior began her lecture about how important it was for everyone's sake to let her know immediately if anything unusual occurred within the convent walls. "We are a community. What happens to one of us happens to all of us. Keeping secrets is being selfish."

And then together they prayed the rosary.

FIFTEEN

Halloween was a most festive time for the children on Lily Lane. They were all in costume, Superman, Howdy Doody, Nurse Ames, Lois Lane. The streets were littered with clowns and fairies, with ballerinas, and cowboys and princesses and one child dressed as a paper clip. Even the children from *Brightside*, the orphanage two miles away, joined in the fun, accompanied by a gaggle of nuns—who hadn't bothered to dress.

The children came in droves, trick or treating, holding out bright, orange plastic pumpkins, already filled to the brim with *Sugar Babies*, and licorice twists, *Neccos*, and *Baby Ruths*. Mrs. Peabody held on to the firm belief that all that candy was not good for children. It gave them cavities and made them wild and fat. It also contributed to diseases, like heart problems and polio.

So Mrs. Peabody gave out apples, the green sour kind, because they were the most nutritious. And then to each child, one penny, which she thought was most generous—especially considering her finances.

Evidently the children did not, because the word got around and the trick or treaters grew fewer and fewer, which did not displease Mrs. Peabody in the least.

So by nine o'clock Mrs. Peabody got ready for bed. She put cold cream on her face, two pink rollers in her gray hair, a powder blue hair net on top of her head, and because the very cheap landlord had not yet put on the heat, Mrs. Peabody wore her brown flannel pajamas, which were decorated with steaming cups of coffee. She had just settled in her bed with the movie magazine she had pinched from Connie Maloney and, with the radio turned down low to Frank Sinatra songs, she drew a sigh of contentment.

Until she heard a knock at the front door.

Now Mrs. Peabody found this very annoying. She didn't have any intention of getting out of her warm bed, putting on her fluffy slippers, trudging into the living room and opening the door to some Johnny Come Lately tricker or treater. Besides, she only had fourteen apples left and she was saving them for the next few weeks.

She continued to read.

The knocking grew to a ringing of her bell, that horrid, shrill sound that always meant some sort of fresh annoyance. The final straw was a barking dog.

She had no choice. She got up, found her slippers and shouted out that she was coming in the most irritated voice she could muster. Maybe the children would be frightened by her. She should have purchased a witch mask, which would give credence to what the Maloney children had told her. That would have put a good scare in them.

But no, the sounds continued, so she flung the door open, prepared to do battle.

To her surprise, no one was there except for a small black and white dog, who was whining to be let in. "Go home." Mrs. Peabody waved her hand. A cold wind passed through her before she slammed the door and headed into the bedroom.

But in her irritation, she forgot to lock it.

The children must have grown tired, so chances were they wouldn't be back, she reasoned. Still Mrs. Peabody was annoyed at being disturbed and decided to make herself a cup of hot milk with a touch of chocolate and a dollop of whip cream on top.

She was headed for the kitchen, when she heard a sound coming from the closet door.

Now Mrs. Peabody lived at one of the end units so there was no question of the sound being one of her neighbors, not on that side of the apartment. It occurred to her that it might be a mouse, something which really frightened Mrs. Peabody. She didn't dare look. Nor did she want to go into the kitchen because that would mean passing the hall closet.

Quickly she retreated to her bedroom, climbed into bed and almost shrieked when she saw a shadow in the hallway. If only the phone was by her bedside, she would immediately call the police. Instead she opened her mouth to scream, but what she saw was the little black and white dog. How had he gotten into her house?

She rose from the bed and then she heard another sound. Only this wasn't the dog, who was now standing beside her, and looking questioningly in the direction of the hallway. Had someone broken into her house and that's how the dog got in?

With a sense of foreboding, she stood frozen, as she saw a hulking figure make its way from the closet.

At first Mrs. Peabody thought it was one of the nuns from *Brightside*, who had somehow wandered into her home. It took her a moment to realize that it wasn't a nun at all, but a man, who was wearing an ill fitted nun costume. And it was too short, coming only to his mid-calf, where she caught a glimpse of blue jeans, dirty white sneakers and beefy arms extending from the cheap material. His puffy face was red and his eyes were blood shot. She could smell whiskey and sweat. He was carrying a large piece of wood.

She recognized the man.

Bill Maloney.

She opened her mouth to scream but nothing came out.

Why was Bill Maloney looking so menacing?

"I want what you took from my house." He snarled as he started to come towards her.

For a moment Mrs. Peabody was so shocked that she couldn't remember what she had taken. Was he referring to the broach she had dropped behind the bureau?

"I didn't take anything," she said, fear bubbling inside of her. "I don't know why you think that I did."

"I know that you did. Give them back to me, you old bat." He started to come towards her. Right away she thought of Violet Rose and then she knew that she was in trouble. Violet Rose had been murdered, so there was a killer on the loose and this killer was obviously Bill Maloney.

"The magazines," he whispered. "You took the magazines."

The magazines, yes, she had taken a few magazines, magazines that were Connie's. But why were those magazines so important that Bill was willing to kill her to get them back? There must be something hidden in them.

"You think that I'm playing with you?"

No, he was obviously not playing with her. She knew that as he stepped forward and she wanted to say, "here are your stupid magazines", but before she could utter a single word, the little black and white dog leaped forward and knocked Bill down and began to bite at his neck and Bill was screaming to call her dog off, except that it wasn't her dog, but when she yelled *Enough*, strangely the dog stepped aside and then stood beside Mrs. Peabody and Bill Maloney ran out the back door.

Mrs. Peabody sank to the floor.

The dog sank beside her.

It had happened so quickly that she thought maybe it hadn't happened at all.

She wasn't sure what she should do—should she call the police?

The dog looked at her with mournful, sad eyes and Mrs. Peabody knew the first thing she had to do—was to feed the dog.

SIXTEEN

ANDREW HAD JUST come home from collecting a nice stash of candy for Halloween, when he heard his father yelling.

"Connie," he shrieked. "Connie!"

She wasn't answering. Andrew knew that she was about to leave for work and maybe was already out the door.

"Connie!" he roared.

"Please, Bill, the neighbors will hear you."

"You think I care about them neighbors? I just been over at the Peabody house."

"What did you go there for? And why are you dressed in that costume?"

"Because I thought she took my magazines."

"And you accused her? Why would she take your magazines? We need her to babysit, Bill, the nights when you're not home. She might not come back…"

"Find someone else. If she took my magazines…"

"She didn't take your magazines."

Andrew felt his stomach burn up. Magazines? The comics he had given to Terrence? Was that what his father was screaming about?

It didn't matter.

Andrew knew something about his father.

Something real bad.

Something he could hold over his father's head. And it proved what he always knew.

His father was an evil man.

"I threw them out," his mother answered, which made Andrew breathe a sigh of relief. At least he wasn't in trouble.

"You what?"

"I threw them all away." He heard his mother open the front door. "Andrew is eleven years old. A few days ago I saw him in the basement, looking at those disgusting magazines. Do you think it's right that he should be seeing half naked women? Is that what you want?"

"What did you do with them?" he screamed.

"I told you I threw them away." She was outside now. "And what about the comic books?"

His father was asking about the comic books. Andrew crept into the hall and saw his father, standing by the front door, his fat face purple with rage.

"I didn't see any comic books," his mother said softly.

"Did you look? You stupid cow," he hollered so loudly that Andrew could hear him, although his mother was half way down the walk. "Who the hell are you to tell me what I can and cannot read?"

His mother kept walking towards the bus stop. Andrew heard his father, come back into the house, slamming the door behind him. Then he heard his father throwing dishes against the wall, one after another and muttering wildly about the comic books tying him to a murder. Andrew stayed quiet, not daring to breathe lest his father take his rage out on him.

For some reason those comic books were important. They weren't just any old comic books. They had to be worth money. And his father wanted them, probably to pay some gambling debt. Yes, he knew his father gambled and he knew his father was in trouble and owed money.

But murder? Andrew had heard some talk about a lady who got killed in the library. Maybe that's where the comic books came from. He had a vague remembrance of seeing them in the children's room.

But if his father thought the comic books were in the trash, then maybe he would give up looking for them.

It didn't matter. Andrew had to get them back from Terrence. Somehow.

SEVENTEEN

SHE HAD SOME left over cold cuts—some low salt turkey and honey ham. She had been saving it to make a sandwich, but, after all, the little dog had defended her against harm and maybe even possible death, so she guessed that she could share her food.

The dog gobbled it up and then she gave him some nice cold water. When he finished drinking, she thought about opening the door and letting him out. But she didn't. For one thing, it was obvious that he was a stray. There was no collar and he did look on the skinny side. It would be nice to have a little company.

But for another thing, the dog had acted as her protector. What if Bill came back? If he was looking out the window and he saw the dog roaming the streets, then he would know that the dog was no longer in her house and he might return.

No, the dog should stay just where he was.

She made sure that both doors were now securely locked. She must have left it ajar when she was handing out treats to the children. Nevertheless, she put on all of lights as she made her way back to the bedroom.

And then she reached for the magazines.

If Bill was so desperate to get the magazines back, there was only one reason why that was so. So sitting on the bed, with the dog beside her, she turned the pages of all of the magazines and to her surprise an envelope fell out of one of them.

It was addressed to Connie Maloney, and to Mrs. Peabody's disappointment, there was nothing inside. And not even a return address. But the envelope was postmarked Ohio.

Who did Connie know in Ohio?

Well, chances are she would never find out.

She should put the magazines down and call the police, tell them that she had merely borrowed the magazines and forgotten to mention it to Connie. She could also say that Bill had broken into her house and had threatened her physically.

But had he? She wasn't quite sure. It was true that his mere presence was threatening. But he could always say that he had found her door open and he came in because he suspected Mrs. Peabody of stealing something.

And just because he was carrying a heavy board didn't mean he was going to hit her with it. If Mrs. Peabody got the police involved, Bill might do something worse.

And if she did call the police, she would have to turn over the magazines, which she was really enjoying. Mrs. Peabody put the envelope aside.

She went into the kitchen and picked up the phone, the little dog trailing behind her.

She put the phone down.

She didn't want to get involved with the police. If she admitted that she took the magazines without telling Connie—she could claim that she had forgotten—but for two days? The police might think she had a habit of stealing—and after all she wasn't Rita Eastman. Hadn't

Kate said something about magazines being missing from the library?

No doubt that the police were looking into Violet Rose's murder and it wasn't going to take them long to discover that she and Violet Rose never had gotten along. Of course, no one in their right mind would kill a person just because they were cut in line while buying honey turkey, or a person wouldn't move aside in church when asked.

But then again, Mrs. Peabody had been the first to arrive after the body was discovered.

No, the thing to do, Mrs. Peabody decided, was to simply leave some of the magazines on the Maloney's front porch in the morning. He wanted the magazines, he could have them. She'd just keep a few, the ones she hadn't read.

And that should be the end of it.

SHE ROSE BRIGHT and early—it was not even six o'clock—and, putting on her housecoat—she didn't bother with her brassiere or her girdle—she went across the street and neatly lay the magazines on the doorstep of the Maloney house. Then she tiptoed away. She figured that she better let the dog out to do his business. She opened the door, the dog went out and then the dog came dashing in, his tail high and wagging.

She decided to name him Oliver, a name she had always loved and planned to use for her first born son, only no child had been forth coming.

Mrs. Peabody supposed she was going to have to feed Oliver—she didn't think a dog would want to eat cereal or buttered toast—so she was going to have to fry up a few eggs and a few strips of bacon.

But just as she was about to close the door, she saw Mr. Wiggins, the milkman coming from his truck. He was headed for the Maloney house, swinging his steel rack and Mrs. Peabody could see the glass containers of milk, the wedges of cheese, the cartons of eggs and a big slab of sweet butter. He used to deliver to her house as well, but when she fell behind, he refused. If she continued to babysit for the Maloneys she could be eating some of that cheddar cheese and maybe even take home a little of the sweet butter. But after what Bill accused her of, she wasn't sure that was going to happen. Except she was returning the magazines, wasn't she?

She watched as Mr. Wiggins gathered three empty glass milk bottles and then he dropped the new items into the aluminum box. Suddenly he stopped and looked down at the magazines. He picked them up and started to rifle through them. And much to Mrs. Peabody's amazement, he crammed them into his pocket and returned to the truck.

She wanted to say something, to catch the truck as it sped away, but what could she say? She could hardly accuse him of stealing, when she had taken the magazines. Besides she didn't want to draw attention to herself.

As she closed the door, though, her thoughts got a bit cheerier. After all, there was no proof that she ever took the magazines in the first place and now there was less proof, because she didn't have most of them anymore. The evidence was gone.

EIGHTEEN

KATE WANTED NOTHING more than to go home after a long day of working in the library, especially since so many patrons came in, just out of curiosity. She longed to sit on the couch and watch *The Tales of Wells Fargo*. She had a crush on Dale Robertson. Well, no one could deny that he was handsome.

All she could hope was that they would rerun it. Because tonight a town meeting was scheduled and she was on the board. She had originally volunteered because she had hoped she'd meet some potential mates. But everyone who attended was either an old woman or a married man.

Mr. Podunk, the totally ineffectual mayor, a tall, thin, balding man, who seemed to care more about his appearance than the fate of the town, began to speak in a monotone voice. He told the small community of attendants that the discussion was whether or not the mansion should be torn down to make room for a playground. Since the meeting was held at the *Finster Mansion*, he looked around in distaste at his surroundings.

"What's the big deal?" Adam Zoha—who owed an expensive jewelry store on the edge of town—and just because he was rich, he felt entitled—bellowed. "Tear the building down and build a playground. The kids need a place and besides this old relic is falling apart."

"We don't need a playground," Lillian Wright popped up. "This is a landmark building."

"This is a dangerous building," Mrs. Peabody said. "Why I almost got killed when that brick came tumbling down last year. Everyone can see that the structure is leaning to the right."

"Let's not forget what happened to that poor writer, Chester Benteen last month," Mr. Stringer said. "He was trying to tell us that the building was lopsided and the writing room was going to cave in. And no one wanted to listen to him and now he's dead, dead as a doornail."

Kate wondered how a doornail could be dead.

"That's because he was smoking that marijuana," Joanne burst out.

"That didn't mean that what he said was invalid," Mr. Stringer argued.

"That's a devil drug, sold by those beatniks, who hang out in Springfield. It's a no wonder that Chester jumped out the window," Joanne said.

"So sad. To have this place connected to a death." Lillian Wright shook her head.

"That's beside the point. We can fix it," Joanne said as she eyed Kate. Kate knew that Joanne wanted to preserve the mansion, which would, no doubt, preserve her job. "It's the oldest building in town. It's our history."

The debate continued with pros and cons and Kate was amazed that the few people who showed up were so passionate. After all, when all was said and done it was just a building and Joanne could find another job. Joanne was her best friend, and she would never want to endure her wrath, so Kate would have to vote to keep the building intact.

The mayor wanted the building to be torn down and

Kate knew that there was some talk about him taking bribes from the contractors who would build the playground.

"Here's the problem," Rita Eastman—who was new to the board—said, "I'm not sure how I feel but what I do know is that brick could have hit Mrs. Peabody…"

"Could have killed me," Mrs. Peabody interrupted.

"And next time we might not be so lucky. If someone gets hurt or killed, they're likely to sue and that might bankrupt our town," Mr. Zoha said.

"I think you're all being alarmists." Joanne frowned. "There is no reason why such a thing might happen. And it's going to cost money to tear it down. Maybe more than to fix it."

"That's a good point," Rita said. "I need to give it some more thought."

"More thought and more thought." Lillian Wright leaped up again. "Because no one wants to do anything."

"If we're going to take a vote," the mayor said, "I will vote to tear this old relic down."

"I say, leave well enough alone." Kate eyed Joanne and then thought her friend was going to owe her big time—although Kate was not comfortable with her vote. Suppose a brick did hit someone? Would she be liable?

Someone like Stanley.

Now it was up to Rita, who would be the deciding vote. "I don't know," she confessed. "I have to think about it. Can I decide and we will vote next time?"

"Let's give Rita time to decide," the mayor said, "She's entitled to that."

So it was shelved to next time and the meeting dragged on. And Kate couldn't help but think if there was any way that she could arrange to have a brick fall on Stanley's head, although she knew that wasn't a possibility and would certainly be considered a crime.

The mayor began to discuss new sidewalks on High Street.

Kate half listened and even found herself dozing as everyone rambled on. The meeting broke up after eight and all Kate wanted to do was take a hot bath, enjoy a glass of cola and watch television, although she had totally missed Dale Robertson and all she could catch would be *The Tonight Show* with Steve Allen. She rose and decided instead of taking the bus, she was going to call a taxi. Sometimes she wished she had learned to drive, but after the accident, the thought terrified her. At any rate she didn't want to hang around downtown, just in case she ran into Stanley.

She was coming out of the telephone booth when Mrs. Peabody headed straight into her. "Are you going home?" she asked in a shrill voice, dangling a black purse from her skinny wrist.

Kate nodded. "I'm calling for a cab."

"Would you mind if I come along? I don't have any money, but since we are both going to the same place..."

Kate did mind. She didn't want to make small talk but she nodded as she saw Joanne coming towards her. "We'll all go together," she said.

Evidently Mrs. Peabody did not like that. She threw a dirty look at Joanne and then said she'd run to the little girls' room.

"Does she have to come with us?" Joanne said. "She is such an old snoop."

Kate agreed but then again wondered what she could

do. Instead she just said, "I suppose we should try and be kind."

"That's your nature," Joanne said. "I'm no good at pretending. Did you see the pocketbook she was carrying? That was mine. I threw it in the trash, because the lining was faded. And what does that old biddy do? She takes it out of the garbage. Oh well, wait until I tell you…" Then Joanne spoke non-stop about her new boyfriend by the name of Malcolm Harris. He was from Ohio and did quite well selling antiques. He was handsome and good looking and seemed very grateful to her, when she cooked him dinner, pot roast, string beans and beets with lime *Jello* for dessert. He was planning to stay for a while and search the area, looking for merchandise.

Joanne said this entire speech without once even looking at Mrs. Peabody in the taxi cab. She addressed her comments only to Kate. Kate nodded agreeably and pretended to be excited, although there was a part of her who wondered what a rich, handsome man from Ohio wanted with a rather plain, skinny, flabby woman with straw colored hair and yellow, uneven teeth. And even more puzzling was the question of why a rich, handsome man from Ohio had joined the *Lonely Hearts Club* to begin with. A man who had so much to offer surely could find a partner in his own neck of the woods.

Was he the man that Mrs. Peabody and she had seen in *Neisers*?

Kate knew she was being hateful, thinking such awful thoughts. And maybe it was because she was worried about Stanley coming back into her life and somehow it didn't seem fair that her friend would have a wonderful future with a wonderful rich man, while

Kate was going to be tied to an ex-con, who had a secret which might forever destroy her reputation.

Maybe even more than her reputation because who knew what sort of person Stanley was now. Prison did horrible things to people and if someone killed once—

As though Mrs. Peabody could read her thoughts, she suddenly spoke. "Just be careful, Joanne. It's a dangerous world out there. Remember what happened to Violet Rose."

Joanne shot a hateful stare at Mrs. Peabody. "Violet Rose? What does Violet Rose have to do with any of this? Surely you're not accusing Malcolm. He wasn't even in town when that happened. He didn't come in until Thursday."

Mrs. Peabody looked as if she wanted to say something and then thought better of it. "Just be careful, that's all."

"We all should be careful," Joanne said and then she stared at Mrs. Peabody in a very creepy manner.

NINETEEN

Mrs. Peabody had just finished her supper of a baked chicken leg, a baked potato with sour crème and butter and some canned peas and was enjoying a piece of chocolate brownie—she had taken several pieces at the bakery, where they were giving up samples—she put them in foil and brought them home to enjoy later—when her phone rang.

Again the call was for her. She could only hope that it wasn't a bill collector. They seemed to be more aggressive as time went on.

She was tempted not to answer but her curiosity won out.

"Mrs. Peabody?"

She recognized Connie's voice.

"Yes?"

"I don't understand. After the last time I saw you, you said you would babysit again on Friday night. Bill has a prior commitment and I need you to be here."

Mrs. Peabody sank on the chair. She didn't feel like babysitting. She wanted to stay home with Oliver and read the rest of her magazines. "I didn't know if you still wanted me."

"I don't understand. Why wouldn't I want you?"

Well, she supposed that now was as good a time as any to tell the truth. "Your husband broke into my house on Halloween Eve. He was very threatening. If it wasn't for my dog…"

"You have a dog?"

"I do now. But that's hardly the point. He accused me of stealing some magazines. Why would I do such a thing? I mean, who steals magazines?"

"I'm sorry about that Mrs. Peabody. Actually I stole his magazines."

That statement rendered Mrs. Peabody silent.

"They were in the basement, and they weren't nice magazines, if you know what I mean. Magazines where women weren't wearing too many clothes. I saw Andrew searching through them one day last week. Well, that was enough. I just threw them in the trash."

Mrs. Peabody recalled seeing the magazines in the street but she thought it best not to respond.

"I told Bill what I did. He was angry, of course, but then again, he's always angry. Anyway, he's not coming home until late tonight, an Elk meeting. He's going with his pal, Adam Zoha. So will you come over? I have to leave in about fifteen minutes."

Mrs. Peabody thought about all the goodies stacked in the cabinet and the colored TV. "I guess it will be all right," Mrs. Peabody said. "But I'm bringing my dog. I don't like to leave him alone."

"That's fine. The boys will love him."

Mrs. Peabody was hoping that Oliver didn't love the boys back. She was hoping that they would be scared of him, thus behaving.

Nevertheless she thought the whole thing very peculiar, the way that Bill had broken into her apartment looking for magazines. What made those magazines so important? Was there something hidden in them?

Maybe something in the envelope that she had found addressed to Connie? Well, whatever it was—it was gone.

And chances are Mrs. Peabody would never know.

SHE DRESSED UP her dog with an old red scarf around his neck. He didn't seem to mind and it made Mrs. Peabody think that somehow that simple act made Oliver hers.

To her amazement the boys were relatively well behaved. She knew they were afraid of her, and Mrs. Peabody had never thought that fear was a bad thing, when disciplining children. She, herself, had been reared by the nuns, literally. She never knew her father and her own mother had died of a rare disease when Mrs. Peabody was in the third grade. She was immediately shipped to *Brightside*, which was nothing more than an orphanage, run by the nuns and she remained there until her eighteenth birthday.

She turned out fine.

It was after ten when the phone rang, for the Maloneys. The boys had already gone to bed, and Mrs. Peabody was enjoying some saltines smothered in *Cheez Whiz*, while watching *The Honeymooners*. She could not imagine who would be calling so late. It was certainly rude. She picked it up.

"Connie?"

"No, this is the babysitter. Connie is at work."

"Oh. This is Adam Zoha. Could you take a message for Bill?"

"Just a minute. I need a pencil."

Mrs. Peabody searched around for a pen and a piece of scrap paper. She was thoroughly puzzled. Hadn't Connie said that Bill was going to an Elk meeting with Mr. Zoha?

She couldn't resist. When she got back on the phone, she asked, "Is the Elk meeting over?"

"What Elk meeting? There is no Elk meeting tonight. It's on the second Tuesday of the month. Anyway, tell Bill I called."

Mrs. Peabody put down the phone.

Bill had lied to his wife and Mrs. Peabody had found out. What was worse was that Mr. Zoha might mention that he called and Mrs. Peabody asked about the Elk meeting. Then Bill would know that she knew that he was up to no good.

Bill was a dangerous man, who had already broken into her house. She didn't want to give him any excuse to be angry at her again.

She looked down at the blank piece of paper.

And wrote nothing.

THE NEXT DAY Mrs. Peabody woke up in a glorious mood. For one thing it was a lovely autumn day in November, and when she took her morning walk with Oliver, she stayed out twice as long.

And the dog seemed to enjoy it as well.

Then to her delight she found seventy-one cents in her jacket pocket, enough for bus fare and a cup of coffee at *Neisers*.

It would be nice to chat with Nellie, who might sneak her a second cup of coffee on the house and, maybe if she wasn't busy, they could gossip for a bit.

The counter was crowded but that didn't stop Nellie from giving Mrs. Peabody a piece of broken brownie.

Mrs. Peabody noticed that he was here again, the very good looking stranger. Only this time he was wearing a leather jacket and a pair of blue jeans. He was eating a hot dog smothered with relish and mustard and drinking what looked like a root beer.

"Mrs. Sotheby is pregnant again," Nellie whispered. "It's her eighth! It's going to be a problem because her husband was fired from the paper mill. He kept showing up for work, drunk."

Mrs. Peabody shook her head, feeling slightly sorry for the eight children.

"Rita Eastman came in. She was caught stealing a spool of red thread and some yellow ribbon. Just putting it in her purse, like there was nothing wrong. I don't understand it. Lawrence is a foreman at the factory, he earns a good living. If you're going to steal, why not go to *Zoha's Jewelry Store* and grab a ring or a bracelet? Not ribbons worth seventy cents."

"See that man at the end of the counter." Mrs. Peabody pointed to the stranger. "What do you know about him?"

"I know plenty," Nellie bragged. "First of all, I know where he's from, the *Lonely Hearts Club*. Joanne Kennedy wrote to him and he answered back. I used to think that was some sort of scam at best, at worst, you could never tell. Could be a serial killer or a black widower, the kind that marry you, and then murder you for your insurance money. But now," Nellie shook her head, "now I'm not so sure."

Of course, Mrs. Peabody knew all of this but, as always, she was hungry for more information. "How did you find out?"

"They were at the drive in movies, last night. I could see them from my window, laughing and talking. They weren't watching the movie. That much I can tell you.

There's nothing special about her, Joanne, I mean. If she could get someone like that, then why can't I?"

"But here's the truth," Mrs. Peabody was eating her brownie slowly, letting it dissolve in her mouth, savoring the chocolate taste, "she doesn't even know him. He's been in town, what maybe a few days…"

"Oh, no," Nellie shook her head. "He's been here at least for a week. I know that as a fact. Clara, the receptionist at the *Roger Roberts Hotel*, is my friend. She comes in here every afternoon at about three for tea and scones. She's English, you know, straight from London. Her husband…"

"What did she say?" Mrs. Peabody interrupted her.

"She said that he checked in a week ago this Saturday. Said he was walking all over town, some sort of antique dealer. From Ohio."

Ohio, Mrs. Peabody thought. And then just like that it flashed through her mind, that empty envelope she found buried in Connie's magazines.

"Hey, Nellie," Pete's voice rang out loud and clear, "I ain't paying you to gab. Your BLT, hold the mayo, is ready, so step to it."

Nellie shrugged and headed for the kitchen.

If what she was telling Mrs. Peabody was true then this man had been here longer than Joanne knew—and even before Violet Rose had been murdered. And did he have any connection to Connie?

Well, Mrs. Peabody thought, *it gave a body pause.*

TWENTY

SISTER REGINA RACHEL was on breakfast duty this week, so there was no question of her sneaking out in the early morning to bring food to Thelma Lou. She was up at four thirty, cracking and mixing eggs, setting the table, putting out the butter so it would be warm and melt on the white toast, finding the skillet, slicing the bacon and letting in Mr. Wiggins, the milkman, making sure that he was delivering what was ordered.

Lately Mother Superior had complained that they were being shorted—the cheese was less than expected, the eggs weren't all there—she thought they might have broken on route and Mr. Wiggins hadn't bothered to replace them—several yogurts were missing and the butter looked as if someone had lopped off a chunk.

Of course, Sister knew exactly why this was occurring—she had been pilfering some of the products to bring to Thelma Lou. But, of course, she couldn't say that to anyone, so she said nothing and let poor Mr. Wiggins—who had six children and a wife in a wheelchair—take the blame.

"Good morning, Sister." Mr. Wiggins was nothing if not cheerful. A good looking man—not that Sister should notice things like that—he had sparkling blue eyes, white teeth and dimples. His hat covered his pitch black wavy hair—and his turned up nose crinkled with he smiled.

"Good morning, Mr. Wiggins."

Mr. Wiggins dropped the bag on the table and began to unload it as he called out the products. "A half a gallon of cream, two pounds of sweet butter, seven containers of yogurt, three pounds of cheddar—the cheddar is good, Sister, real tasty. You want me to cut you a slab?"

"Better not," she mumbled because she thought that Mother Superior might wonder how it happened.

"I also have some nice crisp saltines." Mr. Wiggins beamed at her. "I've been carrying them because some people like to have crackers with the cheese. You think Mother Superior might be interested?"

"I could ask her." The way Mother Superior counted every penny Sister thought it unlikely.

Sister started to put the groceries away and then reached for the envelope that Mother Superior had left on the counter with Mr. Wiggins's name written in perfect cursive. She watched as Mr. Wiggins tore open the envelope, examined the check and shook his head. Sister knew that he had been shorted and she knew that was her fault for taking some of the food and giving it to Thelma Lou.

"Well, I guess that's that," he said in a discouraging tone. "Oh, did you hear the news?"

"The news?" Sister echoed. She never heard the news. The Sisters were to be in their rooms at eight-thirty sharp and radios were not allowed upstairs.

"They caught the person who murdered Violet Rose."

Sister drew a long, deep breath. If they caught the person, then she would not have to be conflicted, she would not be in danger, no one would know. "Who?" she asked, her voice, little and scared.

"I don't know her name. She's that homeless woman that hangs out under the bridge."

Sister felt the room twirl.

"Are you all right, Sister? You look a little peaked."

"She couldn't have done it," Sister said.

Mr. Wiggins shrugged. "I don't know her myself but I'm guessing that she's a little deranged. I mean, wouldn't you have to be if you were a homeless person? Maybe she's on drugs…"

"I don't think so. They don't have any proof. They can't have."

Mr. Wiggins was no longer smiling. Instead he gave Sister a fleeting look of shock and suspicion. "I guess they do. She was holding one of Violet Rose's earrings. She said she found it by the library but I guess the police don't believe her. But think of it this way. If she's convicted, and she will be convicted, if she hasn't confessed already, it might be the best thing for her." Sister must have looked puzzled because Mr. Wiggins continued to explain. "They will put her in jail, which is a heck of a lot better than being on the street. She'll have a warm bed, three square meals, medical attention, if she needs it. How much longer do you think she can survive, especially if we have another brutal winter? Well that's it, Sister. I'll see you on Monday. If you need anything else, well, you know how to reach me." He grabbed his steel rack and slammed the door behind him.

Sister sank on the chair.

Of course, Thelma Lou was innocent. For one thing Sister had been with her at the time of the murder so Thelma Lou couldn't have done it. For another Sister had a good idea of who had been at the library, who had thrown that rock at her.

Was Mr. Wiggins right? Was Thelma Lou better off in jail?

Maybe, but that was hardly the point. Why should she be convicted of a crime she didn't commit, be branded as a murderer, just because she was homeless and had some mental problems?

Sister felt as though she might vomit. But she knew what she had to do. She had to speak to Mother Superior and tell her the truth, that she had been disobedient, that she had stolen food and then accept the punishment. Then she would have to go to the police—and the sooner she did this the better.

She rose, unsteady, holding on to the table. The phone rang, shrill and unexpected. It was five thirteen in the morning. No one called with good news at five thirteen in the morning. Taking a deep breath, Sister picked up the receiver.

"I need to speak to Sister Regina Rachel." The voice was hurried, almost frantic.

Sister was guessing it was the police. Thelma Lou had been cognizant enough to remember that she had an alibi, so now Sister didn't have a choice. And it wouldn't look like she had come forward on her own. Everyone would know that she was a coward.

"Please, it's important!"

"This is Sister Regina Rachel." Her throat felt tight and sore.

"Roselyn, you don't recognize my voice. It's Nora, your sister."

"Oh." A wave of relief washed over Sister and a moment later was replaced with trepidation. "What's the matter?"

"Daddy had a heart attack. He's in the *Springfield Hospital* and he's asking for you. How soon can you get here?"

TWENTY-ONE

WHEN THE PHONE rang and it was for her, Mrs. Peabody's stomach tightened. Lately, she had been getting a lot of phone calls, which was unusual. She didn't like phone calls or unexpected visits because there was always a chance that any news would be bad news.

"Mrs. Peabody?"

"Yes?"

"This is Rita Eastman."

"Yes?" Was Rita going to say something about the fact that Rita had paid for her groceries at the store? Would she insist that Mrs. Peabody pay her back? Well, it wasn't even Mrs. Peabody's idea. Rita offered first.

Instead Rita said something completely unexpected. "I understand from Connie that you babysit."

"Well, actually, that's not quite true. As a favor to Connie, I agreed to watch her three boys now and then…"

"Well, I was wondering if you would consider baby-sitting for Terrence. Sometimes I need to go out at night and I'm not comfortable letting him stay by himself. It would just be for a few hours until Lawrence gets home and maybe now and then at night, when we go out to dinner, or Lawrence has his bowling night…"

Mrs. Peabody was torn. No, she didn't want to baby-sit but the extra money would definitely come in handy.

"I would pay you what Connie pays you, which is

more than a fair deal, because after all, she has three boys and I only have one. And Terrence is a quiet child. He likes to read and draw and mainly stays in his room."

"I guess I could try it. Although I'm an elderly woman and I don't like a lot of noise."

"Terrence is not noisy. Honestly. Can you come over today?"

"Today?" Mrs. Peabody looked at the clock. It was going on three.

"Just for a few hours. Lawrence and I are meeting with an insurance agency."

"All right," she said reluctantly. "But I have to bring Oliver."

"Oliver?"

"My dog."

Rita didn't answer right away. "I guess that's all right, although I think Terrence might be allergic. We had to get rid of the kitten we adopted because Terrence kept sneezing."

"Well, then I guess he really will have to stay in his room," Mrs. Peabody said with a note of finality in her voice.

RITA WAS RIGHT. Terrence was no trouble at all. He stayed in his room and only came out to grab a handful of potato chips and a black cherry soda. But he did shoot Mrs. Peabody a nasty look when he saw that she had helped herself to several chocolate chip cookies.

Once she was sure that Terrence was in his room and wasn't about to come out, she decided to poke around—especially since their television wasn't colored. Not much to see, at least not downstairs. She thought it would be best if she didn't go into the master bedroom because it was right near Terrence's own room and he might emerge suddenly and catch her going through the drawers.

She did open the closet in the downstairs hall and spotted a rather large cardboard box. She opened it and her heart skipped as she saw an assortment of merchandise, all still with their price tags on them.

There were pretty rhinestone broaches, and one ceramic one which featured a small bouquet of roses held together with a pink ribbon, a red and gray beaded necklace with matching earrings, nylon stockings—unopened—two conical brassieres in two different sizes, a cardigan rust colored sweater, several pair of panties, tubes of bright scarlet lipsticks, face make-up—in a brownish orange tint—face creams, sun tan lotions, packs of cigarettes, a leopard belt, a pair of high heel shoes, four Agatha Christie novels, some fountain pens, a paisley scarf, a red shawl, one bottle of vitamin C pills and four baby rattles.

And then there was another box. It was labeled in payment to, but the name was smudged and unreadable. This box contained three bottles of baby lotion, a fountain pen, two golf clubs, and a box of *Fanny Farmer Chocolates*.

For a moment Mrs. Peabody thought about taking something. She would really love one of the rhinestone pins. They would look smashing on her brown dress or even her charcoal winter coat. But no, that wasn't a good idea. Rita might not miss it at first, but she might recognize it, if Mrs. Peabody wore it around her. Or worse still, a store clerk might realize that it was stolen and Mrs. Peabody might be arrested.

But who would miss a pair of nylons?

While she was debating, the phone rang and Mrs. Peabody hurried over to it.

"Hi, sweetheart," a voice came floating over the other end of the line.

"Who is this?" Mrs. Peabody demanded.

"What do you mean who is this? Oh, I get it, Lawrence is home. Just answer yes or say it's a wrong number."

Before Mrs. Peabody could utter a single word, the man—who sounded vaguely familiar—continued. "I'm wondering, you know, about what you told me, about your being pregnant and all." For a moment, Mrs. Peabody thought maybe she should confess that she was not Rita at all. But the moment passed and it was too late. "That wouldn't be good, you know, especially if you weren't sure."

Mrs. Peabody didn't know how to reply. She thought it might be best to say nothing.

"You there, Rita?"

She managed to grunt.

"You can't talk?"

"No," she whispered.

"I'll call back tomorrow after Lawrence goes to work."

Before the man could say another word, Mrs. Peabody hung up.

It was evident what was happening. Rita Eastman was having an affair with some man and she might even be pregnant by him. That woman certainly lived on the edge—she was a thief and an adulteress.

Maybe someone knew. And maybe that someone was blackmailing Rita and Rita was buying the person off with stolen merchandise.

And maybe that someone had been Violet Rose.

But it wasn't really any of Mrs. Peabody's business.

One thing she did know was the peaceful town of Honeyspoon, which used to be quiet and comforting had turned into a horrid place. Murder, robberies, adultery. It was enough to make you sick.

Mrs. Peabody was feeling rather sick, sick to her stomach. She'd have to use the bathroom, which was on the second floor. She held on to the banister—her legs had been bothering her lately. She wondered if it was her arthritis again or something more sinister.

The bathroom was occupied. Terrence had left his door open. She stood in the hall and peeked in. A typical boys' room with posters on the wall of Superman and Howdy Doody and Batman, an unmade bed and a hula hoop and a Davy Crockett hat on the floor.

And something else—something that looked like comic books. Not the newer ones—these looked rather old and rather faded.

Maybe they were the same comic books that Kate had mentioned to Joanne. Comic books which had been stolen from the library. The library where Violet Rose was murdered.

She stepped closer just as the bathroom door sprung open. Terrence came out, his eyes narrowing. He went straight to his room and slammed the door.

Mrs. Peabody decided then and there that she wouldn't be babysitting for the Eastmans again.

TWENTY-TWO

ANDREW WAS THINKING of a way to get those magazines back. They were obviously worth something and why should Terrence have them? The thought that his father had somehow stolen them was slightly disconcerting, especially if they were connected to that dead lady.

And once he got them back what would he do?

Well, he could put them down in the cellar and pretend that they were always there and his father just didn't look in the right place. His father would be so grateful, he might not even stop to question how or if they were moved.

Or Andrew could sell them on the black market. He had no idea how to do this but maybe he could ask David. His father just got out of jail, so he might know the right people.

Or he could turn over his father to the police, which would work fine, if there was some sort of reward. Was there?

No, he wouldn't do any of those things. Of course, he wouldn't do any of those things. If his father stole the magazines, it was because they needed the money, with his mother having to work so hard—maybe if his father sold the magazines, his mother wouldn't have to waitress and that witch, Mrs. Peabody won't be babysitting. He would do the right thing. But first he had to get the magazines back.

He approached Terrence on the way to school, who hardly gave him a chance to talk. Instead Terrence went on about how mean Mrs. Peabody had babysat for him last night. "Thanks a lot for your mother to recommend her."

"Yeah, I hear you. Listen, Terry..."

"I told you not to call me that. My name is Terrence."

"Oh yeah, Terrence, sorry. I need my magazines back."

Terrence laughed in Andrew's face. "You're kidding, right? A trade is a trade. You can't all of a sudden say you want the comic books back. No way, no how."

"But it's not fair!" Andrew was aware that his voice had taken on a whiny tone.

"Stop acting like a baby."

"My mom won't let me use the BB gun." Which was a bold face lie—he hadn't even tried, although he dreamed of shooting a few kids in his class, the ones who had been mean to him, who called him fatty and Mr. Doughboy.

"Yeah, so what? I know all about that. Which is why I traded you. I'm not trading back." He hurried ahead.

Andrew huffed and puffed to catch up with him. "What if I give you something else?"

"Like what? It's not like you have a lot of cool things. You got nothing I'm interested in."

"Yes, that's true. But, but," Andrew hesitated, "but my mother does. She's got this real nice sapphire ring from my grandmother. It's worth a lot of money."

"Yeah, what am I gonna do with a lady's ring?"

"Well, you could sell it. I'm sure it's worth more than a couple of old comic books. Or you could give to it to your Mom, like if she was going to punish you or something, you can maybe bribe her." Terrence bit his lip thoughtfully, as though he was contemplating the thought. Andrew moved right in. "Well, maybe I shouldn't. It's not like it's a fair trade..."

Terrence gave the slightest nod. "Won't your mother miss it?"

"Nah, she never wears it. She just threw it in her jewelry box. She won't even know it's gone."

"Okay," Terrence said, as they approached the school. "I mean, it's not as if I didn't read them already. You got a deal."

BUT WHEN ANDREW searched through his mother's drawer and stuffed his hand inside her girdle, he found more than just the sapphire ring. A necklace with all kinds of pretty stones gleamed up at him. Earrings that glittered and a matching bracelet looked expensive. But it was clearly the sapphire ring that was probably worth a lot of money.

So Andrew began to have second thoughts. Why should he give away the most expensive item? Maybe he could talk Terrence into the necklace or the earrings? Then on second thought, better not. Terrence was somewhat reluctant and he might change his mind completely.

Except when they finally made the trade in the schoolyard—he could swear he saw old eagle eye Sister watching him—the comic books were not in great condition. The Superman comic book had a big black stain on it and smelled like black cherry. And the Batman one had a torn page.

He couldn't give them back to his father, not like this.

So he put them in his desk under the jar of ink and a bottle of glue. By the end of the day, when he stuffed them into his book bag, they were sticky and stained blue.

TWENTY-THREE

WHEN MRS. PEABODY went to bed that night, her head was spinning. She had learned quite a bit babysitting for the Eastmans.

For one thing Rita Eastman was having an affair. She might even be pregnant and not know who the father was. How disgusting was that! And the poor child would grow up, never knowing who her father was, because there was clearly no way to tell.

But then again Rita was a rather disgusting woman, a shoplifter and now an adulterer.

And maybe a thief.

Or a murderer.

Mrs. Peabody had seen the comics herself and they seemed as though they were the ones, which were missing. Had Rita taken them the way she had taken so many other things? Had Violet Rose seen her pilfering them and that's why the cleaning lady was killed? Poor Lawrence!

A mild mannered man, with large glasses, watery blue eyes, a thick, fat head, bushy eyebrows and a prominent Adam's apple, Mrs. Peabody had heard him speak barely five words. Perhaps his lack of what others might consider to be a "manly" side prompted Rita to take up with another partner. But maybe Lawrence wasn't as cowardly as people thought. Perhaps he had a very dark side—maybe he had stolen the magazines and murdered Violet Rose.

Yet someone else had already been arrested, a homeless woman. Of course, she didn't steal the comic books but who was to say that the robbery and the murder were even related? The police could have made a mistake, which, goodness knows, happened enough.

Mrs. Peabody should tell the police about the comic books. But what if they weren't even the stolen ones? Anyway, she learned about the importance of the comic books through listening in to a phone call and she didn't want to admit that.

So as curious as Mrs. Peabody might be—her sense of survival was stronger. So she would do something that was totally against her nature.

She would remain quiet. For the time being.

"Mrs. Peabody?"

She heard someone hammering on the door, which frightened her. Lately she was very fearful and why shouldn't she be? Someone in Honeyspoon had been brutally murdered. And what about the Eastmans? Maybe they knew that she knew—that the man who had called Rita told Rita that he had called and she figured out that it was Mrs. Peabody who had spoken and now Rita knew that Mrs. Peabody knew that she wasn't only a thief but an adulterer as well and maybe she was afraid that Mrs. Peabody was going to tell her husband. And what if Terrence told his father that he caught Mrs. Peabody peeking in the room?

"Who is it?" she asked with a shaky voice. Oliver was by her side, growling. Maybe he would scare the intruder away.

"It's Steven."

"Who?"

"It's the mailman." He sounded impatient and not at all intimidated by the dog.

"Oh."

Steven never rang her bell. This was not good. But at least he wasn't a murderer.

"What do you want?" She opened the door just a crack.

"What do you mean what do I want?" She caught the sneer on his face and smelled tobacco on his breath. Shouldn't he be more polite? Didn't she pay his salary? Never mind the fact that she no longer paid taxes. "I want to give you your mail."

"So stick it in the slot," she ordered as she prepared to slam the door.

"I got a certified letter. You have to sign for it."

Again, that could not be good. He handed her a chewed up pen through the small opening and she scrawled her name, Nancy Adele Peabody.

"It's from *Steigers*," he announced, rather gleefully as he threw a bright yellow envelope into the slot.

"You're not supposed to be reading other people's mail."

A few seconds later the rest of the mail came tumbling in. She picked it up as she ripped open the notice from *Steigers*.

They were suing her for a lousy $23.18. Well, they would have to stand in line. And when she rummaged through the rest of the mail, there was actually a catalog from the same store, trying to entice her with sale items. On one hand they were suing her, on the other, they were begging her to spend more and go deeper in debt.

Darn capitalists.

An advertisement, a cream promising to banish wrinkles. Well, that ship had sailed long ago. An envelope from *St. Hedwig's* for the Sunday collection basket—she hadn't been in that church for years except to attend the funeral of Millicent Hopwood and she only went because after the cemetery the mourners were being treated to a lunch at *The Yankee Peddler*.

And there was one white envelope addressed to *Violet Rose Shaw* at *33 Lily Lane*.

The foolish mailman had delivered the mail to the wrong house again—which might work in her favor since she could deny that she ever received the notices from *Steigers*.

Mrs. Peabody knew exactly what she should do with the mysterious white envelope. Take a bus downtown, return the letter to the post office—and report Steven while she was at it. She might even stop at *Neisers* and tell Nellie what she had learned from babysitting at the Eastmans. That information was certainly worth a piece of chocolate triple layer cake.

Well, maybe not.

But curiosity won over the day and she tore open the envelope.

To her surprise it was just one sentence typed on a green piece of stationary.

I saw what you did.

What did that mean?

Mrs. Peabody put down the letter thoughtfully. Violet Rose had obviously done something. Was that something the cause of her death? Maybe it had never been about the comic books at all. Maybe she was being blackmailed and the blackmailer killed her.

Although it was usually the other way around.

And as far as the homeless woman was concerned, she couldn't have written the letter. Not unless she had access to a typewriter, which was doubtful.

Again Mrs. Peabody thought about telling the police about the mysterious letter. But how could she without admitting that she had opened mail not addressed to her but to a dead woman?

No, it would be best not to get involved. After all, she was at the library when the police arrived to investigate the crime scene. Everyone knew she hadn't gotten along with Violet Rose—although that was hardly Mrs. Peabody's fault. In all the *Perry Masons* she had seen on television, if a person took too much of an interest in the crime, it was usually because they were involved somehow.

Best to mind her own business and hope it wasn't too late.

TWENTY-FOUR

WHEN THE DOORBELL RANG, Kate was watching *Gunsmoke*. She debated on whether or not to answer it because she knew instinctually who it was. She could pretend she wasn't home but it wouldn't matter. Everything she remembered about Stanley told her that he wasn't a man who gave up easily.

He was standing there, barely recognizable. His blue black hair was practically gone. In its place were a few gray wisps and a pink discolored scalp. His lean, tight body had been replaced by a layer of flab around his midriff and a protruding stomach. A slightly misshapen face—as though he had been in a bad fight and had lost—the color of a gigantic beet, looked back at her, the blue eyes faded to a misty gray.

It was the voice she recognized, low and whiny. That hadn't changed. He was carrying a bouquet of withered carnations in one hand, the other hand, which was high in the air, was swinging a bottle of what looked like cheap whiskey.

"Aren't you going to invite me in, baby doll?"

Baby doll. No one had called her baby doll in all those years, and she didn't want to hear it now. It sounded sordid. She didn't want to let him in either. But that didn't matter. He just pushed his way in and sank down on the red vinyl and chrome kitchen chair.

"You look good, baby doll, you really do. What have you been up to? Working as a librarian?"

Kate managed to nod.

He laughed and shook his head. "You? A librarian? Sounds kind of dull. To be honest this whole town seems kind of dull."

"Not at all." For some reason Kate felt she had to defend it. "Actually there was a murder in the library."

His eyes popped. "You're kidding me? Who done it?"

"Some homeless woman who hangs out under the bridge."

"Huh, so even a sleepy little town like Honeyspoon has its dirty laundry. What do you say you get me some soda and a shot glass and I'll fix us some drinks?"

"I don't have soda or a shot glass."

Stanley frowned and she noticed that he was missing several teeth. "Who doesn't have a shot glass?"

"I don't." The doorbell rang and Kate felt a small thread of fear. She didn't want anyone to meet Stanley—whom she was deeply ashamed of—and then wonder about the connection.

"Aren't you going to answer it?"

She better or he would.

Joanne stood there, all dressed to the nines, in a brown shirtwaist dress with an olive green cinch belt, brown tee strap shoes, carrying an oversized brown purse, smelling of *Wind Song Perfume*. "I was wondering if I could borrow your brown cardigan. It's a little chilly out…" She stopped talking when she saw Stanley and her eyes widened as she goggled at him. "I'm sorry. I didn't know that you had a guest. If I'm disturbing you…"

"You're not disturbing us," Stanley rose, slightly unsteady on his feet.

Joanne flashed a smile and opened the door wider, stepping in.

"I'm Stanley Reed, an old boyfriend of Catherine's from New York." He extended a sweaty hand.

"I'm Joanne Kennedy, an old friend of Catherine's. From grammar school actually."

"No kidding."

An uncomfortable silence ensued.

"So, is it all right if I borrow your brown sweater? I'll bring it back tomorrow, I promise. I'm having dinner with Malcolm."

"Hey, I got a great idea." Stanley sank back into the chair, the legs squeaking slightly under his weight. "I'm getting hungry myself. Why don't we double?"

Kate and Joanne looked at each other. Although Kate was curious about meeting Malcolm, she didn't want Joanne to spend any time with Stanley. He was like a time bomb. There was no telling what he might say or do and Joanne tended to be so judgmental.

"That might be fine," Joanne said, a little reluctantly—maybe she wanted to be alone with Malcolm, Kate guessed. "We're going to be at *Valle's* in about a half an hour."

"Well, it's settled then." He winked at Joanne, "We will be there."

Joanne blushed. "About that sweater…"

KATE DIDN'T DRINK. For one thing, she didn't enjoy the taste. For another, it upset her stomach. And thirdly, the one time she did get drunk, well, it hadn't ended well. But tonight she was so all aflutter, and she needed something to take the edge off. So when they arrived at the restaurant—in a cab, which she had to pay for—she ordered a Whiskey Sour and lit up one of Stanley's *Camel* cigarettes for courage.

She was going to need it because she was expecting a long night, which it was. Much to her embarrassment Stanley spent a good part of the evening grilling Malcolm and, although Kate wanted to know more about him, she thought his endless questions were rude.

And it wasn't as if Stanley didn't have a checkered past himself.

But Malcolm answered rather cheerfully. He had grown up in Ohio as an only child. He went to college and became an accountant but he didn't enjoy working with numbers, so he opened a small antique store. He was doing well, but wanted a change so he was looking to settle in a small, friendly town. Like Honeyspoon.

Joanne beamed at this while Kate sat clam like. But still, she could not shake the notion that somewhere her paths had crossed with Malcolm's, although she didn't know how that was possible when he had lived so far away.

When a harried waitress with a wart on her face hurried over, Kate ordered sparingly, just in case she was going to be responsible for the taxi home. Joanne had no such fears. She ordered a salad, a steak with a baked potato and sour crème, green bean casserole and even angel food cake for dessert. And a second highball.

Malcolm studied the menu for a long time and then asked if the restaurant still served their famous French onion soup. They did and he ordered a large bowl and a small salad. Was he trying to save money? Maybe he wasn't doing as well as he claimed.

Luckily, Stanley didn't talk too much about himself and he didn't mention going to prison—which in a small, friendly town like Honeyspoon—that news would spread faster than measles.

When the waitress finally plunked the bill down, Malcolm paid for Joanne—Kate and Stanley each paid for themselves, although Stanley had to borrow two dollars from Kate.

It wasn't until she was safely tucked in bed that night—exhausted and still tense, because who knew when Stanley would show up next—would he come to the library and give plump Margaret a heart attack? Then she remembered what happened when Malcolm ordered.

He had asked if they still made the world famous French onion soup. Except how would he know about the soup unless he had been in Honeyspoon before?

Something was not quite right. That Kate knew for sure. What she didn't know was if the something that wasn't quite right had anything to do with the death of Violet Rose Shaw.

TWENTY-FIVE

Mrs. Peabody decided to take herself downtown and pay some money towards her electric bill. She could go to the library and catch up on the world news, but somehow after Violet Rose's murder, the thought of being there gave her the willies. Not today. Better to stop by at *Neisers* to chat with Nellie. What Mrs. Peabody had learned was worth an entire piece of free prune Danish and it was best to go early in the morning, before the counter got busy with office workers who were on their fifteen minute breaks.

She had plenty to say.

Of course, she would have to swear Nellie to secrecy even though something told her that Nellie could not be trusted. She was always whispering to other patrons, collecting information, which slightly annoyed Mrs. Peabody, especially since Nellie seldom shared any interesting gossip with her. Mrs. Peabody had a good mind not to tell her anything.

Although Tuesday was the day that Pete made coconut cream pie.

Well, she would tell Nellie some things, but not everything. That way she would minimize the danger, somewhat.

She made certain that she wore her oldest clothes downtown. She wanted to look downtrodden and poor, hoping the snotty lady at the electric company would take pity on her. Maureen Hines was dressed in a nifty lemon drop yellow suit, the kind that Mrs. Peabody would buy if she could afford it, even though she wouldn't have anywhere nice to wear it and the yellow would probably make her look sallow. Maureen glared at her, took her money and then she barely touched it as though it had some sort of germ on it. In neat, perfect cursive she wrote out a receipt and then shoved it at Mrs. Peabody. All of this transpired without Maureen saying a word.

Well, at least she didn't say anything about shutting off the electricity.

THE COCONUT CREAM pie wasn't ready. Pete had gotten in late, something about bed bugs, and waiting for the exterminator—which made Mrs. Peabody think twice about eating any of his pies. She had to make due with a half of a honey drip donut and several broken pieces of an oatmeal raisin cookie—which tasted more like oatmeal than cookie.

"Anything new?" Nellie said as she scooted over the creamer and the glass jar of sugar.

"I babysat for the Eastman's last night." Mrs. Peabody looked around but the only one at the counter was Mr. Stringer, who had finally decided to buy his own paper and his nose was buried in what looked like the sports page. "I discovered her stash. You would not believe what that woman has stolen, hundreds of dollars-worth of merchandise."

"I know all about her shoplifting habit." Nellie frowned, as though this was old news and not worth the crumbs she had thrown at Mrs. Peabody. "I've seen her myself, combing the aisles, dropping a lipstick in her purse, or a bottle of pills for stomach problems. I never say anything, I just look away. You know me. I don't like to get involved in other people's business. I keep to myself."

Nellie was about to walk away, which Mrs. Peabody didn't want to happen. Sometimes the waitress was the only person she spoke to for days—except for Oliver, of course, but he hardly counted. So quickly Mrs. Peabody made a decision. "There is something else." Mrs. Peabody pulled on Nellie's red checked apron strings and mouthed, "She has a lover."

"What?" Nellie said a tad too loudly.

With a wave of her hand, Mrs. Peabody suggested that Nellie lower her voice. She began to whisper and Nellie leaned over the counter. Mrs. Peabody noticed for the first time that Nellie had no eyebrows at all, just penciled in with brown, smudged and not terribly even. Somehow that made Mrs. Peabody feel slightly superior— after all, her own eyebrows might be gray but they were thick and symmetrical. "I answered the phone when I was babysitting. A man was on the other end of the line, speaking in loving terms and it wasn't Lawrence." She could have gone on and mentioned Rita's pregnancy but she thought she should draw the line someplace.

"Oh." Nellie put her beefy hand to her mouth. "And here Lawrence is such a hard-working man!"

"Hey, Powers," Pete called from the kitchen, "your scrambled eggs with crisp bacon is up." He shot a filthy look at Mrs. Peabody. "And put another pot of coffee on. I don't pay you to gossip with the customers, especially ones that barely order."

Nellie's only response was a grunt as she wiggled

away. Mrs. Peabody finished the last of the donut, laid down twenty-five cents and a nickel for a tip—with all the information she had given Nellie, Nellie should be tipping her—then she scooted over to the sewing aisle. She needed to buy a spool of brown thread to repair a hole in her stocking.

Standing in the check-out line was maddening. A young girl with bright blue eye shadow and scarlet lipstick on her teeth was examining a box of parakeet seed, flipping it this way and that before she finally screamed for the manager. "Hey, Al, price check!"

Mrs. Peabody looked up and saw Nellie whispering to Mrs. Vogt, who had suddenly appeared from nowhere and was now wide eyed, a shocked expression on her flat face.

Then Mrs. Peabody knew that whatever she had told the waitress would be all over town in just a matter of moments.

SHE WAS WALKING Oliver around the neighborhood. Since Mrs. Peabody had put the scarf on Oliver, he seemed to walk taller and prouder and with more confidence, as though he knew someone loved him and was taking care of him.

And then Rita flung open her door and stomped down to the sidewalk. She was wearing a plaid housecoat, oversized, fluffy slippers, pink rollers covered by a green hair net.

She stood directly in front of Mrs. Peabody, blocking her way, so she couldn't pass. "You old biddy!" she screamed, as she pointed her index finger—perfectly polished with scarlet, her pearl white moons exposed.

Of course, Mrs. Peabody knew exactly what Rita

was referring to, but she decided not to take the bait. "I don't know what you're talking about." Her voice was high pitched, and even to herself, it sounded false.

Rita advanced towards her but retreated when Oliver began to growl.

"You told the entire neighborhood that I'm having an affair," Rita said bitterly.

"Well, aren't you?"

"I am not. I don't know what you heard on the phone."

Mrs. Peabody managed to shrug. "If you're not, then you have nothing to worry about."

"My husband is not pleased and everyone is talking. Why would you make up a lie like that? I just don't understand. I even bought you groceries because I thought she's a poor old lady and that's my good deed for the day. But this…this is unforgivable."

For one moment Mrs. Peabody thought that maybe she had made a mistake, that maybe she had misunderstood. She looked up and noticed people peeking out from their curtains, Mrs. O'Connor with her bratty daughter, Laureen, Mrs. Heartbreaker and Mr. Heartbreaker—who was paralyzed after he dived drunk in shallow water into the Community Field Pool—Mrs. Notewire and her fat cat, Bacall, and Mrs. Tully, holding a glass of what looked like a martini.

Mrs. Peabody knew that she was a busybody, but she knew what she heard and she wasn't going to be called a liar.

"Besides," Rita continued to rave, "what gave you the right to answer my phone in the first place? You were just supposed to be babysitting. Terrence told me that you were snooping in his room."

"I was merely..."

"You're going to hell!"

Mrs. Peabody jerked on Oliver's leash. She didn't know quite what to say, so instead, ashamed, feeling her face flush, she just mumbled, "Sorry."

Then Mrs. Peabody dragged Oliver home, swallowed three Bayer aspirins with a glass of sherry and took to her bed.

TWENTY-SIX

"Mother Superior, may I speak to you for a moment?"

Mother Superior stopped and stared at Sister Regina Rachel. "Can't this wait until after the novena?"

"Well..."

"It's only a half an hour and we're already late. Surely, God comes first and whatever is on your mind will be made better after you pray on it."

"Of course, Mother." Although Sister didn't feel much like praying. She felt as if she should go straight to the hospital and be with her father and her sister, Nora. She had only been there once but her father wasn't even in his bed. He had been taken down for some tests and they were told it might be a few hours. So they left. Mother Superior said that they would return but so far that hadn't happened.

She needed to go to the police first though, and tell them the truth. There was no way that Thelma Lou could have committed that murder because she was with Thelma Lou that very morning.

But she had taken the vow of obedience, so she followed Mother into the small chapel to pray for miracles.

Sister Regina Rachel prayed but her mind was not on the responses. Instead she saw her father in the hospital bed, dying. She saw Thelma Lou at the police station, crying, as the police grilled her and she pleaded her innocence. And then she saw something else. She saw someone stalking her, afraid that she might tell who she saw the morning Violet Rose Shaw had been killed. Someone who was hoping to kill her by throwing a rock at her.

The Mass ended and her stomach tightened as Mother Superior approached her. "Let's talk in my office."

Mother Superior's office was more like a cell, containing a small desk, a few papers held by paperweights, one of the Infant of Prague, one of the Virgin Mother, with outstretched hands. A cross hung on the wall and Sister sat on one straight back chair, while Mother Superior took the other one, behind the orderly desk.

Before Sister could say anything, Mother Superior spoke. "I'm glad you asked to speak to me, Sister. I've been meaning to talk to you."

Sister held her breath. Had Mother Superior found out that she had left the convent without permission?

"As you know, Sister Louis Michael has been my assistant for thirteen years. She's very good at it and I've come to depend on her. Unfortunately, it's going to be difficult for her to continue her duties."

"That's too bad," Sister said, wondering what that had to do with her, and hoping they weren't going to put the sixth graders in with her own class.

"They found something in her." Mother Superior swallowed as her fingers closed around the large crucifix that hung around her neck on a chain. "Actually, it was in one of her bosoms. She's going to need a lot of tests, a lot of treatments, hopefully to arrest the disease before it spreads further. Unfortunately, the prognosis is not good. We don't know enough about this particular sickness. In the meantime Sister Louis Michael will be transferred to Mt. St. Agnes, where she can be cared for while she is fighting this dreaded disease. Of course, she knows that all of this is God's will."

"I'm am so sorry, Mother, but…"

"You may be wondering why I'm telling you all of this. I've spoken to the Bishop and he and I both feel that you would be perfect to assume her duties."

"Me?"

"Of course, you would have to continue with your teaching, as Sister Louis Michael did. I guess I'm going to have to double up the sixth and seventh grades. Poor Sister Bernadette Beatrice! But I can't tell you how impressed I have been with your obedience, with your willingness to work with others. Even when you were struck with that rock, you never complained, never made an issue out of it."

"I'm honored, of course."

"As you should be. But I sense hesitation in your voice. Is that because you're afraid you're not up to the task? Believe me, I've given this a lot of thought, and I've prayed on it. You are a shining example to all of the sisters." Mother Superior flashed a rare smile, her black eyes gleaming like two beetles. "Now what is it, you wanted to tell me?"

"I'm worried about my father. I'd like to go to the hospital as soon as possible."

"Of course. You should have spoken up sooner. I will call Mrs. Boyle and see if she can take over your classroom duties. I won't be able to drive you because the brakes on the van are being repaired. We'll take a taxi and we'll go together."

"Thank you."

"And while we are riding we will pray that your father will be well."

As long as they weren't going to pray the rosary, because hers was still missing.

When Sister stepped in and saw her father, she thought she made a mistake with the room number. She barely recognized him, lying down, oxygen in his nose, IVs hooked to his arm, connecting to beeping machines. Her father lying pale and childlike, his face as chalk white as the sheet that covered his frail body, a body that had been strong and fit after working so many years in construction.

Her sister, Nora, was sitting by his side. Sister hadn't seen her family for over a year. Nora's blonde hair had turned a yellow white, her brown eyes were sunken, her lips narrow and chapped. She had gained weight, mostly in the middle, stick legs supporting a small balloon.

Still her skin was flawless, her nose, small and upturned, her teeth gleamed like Chicklets. She was the pretty sister.

"Roselyn, you've finally come!" Nora went over to Sister and embraced her awkwardly. Sister caught the scent of roses and she pulled away, when she saw the sharp look on Mother Superior's face, knowing that all touching should be kept to a minimal.

"How is he doing?" Sister asked.

"I'm doing fine." Her father's eyes snapped open. "Just a minor one, that's all. I was lucky."

Sister let out a breath of air and the same time her father made a funny, rasping noise.

"You need to stay lucky." Nora bent down and adjusted the sheet. "That means you have to give up your two packs of *Lucky Strikes* cigarettes and your three beers every night. Your life has to be stress free. Remember what the doctor said, how important it is to stay calm."

"Then maybe it's time for good news." It was the first time Mother Superior spoke. "Mr. Randazzo, you're going to be very proud of your daughter. She is going to be my assistant, second in command. I'm going to take her under my wing, groom her, maybe to become a Mother Superior one day!"

Her father broke into a huge grin, exposing his toothless gums. He had lost his teeth years ago and, because the dentures never fit properly, he had given up wearing them. "You make me so proud, Roselyn."

"Sister," Mother Superior corrected him.

"You were always such a good girl. Always did what you were told. Never tried to test me, or bend the rules. Wish it were a family trait." He stared at Nora, who had gotten pregnant in the back seat of a car, had to marry hastily to a gas station attendant, who left her for a stripper in the next town. Since then, Nora had had two more husbands.

"And now God is rewarding you." He began to cough up something yellow and bloody. Nora rushed over, gave him a tissue and a drink of water.

God was rewarding her? Sister wondered when God would be punishing her.

TWENTY-SEVEN

Mrs. Peabody did not know how things could have gotten so out of control in such a short amount of time.

Honeyspoon had always been a quiet, peaceful town but in the three weeks since Violet Rose's murder, the atmosphere had changed. It seemed as if neighbors were growing suspicious of other neighbors, everyone was treading very carefully and people were staying indoors much more. As though no one trusted one another.

Maybe it had always been that way and maybe Mrs. Peabody never noticed that underneath the forced smiles and the "I'll pray for you," people didn't really care, unless it was trouble, because the truth was simply that only trouble was interesting.

But this wasn't just ordinary trouble. It was dangerous trouble. It was time for Mrs. Peabody to mind her own business, and she promised herself to do just that.

Until the phone rang.

It wasn't for her, of course. It never was, unless it was bill collectors. One ring meant it for the Maloneys, Connie and Bill. But since Bill had been so nasty, and so unpredictable, maybe she should find out what he was planning.

"Bill?" Mrs. Peabody's heart thumped as she recognized Rita Eastman's voice.

"I told you not to call me at home."

"I know you did but I just saw Connie headed for the bus stop. Do you know…"

"Do I know what?"

"It's all over town, that I have a lover. That old busybody…"

"Mrs. Peabody?"

"She was babysitting and, when you called me, she must have picked up the phone. You did call me two nights ago, the way you always do at eight o'clock."

"I called you."

"Well, it wasn't me who answered. Mrs. Peabody was babysitting. I should have told you."

"Yeah, you should have told me."

"Anyway, Mrs. Peabody told Nellie…"

"Who the hell is Nellie?"

"You know…"

"I don't know."

"She's that fat waitress with a nose like a hummingbird, who works behind the counter at *Neisers*. Anyway, she told one customer, who told another customer…"

Mrs. Peabody could hear Bill draw angry and exasperated breaths, while she herself was trying not to breathe at all.

"She doesn't know it's you, Bill. I don't think she recognized your voice, or she would have blabbed that also. Exactly what did you say?"

"You think I can remember?"

"Lawrence is furious. He might seem like a mild mannered man but trust me, he has a bad temper. I've told you about that. There is no telling what he might do."

"What *you* have to do, Rita, is deny, deny and deny some more."

Oliver, sleeping at Mrs. Peabody's feet, slightly leaped up and went over to the window. Mrs. Peabody could see Mrs. Notewire's cat, Bacall, right outside her door. She could see the cat and so could Oliver.

"Deny it, Rita. Tell him that old witch is just making up stories because you didn't pay her enough for the babysitting. And do you know why he will believe you? He'll believe you because he will want to. And without knowing who the man is…"

It was at the precise moment, that Oliver started to bark.

Mrs. Peabody hurriedly hung up the phone, but not before she heard Rita say, "Well, I guess now, she knows."

MRS. PEABODY EXPECTED that Bill would come marching over and he did. She took Oliver with her and hid in the bathroom, not answering the door, when she heard pounding, her heart pumping fast in response.

Why didn't a neighbor call the police? Surely, they could see that this was abuse.

Finally after what seemed like an eternity, the knocking ceased. Still Mrs. Peabody waited for a full fifteen minutes. Glancing out the window, she saw that he had gone.

It had started to drizzle, a wet, cold, November rain. She had clothing on the line, sheets and towels. Better hurry.

She was yanking the laundry off the clothes line, throwing it into the laundry basket, when she turned around and saw Bill, standing there in the rain.

His expression was ice cold, his blue eyes glaring, his beefy fists clinched.

Why had she left Oliver inside?

"You're trying to ruin my life, that's what you're trying to do."

Mrs. Peabody knew all about bullies, and she learned long ago in that orphanage, that if you didn't stand up to them, you would be forever a victim. Like dogs, they could smell fear.

"I'm not trying to ruin your life. And you're right, I should have kept what I learned to myself and for that I apologize." Bill didn't look too forgiving so she quickly added. "I could have said other things, but I didn't." The way it sounded, it came out like a threat, which wasn't what she intended.

"So what? You are going to blackmail me? So…if I don't give you money, you'll go to the police?"

Yes, Mrs. Peabody wanted money and she needed money, especially since it was a sure thing that she wouldn't be babysitting anymore for either family. But she had seen enough late night movies to know that blackmailers always turn up dead.

Was that what happened to Violet Rose?

"No, nothing like that," Mrs. Peabody said quickly. "I just want you to leave me alone."

"Leave you alone! What is that, some sort of joke?" He advanced towards her and she considered screaming for Oliver, but he was in the house and she was out here in the rain. Bill stopped suddenly, and then whispered. "You better be careful. I'm more dangerous than you think."

He stared at her some more with those menacing blue eyes and she stared right back until he turned around and walked away.

She didn't doubt for a moment that he was dangerous and she better forget whatever she had learned.

LATER THAT NIGHT when she tossed and turned in her bed—her restlessness didn't affect Oliver in the least, he was sleeping soundly—she began to wonder.

Bill had asked her if she planned on going to the police. But why would she go to the police? Why would they care if Rita was carrying a child that might not be from her husband? That wasn't against the law, at least not in this country.

Then it hit here. It hit here so hard that she gave a little cry of terror and then she bolted upright and began to sweat. All the pieces fell in place with a terrifying speed.

It was all about the magazines she had seen Terrence reading. At first she thought that Rita might have shoplifted them from the library the way she took threads and lipsticks. Taking a few comic books wouldn't be so bad if they weren't classics—if they weren't tied to a murder.

She suddenly remembered another phone call—a nun complaining about the boys trading all the time.

So maybe Terrence traded with Andrew for the comic books. And that made perfect sense when she recalled how ballistic Bill was when he thought that she had stolen his magazines. He wasn't referring to *True Confessions* or *Movie Gossip*. He was referring to the stolen publications.

The publications that would tie him to murder.

And if Bill had murdered once, he could murder again. He himself had admitted that he was a dangerous man. Should she go to the police? Without proof?

They might not believe her. Rita might have already thrown away the comic books.

No, better stay out of it. This time for sure. Besides, hadn't they arrested the homeless lady for the murder?

And just in case, she was going back to church.

TWENTY-EIGHT

ANDREW WAS IN his room, trying to do division—which was an impossible task because he had yet to learn his multiplication tables—when the screaming match began. His parents' arguments were nothing new. Andrew had grown up, hearing them yelling at each other, but there was always a chance that it could escalate into something violent and unpredictable.

Besides, it scared his brothers.

Adam carried little Arthur into the bathroom. "What are they fighting about now?" Adam asked, looking somewhere between resigned and scared.

Andrew shrugged and moved closer to the stairs.

"I saw it with my own eyes," his mother said. "She was on line trying to cash in her S&S stamps. She was wearing my mother's sapphire ring. There was no way she could have gotten that unless you gave it to her! How dare you give my jewelry to another woman!"

"I never gave her any jewelry. It must have been something that just looked like your ring!"

"Except my ring is missing!"

Andrew felt like throwing up.

"You don't think that it's all over town that Rita has a lover. I just never thought," his mother sobbed, "that it was going to be you!"

"It's not me." Even to Andrew, his father's voice sounded weak but with more gusto, he screamed, "I did not give her that ring. I don't know how she got it, but it wasn't from me."

"You're a liar." Andrew heard glass break against the wall.

Arthur started to cry and Andrew went into the bedroom, searched for one of his GI Joe figures, and put it into Arthur's hand. "You can play with this, but just be careful."

Arthur stared at it, as though he wasn't sure what to do and Andrew started down the stairs.

"Don't go down there," Adam begged, looking tearful.

Andrew didn't answer. How could an eight year old boy understand how complicated everything had become?

"You want to throw things. Well, I can throw things too."

Andrew watched as his father hurled a bottle of root beer against the wall, where it hit with a definite crash and dripped brown suds on the orange shag rug.

"I... I... I have to talk to you." Andrew had reached the bottom stair, but his voice was so muffled that neither parent heard him.

"I've had it with you!" His mother was crying loudly now, "I want a divorce."

"A divorce! Don't make me laugh! How the hell are you going to support yourself? With those measly tips you get from those rich snobs from *Lakeshore Lane*? Sure, you can have a divorce, but I'm taking the boys, Adam and Arthur."

Adam and Arthur. "Mommy," Andrew yelled out.

"Go upstairs," his mother ordered.

"It's...it's...it's important."

"Did you hear what your mother said?" His father advanced towards him, expression hard, his eyes narrowing. "Get out of here, you stupid stuttering piece of blubber!"

"William!" his mother gulped.

"Well, that's what he is. I tell you that I'm ashamed that he's my son. Comes from your side of the family, fat, useless wimps. My mother always said, blood will tell. You leave me, you take him." He turned towards Andrew. "Now, get the hell out of my sight." He raised his hand, as though he was going to hit Andrew, so Andrew turned around quickly, running up the stairs, fumbling and falling.

"Big fatso," his father taunted. "Can't even walk up the stairs."

Adam and Arthur were waiting in the bathroom. Arthur had stopped crying and was sitting in the bathtub, playing with the small figure. Adam's eyes were filled with tears. "He's so mean."

Andrew heard the front door slam. He looked out the window, hoping his father had left, but no, it was his mother, and the maniac was still downstairs.

"Wait here," Andrew said. "I'll be right back."

"You're not going downstairs again, are you?"

"No, but I have something to do." He watched as his father stepped out on the front porch and lit a cigarette.

Quickly Andrew tiptoed into his parent's room. It reeked of tobacco and whiskey. He found the telephone underneath the dirty sheets.

He knelt down and dialed 0, then asked for the police.

"Gary Bennis, here. Can I help you?"

"My name is...name is...name is..."

"What is your name, son? Are you in danger?"

Andrew took a deep breath. "Andrew Maloney. And I know… I know…who stole those comic books from the library. And I know who threw that rock at Sister Regina Rachel."

TWENTY-NINE

Although Mrs. Peabody loved her dog, walking Oliver at night was not one of her favorite things, especially when it was cold and damp. Some people just opened the door and let their dogs run wild, but Mrs. Peabody was not about to do that. Oliver might run away, get picked up by the dog pound, get hit by a car. Or return to the place where he had come.

No, best to keep Oliver with her.

She walked around the circle, waiting for Oliver to do his business. If he didn't, then he would often wake up in the middle of the night crying and Mrs. Peabody would have to take him out to the back yard at three in the morning.

Oliver didn't really like to do his business on the concrete. He preferred going on dirt or grass, necessitating Mrs. Peabody to walk in back of the apartment complexes near the corner of the wooded areas.

Right now she was in the area of the Eastmans. For one short minute, she thought about knocking at their back door and apologizing for any trouble she might have caused them, but the minute passed and so did her resolve. Rita might tell Bill and that entire can of worms might come squirming out again.

One moment Oliver was stooping—for which Mrs. Peabody was most grateful—the next second he straightened up and broke free, heading into the woods.

Mrs. Peabody's heart pounded as she called to him. She could see him up ahead. He had stopped and was staring down, probably at a scared rabbit, and she wasn't going to have any of that.

She called again but Oliver wasn't budging.

Mrs. Peabody had always hated the woods. She hated trees that rained leaves on your head. She hated insects that stung you and sometimes invaded your living area. She hated wild animals, who might eat you alive. But her love of Oliver overrode her fear and she made her way slowly down the narrow path.

"Bad boy!" she called out. "You are such a bad boy!"

Oliver didn't even lift his head in response.

When Mrs. Peabody finally approached, she saw in horror what Oliver was staring at. A single, white hand, sticking out from a pile of leaves. A hand with gleaming crimson nails, their little half white moons exposed.

Someone dead.

Someone like Rita Eastman.

Mrs. Peabody stifled a scream and tugged at Oliver's collar, hurrying from the scene.

She knew exactly what she should do.

Call the police. And tell them what? That she had discovered another body, the second time on a site where there had been a murder. And in the case of Violet Rose, she didn't get on with Rita, and even had a very public argument with her.

No, she was going to go straight home. She was going to take to her bed with a cup of strong sweet tea, put on her Patti Page record, take out a copy of *True Confession*, to read about women who had bigger problems that her.

Let someone else discover the body.
Until she heard the sirens.

How could the police have found her so soon? Had someone seen her coming from the woods?

Would she be carted off to jail?

Who would take care of Oliver?

She must hurry, although it mustn't look as though she was running away. Just an ordinary woman, walking an ordinary dog.

The police car stopped abruptly in front of the Maloney resident. Wayne and Gary stepped out of the car and made their way up the sidewalk.

Mrs. Peabody and Oliver stopped, watching as everyone from the neighborhood drifted outside. Kate must have just returned from work. She was wearing a navy skirt and a prim white blouse. Joanne was dressed in a housecoat with purple rollers in her hair, Mrs. Vogt with flannel pajamas, decorated with swirls of cotton candy.

Wayne rapped on the Maloney door with his fist.

"All right, all right," Bill shouted. "I'm coming." And coming he did. In a pair of raggedy shorts, and in a dirty undershirt, he opened the door.

"What the hell do you want?"

"We have a warrant to search the premises."

"What are you talking about?"

"We got an anonymous tip."

"What kind of a tip?" To Mrs. Peabody Bill sounded curious and something else in his tone, something she had never heard before. Frightened.

Wayne didn't answer, just pushed through the door, Gary following inside.

Whispers swept across the crowd.

"What's happening?"

"I think Bill is going to be arrested."

"Finally Constance did the right thing and called the police. That man has been abusing her for years."

"I heard them. Everyone heard them. He was throwing things at her. Could have killed one of the kids."

Bill looked over the crowd and his eyes stopped at Mrs. Peabody. He stared at her for a long while. Now it was she who was scared.

NOT SCARED ENOUGH to not watch the drama from the window when she scrambled inside. She watched, stunned, for ten minutes before she saw Bill coming out in handcuffs. Trailing behind him was Gary, holding the comic books.

But how did the comic books find their way back to the Maloneys when they had just been at the Eastmans? Had the boys traded back? Who had made the anonymous call?

Had it been Rita and when Bill discovered what she had done, he murdered her? Although, Mrs. Peabody thought, he did look genuinely surprised that someone had called the police.

Well, it was none of her business.

And it was going to stay none of her business.

MRS. PEABODY WAS chilled to the bone. After all she was elderly, with a slight heart condition, and it was all too much for her. Seeing the body of Violet Rose, and now the dead body of Rita Eastman, watching Bill get arrested. But maybe this was it—the end of all the trouble.

Two different murders—Thelma Lou had murdered Violet Rose and Bill had murdered Rita because she told the police that he had stolen the comic books. Or maybe he killed her because she was pregnant.

Or just maybe—Rita was being blackmailed and the blackmailer killed her. After all, Mrs. Peabody had seen all those items in a box, which said *In Payment To*, as though Rita was giving items to a blackmailer. Goodness knew Rita had done a lot of unethical things. And Violet Rose? Well, Mrs. Peabody had seen the blackmail note herself, addressed to Violet Rose. She wondered what Violet Rose had done.

Had both women been killed by a blackmailer?

Mrs. Peabody had no shortage of theories, and Rita's body hadn't even been found yet. And when it did?

Mrs. Peabody would be silent.

A HOT CUP of tea and a few shortbread cookies—the kind she kept to be eaten as a special treat when she had a hard day and lately she was having a lot of hard days—then she would take to her bed.

The phone rang. Surely it was going to be for the Maloneys but no, it rang three times without stopping.

She waited, wanting to ignore it. But curiosity won out, although if it were someone looking for information, she wasn't giving out any.

"Hello," she asked with trepidation.

"Mrs. Peabody, this is Connie Maloney." She sounded breathless. "You probably know that my husband is being arrested. The entire neighborhood knows. Mr. Vogt offered to drive me to the police station, but I need someone to stay with the boys. Do you think you could come over and babysit?"

"Now?" she asked miserably.

"Well, yes, now."

"I'm getting ready to go to bed. I've had a very long day."

"I'll pay you double."

Mrs. Peabody hesitated.

"Please, I'm begging you."

"All right, I'll be right over."

Hopefully, Bill would not be coming home with Connie. One thing was for certain. She was bringing Oliver with her.

She found the three boys huddled together on the couch, as Connie dashed out of the house.

Adam was crying, Arthur was sleeping, Andrew was angry.

"Why did the police take my daddy away?" Adam sobbed.

"Because he's a bad man," Andrew answered. "He committed a crime. He stole some comic books."

"Who cares about some old comic books?" Adam gulped. "I can pay for them myself. I have 38 cents saved."

"Why don't we have a nice snack?" In spite of her hammering heart, Mrs. Peabody was rather hungry herself. "Maybe some nice potato chips."

"We don't got any," Adam said, as he climbed off the couch. "But we have some cookies."

"We're not supposed to open those," Andrew said.

"I think your mother might make an exception." She went into the kitchen. "After all, you had a shock and there is nothing like a sweet treat to take the sting out of a bad situation."

The cookies were sugar cookies, not her favorite.

Well, she would take a few home anyway, to eat with her morning coffee.

She brought the bag inside, tore it open, gave each boy two, while Arthur continued to sleep. The boys were chewing the cookies, when Oliver jumped on the couch and grabbed three of them.

"You're a bad dog!" Mrs. Peabody retrieved the bag.

Adam started to laugh. "He's funny."

"He didn't have a good day," Mrs. Peabody commented, as she wondered how long it would be before someone discovered Rita's body.

"Where is it?" Adam asked suddenly.

"Where is what?"

"That silly scarf he always wears, the red one with stars on it."

Mrs. Peabody dropped the cookie she was about to eat and Oliver lapped it up.

She knew exactly where that scarf was.

And it wasn't good. Not at all.

THIRTY

KATE WALKED SLOWLY back home. She couldn't believe everything that had happened. She had never liked Bill Maloney. No one liked him. It was a well-known fact that he was a bully, but a thief and a murderer? Never would she have suspected that in a million years.

Had he really taken those comic books and killed poor Violet Rose, who must have caught him in the act?

What on earth was he thinking?

Well, at least he had been caught. She felt terrible for Connie and the boys. Connie would probably have to go on public assistance and be shamed.

AFTER A RESTLESS NIGHT, Kate decided to walk to work. It was Margaret's day to open and Kate knew that she would be just waiting with baited breath to gossip. Margaret didn't even live in the *Morning Glory Projects*. She had herself a nice house on Blueberry Road. After all, Margaret had a degree from the *Elms College*, which made her a certified librarian. Somehow Kate couldn't bear to listen to the delighted Margaret as she repeated everything she had heard. Feeling sorry for Bill's family would never enter her mind.

The moment that Kate walked out of the house, she saw a police car parked, not in front of the Maloneys, but in front of the Eastmans. Had something happened to Lawrence? Was he in cahoots with Bill?

It was all very confusing.

Mrs. Vogt was standing on her front steps, holding a coffee mug, dressed in a beige shirtwaist dress, which was slightly stained. She had a new hairdo, a poodle cut and her grayish hair was now a reddish orange color—obviously in a failed attempt to look like Lucille Ball.

"Did you hear the latest?" Mrs. Vogt whispered loudly. "I heard it from Doris, my hairdresser."

Kate shook her head.

"Rita Eastman is missing."

Kate managed to shake her head.

"Do you want to know what I think?"

Kate really didn't want to know, but she supposed she was going to know anyway.

"Everyone heard that Rita Eastman was having an affair."

Kate hadn't heard.

"It must have been with Bill. Do you know that he had the audacity to give her one of Connie's ring, a family heirloom? I saw it myself. I think that Rita and Bill were in the robbery together. He knew that the police were closing in, but he loved Rita, so he told her to go on the lam. And she did. She left Lawrence behind, and her poor little boy, Terrence. What kind of a woman would do that?" Mrs. Vogt paused for breath but before Kate could get a word in edgewise—which was just as well, because she wasn't sure what she would say, Mrs. Vogt continued with gusto. "God is going to punish those two. I just know it!"

"It's all very sad," Kate muttered.

"I wouldn't use the word sad. I would say evil. That's what it is, pure evil. And it used to be such a quiet neighborhood."

"Well, maybe it will be again," Kate said without much hope, as she walked away.

She was late so she had to hurry, walking rapidly by the slightly wooded areas, by the small row of ranch houses, by the small drugstore, by the *Honeyspoon Hospital*, by the *Honeyspoon High School*, by *Betsy's Bakery* and downtown, where she saw several young boys playing ball in the street.

It was dangerous being out there, where cars could dash through. They needed a playground, lots of space for older boys, with maybe a basketball hoop. And for the younger children, slides and swings, seesaws and sandboxes. Something like that would be valuable to the town. What purpose was the *Finster Mansion* serving? Concerts and speeches could be held at the *War Memorial*. They didn't need a 27 room crumbing mansion, which was draining the town treasury with its upkeep.

Of course, Joanne would be furious if Kate changed her vote, but what was more important? Joanne or the children of Honeyspoon?

She was at the park now and she spotted Malcolm, sitting alone on one of the benches, wearing a gray overcoat and a red bow tie. She would have said hello but she was in a hurry and he looked deep in thought. Well, why shouldn't he be resting there? He was staying at the *Roger Roberts Hotel* and maybe he just wanted a change of scenery.

Nothing strange about that.

Except a few minutes later, Connie came rushing into the park. At first Kate didn't recognize her. She was wearing sunglasses and a dusty rose raincoat. Instead of a pocketbook, she was carrying a brown grocery bag.

Connie sat herself right down beside Malcolm and

opened the brown grocery bag. They put their heads together and seemed to be studying the pile of papers.

They hadn't seen her and, for some reason, Kate knew that it was important that they did not. She stood behind the tree and watched as they became animated, nodding their heads and talking intently.

What was their connection?

Was it possible that they, too, had met through the *Lonely Hearts Club*, and Malcolm was not only courting Joanne, but Connie was well? Maybe Connie had started writing to Malcolm because she was bored with her marriage—if the rumors were true and Bill was having an affair with Rita and Connie knew it, she might figure, she was entitled to a little romance in her life as well. Malcolm couldn't come to town to court a married woman, so maybe, he was just using Joanne as an excuse.

Did any of this have to do with Violet Rose's murder or Rita Eastman's disappearance?

Kate hurried away, her head exploding with conflicting thoughts.

"YOU'RE LATE," MARGARET SAID, the moment Kate walked in the door.

"I'm sorry. I walked and..."

"Just because I'm opening doesn't give you an excuse to be late. You were probably gossiping with your neighbors, although God knows there is plenty to talk about. Here." She shoved some fruitcake into Kate's hands. "Take this down to the staff room." Since Violet Rose's murder, Margaret had not stepped one foot into the children's library. "At least the murderer has been caught, but I have my doubts about it being that homeless woman. But then again, I can't imagine Bill Maloney killing someone over a few comic books, even if they were vintage, and likely to increase in value. The police said that we won't be getting them back for a while. They have to hold them for material evidence. When they do come back, I'm not going to put them in general circulation. I'm keeping them in our safe deposit box. They have blood on them, that's what I say." She lit a cigarette, put it in her mouth, and let it dangle there.

The front door slammed and Mrs. Peabody limped in. Kate couldn't help but feel sorry for her, dressed in a thin, shabby, brown winter coat, wearing stockings with a snag in them and saddle shoes with a small hole in the toe, shoes that were just a tad too big and kept slipping up and down. The white powder she had slapped over her face made her appear ghostly.

"I haven't had a chance to update the newspapers." Margaret told Mrs. Peabody and then she looked at Kate. "I was by myself this morning."

"That's all right. I didn't see yesterday's anyway." She hobbled over to the reading room.

Margaret took Kate aside. "She doesn't look well. Rather peaked."

The door flew open again and Joanne marched in. Kate was rather surprised to see her, especially after having just seen Malcolm with Connie in the park. Had Joanne seen him as well? Did that count for her grim expression?

"Shouldn't you be at work?" was the only thing Kate could think of saying.

"I'm on my way." She glanced at Margaret. "Can I talk to you for a moment? Private?"

Margaret sneered and turned away, dropping ashes

as she left. Kate and Joanne walked towards the reading room.

It must be about Malcolm, Kate thought, *and I'm going to pretend I never saw him, because that's the right thing to do.*

But it wasn't about Malcolm. Not at all.

"I just want to remind you that two weeks from Wednesday night is a community board meeting. And they are going to be voting on the destruction of the *Finster Mansion.* It is really important that you vote to keep my building standing."

Kate hesitated because the more she thought about it, the more she was convinced that the city needed a playground more than one more decrepit mansion. "Well, I don't know. Everything is so confusing, with Bill being arrested…"

"What does Bill have to do with the voting? He's not on the committee. Oh, I know what you're thinking. You're thinking that Malcolm is going to ask me to marry him, and we're going to move far away, and I won't need this job, so what's the harm?"

"Well…" No way was Kate going to tell Joanne what she saw.

"Please stop saying well. I don't see that happening anytime soon. In the meantime, I need a job. How would you like it if they closed the library?"

"They're closing the library?" Margaret came running over.

"No such luck," Kate mumbled under her breath.

THIRTY-ONE

As soon as Mrs. Peabody became aware of the missing scarf, she wanted to immediately go and retrieve it. But, of course, that wasn't possible because she could hardly leave the boys alone and, by the time, Connie came home it was after eleven.

"They're going to keep Bill in jail," Connie sobbed as she sank into the sofa. "He admitted that he stole a few comic books from the library to settle gambling debts. But he didn't kill Violet Rose. No way! He never saw her there. I thought they had the woman who did it. And they're accusing him of hurting Andrew's teacher. Why on earth would he do such a thing? None of it makes any sense!"

"I'm sure things will turn out all right," Mrs. Peabody said, although she was sure of no such thing, especially because Bill had a reputation of being violent and unlikable.

"They're going to arraign him in the morning and set bail. But who can afford bail in a murder case? What on earth am I going to do? With Bill in jail, how can I feed my children? And even if he gets off on the murder charge, he will go to prison for the robbery." She put her face in her hands and cried loudly.

Mrs. Peabody wasn't sure what to do. She had never been good at comforting people. Besides, she had to leave, go back into the woods and get that darn scarf. And the later it got, the scarier the thought became.

She should go home and get a flashlight.

"Bill wants me to call my brother and ask him for money. But Jeffrey has always hated him. He won't give us a dime! What am I going to do?" Connie repeated, in a quivering voice, through her sobs.

Mrs. Peabody didn't know. What she did know was that she needed to leave, after she got her babysitting money.

"I'm so sorry," was all she could think of saying awkwardly, "but Oliver needs to be walked."

Oliver was curled up on the rug, sound asleep.

"Thank you so much for coming."

Mrs. Peabody rose and grabbed her coat. She stood in front of Connie.

"Oh, the money." Connie reached her hand inside her purse and took out a wallet, which looked thick with coupons. She handed over a dollar and fifty cents.

At first Mrs. Peabody didn't retrieve it. After all, she had been promised double. But then looking at Connie's tear stained face, Mrs. Peabody felt a stab of regret. No doubt Bill was going to be put away for a long time and what *was* Connie going to do? Well, who told her to marry such a bully in the first place? And more importantly why had she chosen to have not one, not two, but three children with him? Mrs. Peabody supposed that the Catholic Church was somewhat responsible, the way they didn't allow birth control. And Bill didn't look like a man, who would take no for an answer.

Mrs. Peabody took the money and when Connie went to check on her boys, she left the sugar cookies she had intended to take home, on the coffee table.

Connie and the boys needed them more than her.

Mrs. Peabody was slightly relieved when she stepped out on the porch and saw that the Eastman house was surrounded by people. That meant that she couldn't return to the woods, which she had been dreading.

She peered around nervously from the street as the local reporter, Mike Stone, stuck a microphone in Lawrence's face. "How long has your wife been missing?"

"I came home late last night. I didn't want to wake Rita, so I slept on the couch. This morning my son told me that his mother wasn't in the bedroom and it looked as if she never slept in her bed. She must have gone out and never came home. I don't understand it. She would never leave my son alone. Not in a million years. Something terrible has happened to her," he said with a strangled cry.

"How well do you know your wife, Mr. Eastman?" Mike asked.

Lawrence paused and looked out at his neighbors. "Well enough," he said dryly.

Mrs. Peabody hurried inside out of the cold. Lawrence might know Rita well enough but what he didn't know was that she was dead, right in the woods behind him.

Mrs. Peabody rose early to look for the scarf but a glance out the window told her that was not possible. Still a gaggle of people stood outside, the media, and neighbors so it wouldn't be too long before someone found the body. If they hadn't already.

If she were caught near the scene, trying to pick up the scarf, she might really look guilty. Especially since she had such a public argument with Rita.

The best course of action would be the truth, or at

least part of the truth. She would tell them that Oliver had run off and, for a few minutes, she did not know where he was. She called for him and finally, he caught up to her. She hadn't even noticed that the scarf was missing, until Adam Maloney commented on it last night.

In the meantime, she wasn't going to just sit around looking anxious. She'd take a walk downtown, go to the library's reading room and read about someone's else troubles for a change.

THE NEWSPAPERS WEREN'T READY, probably because the librarians were too busy gossiping. Well, she would just have to make do with the New York ones, although they were rather boring, mostly politics and she had no interest in that.

Except today she spotted a photo of a man who looked familiar, Stanley Reed, who resembled Kate's current boyfriend, whom she had seen leaving Kate's apartment. A brief article stated that he was being released from prison, where he had served fifteen years for manslaughter.

Manslaughter was just another way of saying—murder.

Well, that explained a lot, like why Kate left New York so suddenly but now Stanley was back and what did that mean? He was a convicted killer, but he couldn't have murdered Violet Rose because, after checking the dates, it was obvious that Stanley was still in jail. What about Rita? Why would he kill someone he barely knew? If he was going to murder someone, wouldn't he murder Kate? It was all a big fat coincidence.

Maybe.

Mrs. Peabody wished there was a place where she could find out more, where you could just type in a name and all sort of information would pop up. Maybe there might be other articles, but she'd have to ask Margaret—who was always so smug and grumpy and never wanted to help setting up the microfilm—which Mrs. Peabody found confusing. Perhaps Margaret found it confusing too.

She put down the paper just as Nellie burst into to the library, her brown eyes popping, a geranium pink tinge appearing on her sallow complexion.

"They found Rita Eastman's body!" she announced rather gleefully.

Margaret gasped and Kate paled.

"And guess what? This time the murderer left a clue!"

Mrs. Peabody kept the paper in front of her, not really seeing any of the print. Her stomach began to cramp with a prickle of fear. She needed to use the bathroom, but it was not the sort of bathroom trip she wanted to make at the library. In a while the police would come calling. It was such a small town, no doubt, Nellie would tell them where to find her.

And just as she feared in less than a half an hour, Wayne walked in and right over to her.

"Mrs. Peabody," he said in a loud voice. She had always been somewhat frightened of the arrogant Wayne, although he had no right to be snooty. Why he had been born and raised in the flats—a poor side of town. No one knew who his father was and his mother, like Violet Rose, cleaned houses for a living. "We'd like to speak to you."

Mrs. Peabody thought it important that she not show she was frightened. "Who is the we?" she asked.

Wayne ignored her question. Instead he looked around at Mr. Kitchenmaster, who was pretending to read a *Reader's Digest*, and Margaret, who was standing right near the entrance of the reading room, looking at the card catalog, at Melissa Sharon, who was sitting with a pad of yellow paper. Someone said she was writing a novel, hoping it would be the next *Peyton Place*. Well, she would have a lot of material.

"Not here," Wayne said. "We would be better off going down to the police station."

"I don't understand." She did her best to sound confused. "What is this about?"

Again, he didn't answer her questions. Just said, "More private."

"I guess I have no choice." She picked up her coat and wished that she had used the bathroom in the library, because God only knew what the bathroom at the police station was like.

They couldn't arrest her. She had done nothing wrong.

Neither had Henry Fonda in *The Wrong Man*, and look what happened to him.

What would become of Oliver?

THE POLICE STATION was only a few blocks from the library so they walked. She trudged behind Wayne, freezing in her thin coat. If she knew what was to come, she would have worn a sweater.

Wayne led her in a small cell like room. He offered her coffee and she accepted, wishing there was something to go with it, a piece of toast, or a muffin. She tried to read his expression. He seemed friendly when he offered her a piece of gum. She said no although she would have liked something to chew but they might pull her dentures out.

He shoved a piece of *Black Jack Chewing Gum* into his mouth and then sat down across from her and reached into a drawer, pulling out Oliver's scarf. "Do you recognize this?"

No sense in lying. "Yes, that's Oliver's scarf! Where did you find it?"

"Beside the dead body of Rita Eastman."

She managed a slight gasp.

"Did you know that Rita Eastman was dead?"

"Not until Nellie came into the library and announced it. What happened to her?"

"She was strangled."

"Oh my God!" Mrs. Peabody hid her face into her hands. She didn't have to pretend to be upset and shocked. All of this was too much for her.

"Do you know how the scarf got there?"

"No, except," she paused. "Yesterday I was walking Oliver by the woods in back of...in back of the Eastmans and he just ran off. I guess I wasn't holding the leash tight enough. I called for him and after several minutes he came back. I didn't realize that he wasn't wearing his scarf. Last night I babysat for the Maloneys and Adam, the little boy, asked me what happened to it. Then I realized it was missing."

It was hard to tell whether or not Wayne believed her. His face didn't change as he chewed. "I understand that you and Rita Eastman had an argument. That you spread the rumor that she was having an affair."

Mrs. Peabody lowered her eyes. She could hardly

deny what everyone knew. "I told one person, Nellie, the waitress at the counter, who works at *Neisers*. I told her in confidence. But Nellie is a blabbermouth. She spread the gossip, not me."

"Rita was pretty mad at you, right?"

"She said some things to me, that weren't very nice. But I understood, really. I should not have said anything. I was wrong." Wayne's stern expression did not change with her apology.

"You found this information out while babysitting. Right?"

"I answered the phone."

"I wonder if you found out anything else, anything else that might be helpful."

Mrs. Peabody breathed a sigh of relief now that the emphasis was off of her. While she was deciding whether or not she should mention the fact that she knew Rita was pregnant—something they might learn soon enough—Wayne interrupted her.

"Did you ever hear Bill threaten Rita?"

"Never."

"Did you ever see him hit Connie?"

"No, but I heard them arguing. Everyone heard them arguing."

"Mrs. Peabody," Wayne shoved another piece of gum in his mouth, "I'm pretty good at my job. I can read people well. I know that there is something you're not telling me."

Mrs. Peabody drew a deep breath. "There is one thing. I just learned that Kate Tringali's boyfriend is a murderer."

THIRTY-TWO

Sister Regina Rachel left her father's room, feeling confused and sickened. How could she possibly admit what she had done, sneaking out in the early dawn, breaking the rules of the convent, when everyone was talking about what a good nun she was, about all the faith they had in her.

Yet having Thelma Lou blamed for a murder she couldn't have committed, how could she allow such a thing?

She once read long ago—when the books she chose didn't have to be approved by Mother Superior—that when you have a difficult decision to make and you're vacillating, it's because you are unclear about your value system.

So what was more important?

Not destroying the faith her family and her convent had in her or freeing Thelma Lou from suspicion?

It was not a hard choice.

She was going to come clean.

Only not right now.

They passed by the busy cafeteria, their long cloaks dragging on the ground. Sister's eyes lingered for a moment on the doctors and nurses and visitors, sitting down at small tables, enjoying lunch, ham and pickle sandwiches, tuna salad stuffed into tomatoes, coffee with cinnamon buns. They all looked so relaxed, so carefree that she longed to ask Mother Superior, if maybe they couldn't go in also, for maybe a spot of tea and a banana muffin.

She didn't dare. First of all, even tea and muffins cost money and money spent on just one or two nuns were frowned upon. Everything had to be disturbed equally around the entire community.

It wouldn't matter anyway. She couldn't pretend they were normal, two friends, catching up. When people, Catholic or not, saw nuns in their habits, they became uncomfortable and awkward, probably afraid that they were going to be judged.

As though Sister was in a position to judge anyone.

Well, at least she had the day off from teaching, so rare. One never got a day off unless she was hospitalized. She thought about spending part of the day in the chapel, praying for courage and then maybe baking a batch of chocolate chip cookies for the convent.

But these hopes were dashed as soon as they settled in the taxi.

"It's barely eleven thirty," Mother Superior said. "That's wonderful! I was able to get Mrs. Boyle to take over your class, but she doubted that she could spend the entire day. She has some trouble at home. Her daughter, Susan, is being tested for polio. Mrs. Boyle thinks she might have contracted it swimming in that filthy lake by *Bear Paw Amusement Park*. I told her that we would keep Susan in our prayers. We mustn't dawdle. Driver, driver," Mother Superior rapped on the back seat, "why are you taking the long way around? Maybe so you can increase the fare. We weren't born yesterday, you know. And you should have some respect for the religious."

So much for a quiet afternoon, Sister thought.

SHE FOUND HER classroom in the lunch room under the supervision of a harried Mrs. Boyle.

"I'm so glad you're here," she said. "They have given me a terrible time!" Mrs. Boyle wasn't known for her classroom management skills—even worse than Sister's—and the most that you could say for her is that she was usually available at the last minute. "A terrible time for me and poor Andrew Maloney."

Sister spotted Andrew in the corner at a table by himself, gloomy and looking as though he had been crying.

"He's very upset," Mrs. Boyle had to scream in order to be heard above the din. "You know his father was arrested last night. Evidently, someone called in an anonymous tip and they found comic books in the basement. Mr. Maloney had stolen them to pay off some gambling debts."

Sister's heart gave a hard jolt. It was all right then. Mr. Maloney had been arrested and there was no need for her to speak up, to admit that she had been with Thelma Lou, and that she saw him run from the library. They didn't need her testimony.

God was good.

"He denies killing that cleaning woman, of course, but someone said that they actually saw him hit you on the head with a rock. So that mystery is solved. But can you imagine? I mean, why would he do such a thing?" Sister knew very well why he would do such a thing. Because she saw him running from the library. "Poor Andrew, he's taking it hard."

A group of boys, Peter, Norman, Mark and Frankie, looked up and suddenly Frankie yelled out in Andrew's direction, "Your father is a jailbird! You're going to be a jailbird too, because the apples don't fall far from the tree!"

Andrew let out a wail.

"Thank you for coming," Sister said, "and please know that we are all praying for Susan."

"Thank you."

Sister watched as Mrs. Boyle exited and then Sister marched over to Frankie and slapped him hard across the cheek.

His expression went from shock to mortification to pure loathing as his face flushed and the mark where Sister had slapped him started to redden. The other boys looked away, a little nervous, except for Peter, who seemed as though he wanted to laugh between mouthfuls of his lunch. She fought the desire to slap him also.

The noise in the lunch room ceased and the only sound was the scraping of forks as the children finished their chicken a la king.

"We don't make fun of people's misfortunes," Sister said. "Instead we support them and we pray for them. Does everyone understand?"

"Yes, Sister." The response was weak.

"Louder."

"Yes, Sister."

"Finish up quickly. We have a lot to do this afternoon." Although what she was going to do with them, she had no idea.

She walked over to Andrew and sat down across from him. He was moving around his chicken a la king with his fork. "I'm so sorry about your father. I know how hard this must be."

"It's all my fault!"

"That's ridiculous, Andrew. Your father committed

a sin. He went against the Bible. But God will forgive him and, if he did throw the rock, which injured me, then I forgive him as well. You must also."

"He didn't kill anyone," Andrew shouted out. "Just because he makes coffins people think that he doesn't mind being around dead bodies!"

"That's for the police to decide," Sister said quietly. "In the meantime, I know your father would want you to continue to do well in school and to pray for him."

"My father doesn't believe in God," Andrew mashed his cut up chicken so forcibly that a small piece of white meat hit her in the eye. "And neither do I." He wiped his face.

"You will," Sister answered.

IT WASN'T RIGHT, the feeling of being so light hearted, when she should be pitying Andrew and his family. Because she felt guilty about being happy, she was irritated, which is why she slapped Frankie. But Frankie was a bully and he had it coming.

God had heard her prayers. There was no need to admit that she left the convent, to give food to Thelma Lou, that she saw Bill Maloney leave the library at the crack of dawn. All she could hope was that Bill would deny hurting her, so no one need know that she had left the convent and seen him leaving the library.

So grateful was she for the miracle, she offered to help Sister Maria Dominic prepare supper.

Sister found a certain satisfaction and peace when she chopped vegetables, dicing cucumbers and carrots, onions and tomatoes, tossing them all in the big salad bowl. It was simple work, a mindless chore.

From the other room the radio played Connie Francis singing *Together*, and then a grim announcer spoke on the five o'clock news.

"An arrest was made in the library theft. William Maloney of 11 Lily Lane confessed to stealing rare comic books from the children's room. Following an anonymous tip, the police confiscated the comic books hidden in the Maloneys' basement. Maloney, however, has denied killing Violet Rose Shaw, who came in early that morning to clean the library. The woman they were holding, Thelma Lou Edwards, was released. The police speculate that the cleaning woman arrived around seven thirty to do her work and caught Maloney as he performed the robbery. Not expecting to see Shaw, Maloney panicked and murdered her. Maloney is being held without bail at the *Springfield Correction Center*."

Suddenly Sister felt dizzy and nauseous. She reached out to the counter, to hold herself, but the salad bowl tipped over and fell on the floor with a definite crash.

"Sister, are you all right?"

"She just fainted."

"She hasn't been right, since she was hit with that rock."

"Let's put her on the sofa."

"Does anyone have any smelling salts?"

"Why was she even in the kitchen, prepping for dinner? It's not her duty. She is supposed to be cleaning the bathrooms."

"Look, she's as white as a sheet."

"Should we call an ambulance?"

"I'm all right," Sister said. "Please just give me a minute." She closed her eyes, with one thought running through her brain. Bill Maloney was not lying. He could not have killed Violet Rose. She saw him leave the library at five forty-five, hours before the murder occurred.

So maybe Thelma Lou was guilty after all.

"It's all been too much for her. Her father's heart attack, her own assault, having that awful boy in her class, the son of a murderer! Why he could be a bad seed himself!"

"He's not a murderer," Sister whispered, but no one was listening.

"I'll help you to your room." From a distance Sister could hear the loud, competent voice of Mother Superior. "You'll feel better after you have rested and had something to eat."

But what Sister knew it was only a matter of time before Bill used her as an alibi. And she would not feel better until she told the truth, and maybe not even then.

THIRTY-THREE

Mrs. Peabody could never remember being quite so bone tired. After all, she wasn't a young woman and although she had always found gossiping entertaining, this was way too much for her. Maybe there was something seriously wrong with her. Maybe she had an iodine deficiency and she needed Goiter pills. But she didn't have any extra money to be visiting a doctor.

There was no doubt that she was under an awful lot of stress.

Just thinking about what a dangerous man Bill was gave her the willies. Why she could have been a victim herself! Hadn't he broken into her house and threatened her? The stare he gave her when he was being arrested was chilling. Hopefully, he would never get out and go straight to the electric chair.

After her talk with the police, Mrs. Peabody went immediately home. She wasn't in the mood to chat with anyone, including Nellie, who had betrayed her by sending the police towards her.

She let Oliver out in the back yard, watched him as he did his duty, then she let him in and was preparing tea—and the last of her shortbread cookies—after all she had been through, she deserved a treat—when the doorbell rang.

She stood frozen by the stove, holding her breath. She couldn't remember the last time the doorbell rang—

with the exception of Steven, but the mailman had come and gone a long time ago. No one ever came to visit her, she wasn't that important and whoever was on the other side of the door probably wasn't friendly.

Was it the police with more questions? Did they know she had been lying about finding Rita's body?

She tiptoed out of the kitchen and peeked in the window, Oliver trailing behind. She saw a car parked directly in front of her unit, a *Chevrolet Bel-Air* two toned car—in beige and bronze. Mayor Poduck was standing on her stoop, dressed in a gray overcoat with a bright red scarf and a black hat.

What possible reason would the Mayor have for visiting her?

She opened the door a crack, and Oliver, sensing her nerves, began to growl.

"What do you want?" She hoped she sounded more irritated, than scared.

"I'd like to talk to you, Nancy. May I come in?"

She couldn't picture the Mayor, with his fancy clothes, and his expensive after shave, sitting on her sofa, his feet on the threadbare carpet, his eyes on the chipped knick-knacks.

Oliver growled again.

"It's a friendly visit," he said. "So you can call the dog off."

Who knew what he wanted, but denying him access wouldn't be good. She opened the door wider.

He stepped in and looked around. She caught a flash of pity in his expression.

"Do you mind if I sit down?"

She nodded and he perched on the edge of the lazy boy chair which Louie bought five years before his death. Now there was nothing lazy about it. The cheap leather had ripped, the stuffing bursting out and if you leaned too far back, you could get a nasty jolt.

The Mayor didn't look as though he wanted to lean back. Instead he was staring at his right hand, at the small, diamond pinkie ring he wore next to the gold wedding band. "You heard about Rita Eastman."

"I had nothing to do with that!" The moment she said it, she realized that it was the wrong thing to say.

"I'm sure that's true and it would never occur to me that you did."

"Well then..." she said in a puzzled tone of voice.

"Her death leaves an unoccupied seat on the city board. Eventually, we're going to have to have an election to replace her but that probably won't happen until the first of the year. In the meantime, there are many issues that need to be resolved and I'd like to ask you if you would consider the position of an interim board member."

Mrs. Peabody was flabbergasted. No one had ever asked her to do anything, to be on any board, why she was never even picked in school, when choosing teams. She couldn't imagine that she was being considered for such an important position!

"Of course," Mayor Poduck cleared his throat, "this is entirely volunteer. We won't be able to pay you. But we do provide lunch and soft drinks at our weekly meetings and free parking..." he hesitated, realizing that she probably had no car. "We are considering you for a variety of reasons. You have lived in Honeyspoon your entire life, you know the people and you seem to be devoted to our town. Since I've been the mayor, you have never missed a meeting. You have very strong opinions on some of the issues and I feel you would be an asset to the board."

"Well," Mrs. Peabody found her voice. "It's an honor to be considered. I love this town and I want to do everything in my power to help it grow. So, of course, I would be happy to serve."

"Wonderful! The next community meeting is a week from this coming Wednesday." He jerked open his brief case and took out several folders. "These are some of the issues, we will be voting on. If you could just read the data, that way you would be up to speed. And, of course, if you have any idea of how Rita might have voted, well, you might want to consider that."

"Of course." Mrs. Peabody reached out to the folders. She would take them to bed and read them thoroughly. She would know every issue backward and forward. She would be the best board member ever. So when it came time for the election, she would be considered as a permanent member.

"There is one thing." The Mayor's lighthearted tone seem to change to cautious and heavy. "Most of the board members thought you were an excellent choice but…"

She had an enemy. She always had enemies. But that never seemed to matter. Until today.

"What you need to understand is that a lot of things we discuss as board members are quite confidential and can't be leaked. I hesitate to bring this up, but you do have a reputation for gossiping."

"Yes, I do." No sense in denying it. "But you can count on me. I won't breathe a word of anything that's being said."

"Very good." He scrambled to his feet, smiled and

then extended his red and rather sweaty hand. "Welcome aboard."

"Would it be all right, I mean, can I tell people that I'm on the board?" she asked timidly, "Or that a secret also?"

"Of course not. Eventually, we will be giving you a key to the *Finster Mansion*, where the meetings are held. I know Rita had one, of course, but I can hardly ask Lawrence at this time, if he'll give it back. Well, thank you. I think you will be a nice addition."

Mrs. Peabody walked the Mayor to the door and waved goodbye as she stepped out on the stoop. She was hoping someone saw him visit and wondered why such an important man came all the way up to the *Morning Glory Projects*.

If only there was someone she could tell, someone to brag to! Someone like her husband, Louie, who always called her a bird brain, with the sense of a wet dishrag. She wanted to scream out, "I'm a smart woman and I'm going to have a hand in shaping this city!"

Once when Louie had too much cheap whiskey to drink, he confessed that the only reason he married her was because she was an adequate cook. She hadn't cooked an entire meal, since he fell off that roller coaster.

Mrs. Peabody stared at the phone. Who could she call?

Then it came to her. Kate Tringali. That would be easy enough to do, and it wouldn't seem like bragging. She could ask Kate, as a fellow board member, if there was anything she should know, anything she would need help with. Except—Kate should probably be the last person she should call. Because suddenly just like that, Mrs. Peabody knew that Kate was the person who had objected to her being put on the board. Well, why not? Mrs. Peabody had told the police about Kate's boyfriend and, even if the police hadn't relayed that information, all Kate would have had to do was look at the newspaper that Mrs. Peabody had been reading.

No, not Kate.

Nellie? She would think it might be peculiar if all of a sudden Mrs. Peabody called her on the phone. Why, Mrs. Peabody didn't even know her number, she'd have to look it up in the phone book. Besides, Nellie knew everyone's business and she would try to soak Mrs. Peabody for information once she started to attend the meetings.

Not a living soul could Mrs. Peabody tell. Well, maybe Mildred in Iowa. She hadn't spoken to her sister in two years, but blood was blood. Besides Mildred was having some arthritis and Mrs. Peabody should really call to find out how she was feeling.

It was a long distance call, so she couldn't stay on long. She could call collect. No, that wasn't right. She could wait until seven at night, when the long distance calls were cheaper. But she was too excited.

She picked up the phone and, at the same time, it rang. The next thing she heard was Bill's voice.

"Do you have any idea how long I had to wait on line just to make this damn call?"

"I'm sorry," Connie said, not sounding sorry at all.

"You gotta get me out of here. You don't know what it's like, being locked up with common thieves, and drug addicts, and killers. I'm afraid for my life. Did you talk to your brother?"

"Yes..."

"Well?"

"He's thinking about it."

"What the hell does that mean? What is there to think about? He's got plenty of dough. Let him take out a second mortgage on his house. I'm his brother-in-law for Christ's sake, the father of his nephews. That's gotta count for something, even in your crazy family."

"I'll ask him again."

"You know I've been thinking, Connie, thinking about those comic books. I hid them in the cellar. Then I went looking for them, cause I got a buyer. I was going to pay off my debts and guess what? They were gone."

"I didn't take them, Bill."

"Then I look again a few days later, and they're right back where I left them, although a little worse for the wear. I mean, someone spilled ink on them, almost on purpose, just so I couldn't sell them."

"I didn't take them," Connie repeated.

"Who said you did? Now, I'm thinking about that anonymous tip. You tell me who is the only person who could have done that, the only person who knew I had those comics?"

Connie was silent.

Mrs. Peabody wanted to sit down, but she was afraid of making noise.

"I'll tell you who. That long nosed witch that you got babysitting for us."

Mrs. Peabody quietly sank to the floor, praying that Oliver wouldn't bark.

"But she's only been in the house a couple of times and the last time was *after* you were arrested."

"You leave the doors open, don't you? She could

have easily sneaked in, when the boys were in school and you were grocery shopping."

"Why would she do such a thing?"

Yes, why would I do such a thing, Mrs. Peabody wondered.

"Because she's a snoop, that's why. And maybe she wants to take the blame off herself, because she killed Violet Rose and Rita Eastman. Maybe she's some kind of serial killer living right on our block."

"I think you're getting carried away, really."

"Well, someone killed those ladies and it ain't me. All right, I admit I took those comic books. But no cleaning lady was there. And why would I ransack the library? I knew where they were and I was hoping no one would even notice that they were missing. That old bitty probably stole your ring and put it in Rita's jewelry box. You know Nicky McDonald up at *Fern Tracts*? He got arrested because he was pissing in front of the library. I saw him for five minutes when they were filling out the paper work. You wanna know what he told me? He told me that he saw Peabody at the police station, holed up in a room with Wayne. God knows what she was telling them. You got to get me out of here, Connie."

"I'll do what I can."

"Yeah, here is another thing. Those people I owe a little bit of money to, maybe they're setting me up, trying to railroad me for a crime. They are not the kind of people who will let things go. Tomorrow I gotta be out of here by tomorrow, because then they're moving me upstate. And if they didn't set me up, they're gonna get me in prison. I'm not safe here. You gotta do something."

"I'm sorry, really I am." Connie sounded scared. "I'll do what I can."

"Yeah, you better."

The line went dead and Mrs. Peabody held the phone for a long time. The elation she felt about being a board member had oozed out of her like air in a balloon, deflated and useless.

If Bill got released from prison, he would definitely come after her. She was in danger, but she couldn't explain that to the police without telling them how she found out.

She knew who must have moved those books—Andrew. He had given them to Terrence and then they traded back. Hadn't that nun complained about that on the phone? Was Andrew the one who had called in the anonymous tip, on his own father? That certainly wasn't nice. But then again, the entire family wasn't nice.

Yes, she had her suspicions but since most of them had come from listening in, and she couldn't reveal what she knew.

She'd have to keep a low profile and as a board member that might be hard to do.

THIRTY-FOUR

IN HIS ENTIRE eleven years, Andrew had never remembered feeling so miserable.

What had he done?

When his father first got arrested, he couldn't have been happier. The entire atmosphere of the house had changed. He and his brothers were able to laugh, play, tease each other, without worrying about when his father would come home, sweaty and angry at something someone did to him at work. He would lash out at whoever happened to be in sight.

Andrew thought his mother would be relieved also.

He never expected her to be so hysterical.

She wouldn't stop bawling, which made no sense to Andrew at all. You would think she would be thrilled to have her husband locked away, the way he treated her, always ordering her around, always barking at her. His father was a bad man. Even if he didn't kill those ladies, he stole from the library. And he had hurt Sister Regina Rachel for no reason at all—although Andrew wasn't especially fond of his teacher—she was on the mean side. But Andrew had never told his father this, and he doubted very much if his father had hurt the nun to defend him. It was a good thing that his father was out of their lives.

Andrew found his mother, sitting on her unmade bed, holding a lit cigarette.

"Do you want me to make you some tea?" he asked.
She shook her head and took a puff of the cigarette.
"It's going to be all right, Mommy. You'll see."

He expected her to look up, to give a weak smile, to offer some sort of reassurance. After all, he was the kid here. Instead she squashed the half smoked cigarette into an ashtray, which was already overflowing with butts, and reached for the pack.

"You don't understand." She put the new cigarette in her mouth and flicked the match lighting it. "Your father is going away for a long time. Even if they don't charge him with murder, they got him on the robbery. Although how much could those stupid comic books be worth anyway? And they're accusing him of hurting a nun. And maybe even murdering Mrs. Eastman. They're just trying to railroad him. They don't know your father." She gulped and took a long puff. "He could never murder anyone. He is a good, kind man."

And then Andrew knew something that he had suspected for years. His mother was nuts. She had to be nuts. Everyone knew that his father was nothing but a bully. He had no friends, not like Terrence's dad who sometimes went fishing with a bunch of guys.

"Your father is not coming home and you know where that leaves us? It leaves us in the poor house, that's where!"

The poor house? Where was that? Down by the flats, where it was dark and shabby, where the rats walked through your living room, where bugs suck your blood at night when you're trying to sleep, where windows are boarded up, where kids had to search through the trash for a scrap of food?

"Your father had a good job, building caskets. Now

and then he got in a little over his head, when he was betting on the horses, but there was always a steady paycheck and health insurance."

"But you work."

"I barely make enough in tips to buy groceries. Your father paid all the big bills." His mother took another deep, long puff. "What are we going to do without health insurance? Adam is supposed to have his tonsils out. I can't even afford the penicillin and what about Arthur's asthma? If I can't support you kids, do you know what's going to happen? They'll send you all to *Brightside* and you'll be orphans."

Brightside, orphans, the poor house. Andrew burst out crying and fled to the bathroom.

Parents were supposed to take care of you. Weren't they supposed to comfort you and tell you that everything was going to be all right?

Yet he couldn't blame his mother. It was all his fault. He should have never called the police. And if his father should guess what Andrew had done, there wasn't a doubt in Andrew's mind, that he would get the beating of his life.

If his father was really a murderer, then what would stop him from killing his own son?

Andrew wished that there was someone he could talk to. Maybe a priest. Maybe he could go to confession to Father Preston, who was nice, and never gave a lot of penance and never judged.

But what sin had Andrew actually committed? Honor your father and your mother shouldn't count if you were honoring a criminal.

He didn't feel bad for his mother anymore. She was just as bad as his father. But he did feel bad for his little brothers. They were all going to end up as orphans because of him.

He cried some more and didn't stop until Arthur knocked on the door and said he had to use the bathroom or he was going to pee in his pants.

Andrew dried his tears and then decided there was only way to make things right.

He was going to run away.

THIRTY-FIVE

AFTER A GOOD night's sleep, Mrs. Peabody rose, feeling healthier and stronger, and convinced that she had nothing to worry about.

Bill was a thief. There was little doubt about that. All the evidence had been collected and, in spite of his vehement denial, he was probably a murderer as well. He was going away for a long time, so he was no longer a danger to her.

As long as no one let him out on bail.

She wished that she could go to the police and tell them that Bill had threatened her. Except he hadn't really threatened her at all—if she didn't consider the Halloween Eve incident, which the police might dismiss, since she hadn't said anything at the time—and the only reason she was frightened was because she had overheard the phone conversation. But again she could hardly tell that to the police.

But what she could do was to appeal to Connie, telling her that everyone knew her husband had been arrested on an anonymous tip. Only she wasn't the person who called, that she would never do such a thing, even though she knew that Bill didn't like or trust her. Mrs. Peabody would convince Connie that she was fond of the boys and wouldn't put their father in jeopardy.

She would also slip in the information that she was now on the board and she knew how hard it was to be a single mother. So if Connie needed assistance of any kind from the town, she would fight for her—probably wouldn't do much, but Connie wouldn't know about that.

Feeling quite good about this decision, Mrs. Peabody put on her good winter coat—a beige one with only one spot near the hem—her wool olive green scarf, her second best dress—a gray shirtwaist, she was saving her pink polka dot dress for the first board meeting—her black gloves, her brown pillbox hat and her pearl clip on earrings. She kissed Oliver goodbye and marched over to the Maloneys.

But no one was home.

MRS. PEABODY TOOK the bus downtown and stopped in at *Neisers* for a cup of coffee, planning to casually mention her appointment to the board.

She had barely sat down when Nellie zoomed over with a cup, a saucer, a pot of coffee and a big grin on her round face.

"I heard you were down at the police station. What happened!?" she asked breathlessly.

For a moment Mrs. Peabody thought about not saying anything, but the moment passed. "My dog dropped his scarf by the dead body of Rita." She eyed the strawberry crème pie.

Nellie gasped. "Oh my God! I still say all of this, the murder of Violet Rose and then Rita Eastman, it all has to do with Russia. Why we could have Communists living right in our midst!"

"Put her coffee on my tab." Mr. Radcliff plunked down right beside Mrs. Peabody. He was quite bald, reminding her of a hard-boiled egg. She could smell his cologne, *English Leather.* Louie used to wear *English Leather.* Mrs. Peabody hated the smell. "Is there anything else you're planning to eat?"

Mrs. Peabody hesitated, not sure what was happening.

"My treat," Mr. Radcliff said quickly.

"Well, I was going to have lunch. A grilled cheddar cheese sandwich with an order of crispy French fries."

Mr. Radcliff nodded and Nellie frowned. Mrs. Peabody had never ordered a sandwich before. Nellie looked dumbfounded, but, with the next statement, her expression changed.

"I heard you're on the city board," Mr. Radcliff said.

"Really?" Nellie muttered as she walked away and Mrs. Peabody thought—was jealous—because everyone knew that your best friend would never tell you that your face was dirty because then you would wash it and look better than her.

"So I want to talk to you about the sidewalks on High Street. You are probably not aware…"

Mrs. Peabody was going to nip this in the bud. She didn't want anyone to think for one moment that she was a dotty old lady, who could be pushed around for a sandwich and an order of fries. "I am very aware of all the issues facing the city council. I was up half the night, reviewing the files."

"Then you know that I'm one of the bidders on the job. I will admit I came in a little higher than some of the others…"

"A great deal higher." Mrs. Peabody added two teaspoons of sugar from the sugar jar.

"But this is what you need to understand. I was born and raised in Honeyspoon. I love this town and I want to do good by it. You hire one of those big companies from Springfield or Hartford and they will probably do a rush, second rate job and we'll have to replace the walks in ten years. You can count on me to do excellent work. Just ask any of my customers."

"All right, I've heard you." Mrs. Peabody took a sip from her coffee, which was rather bitter. But she could hardly complain, when she wasn't paying for it. "I will consider what you told me."

"Thank you."

Mr. Radcliff laid down a five dollar bill and Mrs. Peabody was half way finished with her grilled cheese when Mr. Kitchenmaster came in and told her he heard she was on the city board. Therefore she needed to do something about the teenagers that hung outside the ice cream parlor, whooping and hollering till all hours. "It's not fair to me and my neighbors. I'm an old man. I spent years on my feet, distributing your mail. Now it's time to take it easy. I need my sleep."

"I'll see what I can do," Mrs. Peabody said rather cheerfully, after he agreed to buy her a piece of that strawberry crème pie. She doubted she could do anything at all.

Mrs. Peabody was certainly enjoying all the attention and the free food—who would have thought—but—in the end, she wanted to do the right thing. If it got around that she could be bribed by a cheap lunch at *Neisers*, then she would never be elected to a permanent position.

She was enjoying the pie and a second cup of that bitter coffee when Joanne Kennedy marched in. She was dressed in a smart wool coat, a Scottish plaid, and wearing matching red leather gloves and low heel black Mary Janes.

Suddenly Mrs. Peabody felt old and poor. She wished she had money to buy new clothes.

Well, maybe someone would buy them for her.

Joanne sat down beside her and ordered a cup of *Sanka* and a fruit salad.

"How are you today, Mrs. Peabody?"

Mrs. Peabody thought that the question was very peculiar. Joanne Kennedy had never spoken one word to her and couldn't care less how Mrs. Peabody was feeling.

"I'm fine," Mrs. Peabody said, trying to sound curt, but her comment only came out as muffled because her mouth was full of sugared strawberries.

"I hear you have been given a position on the board."

Mrs. Peabody didn't bother to answer.

"I know you're going to be voting on some very important issues."

Mrs. Peabody decided it would be best to end this painful conversation. "What is it you want, Joanne?"

"About the destruction of the *Finster Mansion*..."

"I haven't quite made up my mind about that," which was a lie but Mrs. Peabody was not in the mood for a debate. She was feeling quite nauseated from having such a large greasy lunch so early in the day.

"What I know is at the last community board meeting, you were very vocal about wanting to tear the mansion down. Just because a brick might have fallen on your head..."

"It could have killed me."

"That's true." Mrs. Peabody could tell that Joanne was doing her best to sound sympathetic, but she wasn't a good actress and her voice was shrill. "But we did have someone inspect the building. If you don't believe me, you can ask Mr. Vogt. He'll tell you that it's perfectly safe now."

Mrs. Peabody was tempted to say, *of course he will agree. It's his job, which is on the line also.*

"I work there, you know. And if the mansion is torn down, then I will be out of a job. I know you have spoken in favor of the demolition but just between you and me," Joanne leaned forward and Mrs. Peabody could see that Joanne's bright scarlet lipstick had migrated to her teeth and her heavy make-up had settled into her pores. Seeing Joanne so vulnerable made Mrs. Peabody feel just a tiny bit superior, "Kate doesn't really understand. Her job at the library is secure. But me, at my age, it would be hard to find another place of employment. With all these young girls coming out from the *John Powers Secretarial School*, knowing how to operate electric typewriters and tape recorders, I don't know if I could find another job so easily."

"With all due respect, Joanne, the issue is larger than just your job. Children are playing in the streets and when you measure that against a crumbling mansion…"

"It's not a crumbling mansion! I just told you! It's perfectly safe! Just because it's old doesn't mean that it's useless. You should know that." Mrs. Peabody winced and Joanne quickly added. "I didn't mean that the way it sounded. But the *Finster Mansion* is a place where the arts are respected and encouraged. Young people submit their paintings to the gallery on the second floor. I was in charge of the renovation in the attic where we created a writing room for people of all ages to come and find some solitude as they write. The stage in the ballroom gives local playwrights a chance to see their work performed and actors a chance to stand in front of an audience. And then there's the speakers platform. We invite professors from all over the state to come and speak. Maybe we could create a playroom in the cellar for the children," Joanne said hopefully.

"I don't think children should be in the cellar." Mrs. Peabody took a final sip of her coffee, which was now ice cold.

"Just promise me that you'll think about it."

"Of course. I will be giving a great deal of thought to all the issues in front of me." Suddenly Mrs. Peabody was very tired and she wondered just what she had gotten herself into.

"I mean, it's very obvious why the mayor put you on the board. I mean, he wants to tear down the mansion and he knows that you feel the same way, and since you will be the deciding vote…"

Yes, that does make sense, Mrs. Peabody realized with a plummeting stomach. It wasn't because he thought that she was smart or would do a good job.

Joanne reached inside her pocketbook and took out a quarter. She put it beneath Mrs. Peabody's dessert plate. "But I know that you're not about to be pushed around by any man. The tip is on me," she winked.

Mrs. Peabody was feeling discouraged—her head was aching from conflicting thoughts.

She decided to walk home and save the bus fare. It was a crisp fall day, the sort she liked. The leaves were changing, gorgeous colors, golden yellow, rustic red, burnt orange, crunching under her feet. She wished that she felt better.

Thanksgiving was soon upon her and the holidays

were particularly lonely for Mrs. Peabody. Well, maybe serving on the board, she would make new friends.

Well, maybe not. Maybe just new enemies.

At least this year, she had Oliver with her. She'd make a special Thanksgiving feast for him.

And while she was thinking of what groceries she could afford to buy, she saw Andrew Maloney, walking slowly in front of her.

That struck Mrs. Peabody as odd. Shouldn't he be in school? He was wearing the *St. Hedwig's* uniform. Perhaps he told Connie that was where he was headed and had something else in mind all together.

She could have crept behind him and not said a word, but, after all, she had babysat for him on a couple of occasions and she was feeling rather motherly. Andrew, poor child, needed some guidance, since Connie was such a mess and Bill was in jail.

"Andrew, what are you doing out of school?"

He stepped in front of her, stopped, and glared at her. The confusion on his face suddenly changed to anger.

"Are you in trouble?" she asked.

His eyes narrowed. "I'm just fine."

He didn't look just fine and she was about to say so, when she saw Mrs. Vogt approach in her station wagon. She stopped the car.

"Leave me alone!" Andrew turned around and kept walking.

"I heard how rude he was to you." Mrs. Vogt leaned out the window. Her new look, the dyed red hair and Lucille Ball hairdo made her look like a sick poodle. "The apples don't fall far from the tree, if you know what I mean. Would you like a ride home?"

Mrs. Peabody would have liked a ride home but she

didn't want to ride with Mrs. Vogt, who was a known troublemaker and would probably pump her for information.

So she declined and trudged on.

THE FIRST CLUE that something was wrong when she opened her front door and Oliver was nowhere to be found. He was usually at the front window, watching and waiting for her. Had he fallen ill? A cold panic set in.

The second clue was that the house smelled different, like the carnations, something she never used because it reminded her of Christmas.

She found Oliver underneath the bed, cowering, a puddle of urine on her scattered dusty rose rug.

"Bad boy!" she shouted.

Oliver whimpered.

She could tell that the poor dog was shaking. Something had scared him.

Then as she looked around she knew. Mrs. Peabody was a very organized woman. She would never have left her closet door open. Her jewelry box had been moved to the far end of the bureau.

Someone had been in her house.

Were they still there? Hiding in the closet?

It took her several minutes to coax Oliver out from under the bed, to put the leash on him and flee out the front door.

Then she saw Mrs. Notewire, chatting with Mrs. Vogt.

"Call the police," she told them. "Someone broke into my house."

THIRTY-SIX

"It's your boyfriend." Margaret handed Kate the phone, as Kate was writing out the overdue notices.

"Stanley, why are you calling me here?" she whispered. "I told you I'm not supposed to receive personal calls at work."

"Because I didn't appreciate being questioned by the police. Someone told them that I was a felon, that I had served time for murder."

"Well, it wasn't me. Why would I do that? You think I want people to know something like that?"

"All I can say is that this small, cozy town is full of blabbermouths. I thought they caught the guy who murdered those two women. What the hell do they want with me?"

From what Kate knew Bill was admitting to the theft—which he could hardly deny since they found the comic books in his house—but denying the murder of both Rita and Violet Rose. But she didn't want to say any of that. She didn't want to engage in any further conversation, especially when Margaret was stacking books on a nearby shelf, pretending not to listen.

"Honeyspoon is not all it's cracked up to be. I got a good mind to go back to Staten Island."

Oh please, please, she thought, *go back to Staten Island.*

"We'll talk about it tonight when I come over for dinner."

"No, I won't be there. I have a board meeting," she lied.

"Yeah, I would like to come to that board meeting, see what the hell is going on in that town of yours."

"It's a closed meeting." Kate saw Margaret raise her eyebrows. Did she know that Kate was lying? "I'll call you later. I have to get back to work."

"Don't put yourself out."

Kate had no intention of putting herself out, especially for someone like Stanley. She hung up and took the cart, planning to return the checked in books to their proper place. She enjoyed this job the best. She loved going in the quiet aisles, the smell of the old volumes, the history of the library.

That made her think of Joanne and the *Finster Mansion*. She wasn't sure which way she was going to vote but that was the least of her problems with Joanne. She had been wrestling with whether or not she should tell her friend that she had seen Malcolm with Connie.

If Stanley were lying to her—and who knows, he probably was—wouldn't she like to know?

She was putting back Mickey Spillane novels, when she noticed that something had dropped under the bookshelf. She bent down and slid the item towards her. It was a library card and Kate felt her heart skip a beat when she saw the name on it.

Chester Benteen. Wasn't he the man who had jumped from the *Finster Mansion*? Attached to the card was a small piece of white paper, where he had written down the Dewy Decimal number of a book, which he was obviously searching for. Kate could tell from the number that wasn't a fiction book—and she couldn't help but wonder.

She crumbled the paper and crammed it into the pocket of her cardigan, intending to look up the number, when she approached the front desk. But Margaret called out to say she was going to the ladies' room.

Kate took the opportunity to call Joanne and suggest that they meet for lunch.

"That sounds great," Joanne quickly agreed. "Although I can't eat very much. I had breakfast at *Neisers* with that awful witch and I actually left her tip."

"How about *Danny's Diner*?"

"Oh no. All the high school kids go there for lunch. We'll never get a booth. Why don't you bring a few sandwiches and we can eat here. I'd like to show you the writing room which I helped to renovate. You never did see it and it's been years."

Kate was guessing that was not going to be easy.

"So get me a green salad with no dressing, lots of onions and a large *Tab*. And could you stop by *Chester's Drug Store* and pick me up a pack of *Pall Malls*? I'm all out."

"Yeah sure," Kate said with no enthusiasm whatsoever.

WALKING INTO THE *Finster Mansion*, Kate could understand why Joanne might want to save it. It belonged to another world, a lovely old world, with its nooks and crannies, turrets, sweeping staircase, its high ceilings. They didn't build houses like that anymore. People didn't want to spend the money on construction, on high taxes, on the upkeep of the property. Maybe voting to keep the mansion a landmark was not such a bad idea, after all.

She found Joanne at her desk—which used to be the large pantry—it even had a dumbwaiter in the corner. Joanne's head was bent over some papers, but she looked up when she saw Kate.

"How much do I owe you?"

"Seventy four cents."

Joanne was reaching in her pocket when the phone rang. She frowned and picked it up. "Yes, Mr. Vogt. Right away." She hung up and grabbed her steno pad. "He wants me to take a letter. Honestly. He has no respect for the fact that I have to eat lunch. It's so annoying. Will you be all right here? I won't be long."

"Sure, I'll be fine." Except Kate was hungry herself and needed to get back to work within the hour. She was tempted to start eating but thought it might be rude. Instead she ripped open the bag, put Joanne's cigarettes, soda and green salad on her desk with a napkin and took out her own chicken salad sandwich. She noticed a percolator in the corner.

She'd pour herself a cup of coffee and wait for seven minutes. If Joanne didn't come back then, Kate would start eating.

She rose and passed Joanne's desk and her eyes traveled to a bank statement. A quick glance told her that Joanne had been writing to the bank on a yellow legal pad.

Kate wasn't nosy by nature but she couldn't resist the temptation to peek. The bank paper was peppered with minus signs and Joanne was asking the bank to reconsider her request for a loan.

None of this made sense. Joanne had a good job with excellent benefits. She spent money freely on clothes, cosmetics, trips to Cape Cod and even a cruise to Bermuda.

Well, maybe too freely.

She heard Joanne approaching and Kate scooted back to her chair.

"I can't believe him!" Joanne sank into her own chair and took a stab at her lettuce. "He expects me to have these letters out tonight. What can I do? He's the boss."

She chewed slowly. "So have you given it any thought?"

For a moment Kate couldn't remember what she was supposed to be thinking about.

"Voting to keep this a landmark. Kate, I need my job. I mean, I really, really need my job."

"I know."

Joanne's eyes immediately rested on the bank statement. "You read it?" She took another stab at her lettuce and a piece of tomato flew across the room. "I can't believe you would do such a thing?"

"It was right there and I was going for coffee. Listen, I think I know where your money is going."

"What?" Joanne pushed the salad aside and, reaching for a match, lit a cigarette.

"I have something to tell you. It's about Malcolm."

Joanne blew a smoke ring.

"I saw him and Connie in the park together."

Joanne's ruddy face paled. "Connie?"

"Connie Maloney."

"I hate that woman! Do you know that she was the one who introduced Helen to Bruce? If it wasn't for her—" Joanne stopped suddenly. "You saw them in the park together? Well, maybe they just ran into each other."

"I don't think so. They looked quite friendly. Like they are meeting there, obviously something that they planned. They were bending over some papers. It was obvious that they had met before."

Joanne took a quick puff of her cigarette. "What are you saying?"

"I'm saying that maybe he's playing both of you. I know that Connie is a married woman and maybe he's taking advantage. So if you've been giving Malcolm money, you should stop."

"And this is coming from a woman who is dating a felon, someone who served time for committing murder."

"It was manslaughter," Kate said quietly, wondering how many people now knew about Stanley's checkered past.

"Murder is murder, whatever you call it. Is that why you left New York? Because you got tired of visiting him in jail?"

"Joanne, I'm just trying to be a good friend."

"And this is you trying to be a good friend, reading my bank statements, spying on my boyfriend, accusing him of two timing me with a married woman! Who just happens to have a murderer for a husband! Get out!"

"If you would just…"

"Get out!"

Kate rose and took her sandwich, stuffing it into her

pocketbook. She hated confrontations, but she felt that she had done the right thing.

Maybe.

THIRTY-SEVEN

Mrs. Peabody waited outside with a motley group of neighbors and when she saw Gary emerge from the police car, she knew that she was not going to be taken seriously.

"What seems to be the problem?" he asked in an irritated tone of voice, as though she had interrupted him from doing something far more interesting.

"Someone broke into my house."

"And you know this because..."

"Because my dog was hiding under the bed." She looked at Oliver, who was standing beside her, shaking, with his tail slopping steeply downward. "He never does that."

Gary shrugged. "You got him from the street? Those kinds of animals have all kinds of issues. Maybe he saw something he didn't like out of your window."

"Things in my bedroom had been moved."

Gary smirked and Mrs. Peabody felt like slapping him. "Was anything taken?"

"I don't know. I wasn't about to look. Why the intruder could be hiding in the closet!"

"Mrs. Peabody, I don't want to be rude..."

"I think you do."

"But we're working a double homicide here."

"I thought those two murders had been solved," Mrs.

Notewire piped in from behind, holding her cat, who spit at Gary.

Gary ignored Mrs. Notewire and her cat. "Just because your dog was hiding and you forgot where you put your dentures…"

Mrs. Peabody felt herself reddened with anger. "This has nothing to do with my dentures!"

Mrs. Vogt stepped up. "That's just the point. Two people in this town have been murdered! Why Mrs. Peabody could be next! I can't believe that you're not taking this seriously. What kind of a person are you? Ignoring her just because she's an old woman."

"I am not an old woman," Mrs. Peabody said—although she knew that was exactly what she was. "And it may interest you to know that I am now on the city council. There are all kinds of bills coming before me and my vote will count. One of them just might be a raise for the police department." She knew no such thing but she relished the way that Gary turned slightly green. "If you're not servicing the community, I hardly think you deserve more money."

"I'll look inside," Gary said.

Mrs. Peabody followed him to the front stoop and then stopped. If someone was hiding in one of the closets, why should she be the one who got shot?

She was ignoring the murmurs from the neighbors.

Gary came out a few minutes later and shook his head.

"Nothing seems amiss," he said pompously. "Are you sure you're not imagining all of this?"

"I'm quite sure."

"Well, if there are other problems, you can call on us."

"That's what we're paying you for."

She walked into the house, while Gary was still outside. Everything seemed the same—except for that smell now mingled with the cologne Gary was wearing—*Old Spice*—except for Oliver hiding—except for her jewelry box being moved.

She had not imagined it.

Gary said that they were working on a double homicide. Did that mean that the cases hadn't been solved? That they were beginning to believe that Bill was not responsible for the murder of Violet Rose or Rita?

"Let me ask you a question," Gary appeared suddenly. "Do you know the whereabouts of Andrew Maloney?"

"Why would I?"

"Because someone saw you talking to him. And now he's disappeared."

Mrs. Peabody held her ground. "And I suppose that someone is Mrs. Vogt." She shot a nasty look at Mrs. Vogt, who had the good sense to lower her eyes meekly. "Yes, I was speaking with him. But why on earth would that implicate me in his disappearance? He probably ran away. Considering his home life, I could hardly blame him."

Gary didn't bother to reply. Instead he just left. And Mrs. Peabody was alone.

Maybe Mrs. Vogt was right. If Bill wasn't guilty, then there was a killer roaming around. She checked all of the windows and made sure they were locked securely.

And then she took a nip of sherry.

THIRTY-EIGHT

Sister Regina Rachel didn't feel like prepping for dinner anymore. She felt dizzy and nauseous. Mother Superior held her up and walked her up the steep staircase.

"You poor dear. You came home from the hospital too soon. I think that bump on the head was too much for you," Sister Bernadette Beatrice said.

Sister nodded and slowly made her way up the back staircase to her room. Resting during the day alone was forbidden—at least without the permission of Mother Superior, which she clearly had now. But she was about to get into a lot more trouble and besides, everyone was still blaming the bump on her head.

Well, they wouldn't be doing that for long. Once she spoke to Mother Superior, the entire convent would be buzzing. Nuns liked gossip, even more than lay people. Their own lives were so dull, so routine, with little hope that anything would change in the future.

Sinking on her small cot, Sister made a decision. She was going to confess everything to Mother Superior immediately after supper. Before they said the rosary. She would tell Mother Superior that she had sneaked out of the convent to give food to Thelma Lou. She would confess that she lost her rosary beads—which would soon become apparent. Mother Superior wouldn't care about the rosary beads. Not when she heard the rest of what Sister had to say.

She couldn't let a man go to prison for murder or let the real killer get away and watch someone else get hurt. That would be unforgivable.

Disappointing Mother Superior and her own father paled in comparison.

Didn't it?

Sister didn't want to eat dinner but skipping it was not an option. Then she'd have to tell Mother Superior first and she wasn't quite ready to do that.

She sat down and picked at the salad she had helped make. She played with the heavily buttered whipped potatoes and the well done roast pork.

No one noticed that she wasn't really eating, that she wasn't really talking. They were gaily chatting about the upcoming bake sale.

"I think we should make brownies." Sister Immaculate Conception added another pat of butter to her potatoes.

"No, I don't think so." Sister James Elizabeth salted her string beans. "Cupcakes are much easier because you don't have to cut them in even pieces."

"But you have to ice cupcakes," Sister Theresa Maria said. "And they become harder to pack. The frosting gets all over the wax paper." She was cutting her pork into small little bites, because her dentures did not fit properly.

"How about cookies?" Sister Patrick Louise poured herself a big glass of milk.

The doorbell rang and suddenly everyone stared towards the front hall.

"Who can that be calling at the dinnertime hour?"

Sister Immaculate Conception said, her mouth full of potatoes.

"Some disgruntled parent no doubt," Mother Superior said, sitting at the head of the table. She frowned at Sister Hilda Anthony, as though being the principal made her responsible for all the disgruntled parents.

"I'll get it," Sister James Elizabeth, Sister Bernadette Beatrice, and Sister Immaculate Conception said in unison as they all rose.

"Sister Theresa Maria will answer the door," Mother Superior said.

The nuns fell silent as they watched Sister Theresa Maria leave the room. They sat staring at the doorway, Sister Regina Rachel included. She was sweating underneath her habit. She had a bad feeling.

Sister Theresa Maria trudged back into the dining room, her face all aflutter. "It's the police," she whispered and all ten nuns leaned forward in order to hear. "And he's got that homeless woman with him."

The dizzy feeling was worse and Sister Regina Rachel held on to the table to stop herself from falling over.

"They want to speak to Sister Regina Rachel."

Twenty eyes settled on her.

"You tell them that Sister is eating dinner now and they may speak to her when she's finished."

Which wasn't going to be anytime soon because Sister thought she might vomit.

"You can ask them to join us, if they like. We have plenty."

Sister Theresa Maria left the room and Sister Patrick Louise leaned over and whispered to Sister Regina Rachel. "Do you have any idea what this is about?"

Sister shook her head, which, of course, was a lie.

She'd have to confess it, but what was one more lie when combined with all her other sins?

A few moments later Sister Theresa Maria came in with Thelma Lou, trailing behind. "The policeman said he would wait in the vestibule," Sister Theresa Maria said.

"As he wishes." Mother Superior pulled up another chair, went into the kitchen for a plate and utensils and then heaped the dish with meat and potatoes and string beans and three rolls with three pats of butter.

Most of the nuns were quiet as they leaned back and Sister knew that it was because Thelma Lou smelled. Sister was thankful that Thelma Lou did not say anything. Indeed she didn't even acknowledge Sister. Instead she stuffed her mouth, not bothering to close it as she chewed, exposing missing and rotten teeth. The napkin had fallen to the floor.

The nuns watched Thelma Lou and then watched Sister, wondering no doubt what was happening because this was probably the most exciting thing that had occurred in the convent in years.

There was dessert and it wasn't even a dessert that Sister might have liked. Stewed Pears.

Still Thelma Lou didn't speak, not even to say thank you when Sister Immaculate Conception cleared her dinner plate and placed the stewed pears before her. The nuns might have thought she was mute.

Sister wished that she was mute.

Finally it was over and Mother Superior gave the signal. Everyone rose, said a quick blessing. Mother beckoned to Sister and she followed. Thelma Lou took a last spoonful of the pear before shuffling out of the room.

Quietly, they entered the vestibule.

"Good evening, Sister." The policeman was leaning against the wall.

"Good evening, Wayne." Mother Superior turned towards Sister.

"I'd like to speak to Sister Regina Rachel alone, if I could," Wayne said gruffly.

"I'd like to be in a monastery in Italy right now, but that's not going to happen. There are no secrets from me in this convent. I'm Mother Superior and anything you have to say to Sister Regina Rachel, you can say to me."

Sister needed to sit down before she fell down and she wondered if she could ask if she could plop in one of the two straight back chairs. Better not. Instead she took three, long, deep breaths and said a silent prayer.

Wayne reached in his pocket and took out a pair of rosary beads. Sister recognized them right away, "Thelma Lou, would you like to tell the nuns where you found these rosary beads?"

Thelma Lou looked at Sister with watery blue eyes, almost as though she wanted permission. But Sister didn't nod. She was afraid to move her head.

"You didn't steal them, did you, Thelma Lou?" Wayne probed.

"No!" Thelma Lou's voice came out hoarse and raspy. Too many cigarettes.

"And where did you find them?"

"I told you. On the street going to the library."

"They belong to one of my nuns," Mother Superior walked over and took a closer look. "I recognize them. They were blessed by the Pope and the Bishop gave each of us a pair when he returned from the Vatican. I'm assuming that they belong to Sister Regina Rachel. But how did they get to Elm Street by the library?"

Sister opened her mouth to answer, but nothing came out. She flattened herself against the wall.

"She's been real kind," Thelma Lou said. "Bringing me food almost every morning."

"Every morning?" Mother Superior's face went from pink to purple in a matter of minutes. "Well, that is certainly something that I'm going to have to discuss with Sister because obviously, rules have been broken." Sister felt Mother Superior's eyes boring into hers. "But that's hardly a matter for the police. I don't know why you had to come here during dinnertime and dragging this poor, unfortunate woman with you."

"I am not a poor, unfortunate woman," Thelma Lou protested.

"Thank you for bringing back the rosary beads." Mother Superior held out her hand.

Wayne kept his palm tightly clenched. "Unfortunately, there is more. Go ahead, Thelma Lou."

Thelma Lou turned towards Sister and muttered, "I'm sorry."

"Go ahead, Thelma Lou," Wayne said, this time louder.

"Sister, I chased you, because I saw you drop the rosary beads. Except I don't walk so good. My knees, they're all swollen. I saw you in the distance in front of the library. You stopped, so I stopped. And I saw a man running out, carrying a paper bag. I got scared because I knew it was too early for the library to be open, so the man, he shouldn't have been there. After he ran away, you left, Sister, and I couldn't catch up with you. Sometimes Father Preston brings me the evening papers, the next day, the *Honeyspoon Herald*. Yeah," she turned towards Mother Superior, "I can read. So I know that the guy running away was William Maloney."

"I see," Mother Superior said dryly. "So that places him at the scene and means that he's guilty of killing that cleaning woman."

Thelma Lou looked at Wayne, who was looking at Sister Regina Rachel, who didn't want to meet their eyes.

"And what time was this, Thelma Lou?" Wayne asked.

"Sister always comes early at about five o'clock. But it said in the paper that the cleaning woman was killed just after she started her shift, which would be about seven."

"So you see," Wayne said, "Bill Maloney could not have killed Violet Rose Shaw. Not if what Thelma Lou is saying is correct." He turned towards Sister Regina Rachel. "Is this correct?"

Before Sister could answer Thelma said, "He could have come back."

"And why would he?" Wayne challenged her.

Then Thelma Lou shrugged. "I found the earring later that morning. I didn't know who it belonged to. I just thought it was pretty, you know, in the shape of a lilac, my favorite flower."

Wayne turned towards Sister. "Do you think Bill Maloney saw you, Sister?"

"I suppose he could have," Sister said softly.

"And do you suppose he might have thrown that rock?"

"It's possible," Sister whispered.

"Sister, I am going to need you to come down to the

police station and sign an affidavit. Can you do that tomorrow?"

"She'll be there," Mother Superior said.

"Thank you for your time." Wayne had his hand on the door.

"I'm sorry," Thelma Lou mumbled to Sister. "I just had to go to the police. I couldn't let that man be accused of something he might not have done."

"You did the right thing." Mother Superior walked them to the front door while Sister stayed inside, staring longingly at the chair. She should sit down before she collapsed. Better not. She didn't deserve it.

Mother Superior returned. Sister could never remember her looking so cold, so angry.

"I'm sorry," was all Sister could think of saying.

"You're sorry? Those are empty words. You knew that man was innocent and yet you allowed him to go to jail."

"He did steal some comic books," Sister mumbled. "And he might have hurt me with that rock..." It was a weak defense.

Mother Superior thought so too. "Nevertheless, he was accused of murder and you never came forward. What if the killer had murdered someone else when everyone believed they had the murderer locked up? If it wasn't for that poor, unfortunate homeless woman, no one would be the wiser. She has a stronger moral compass than you have, a bride of Christ."

"I was going to tell you, Mother. Tonight. It has been weighing on me."

"And now you want me to feel sorry for you because you feel guilty."

"No."

"This is going to be in all the papers. You know that. People will be talking, the parents of our students, wondering what sort of woman is teaching their children. And what about your father with his bad heart? The Bishop himself will be questioning my judgment, offering to make you my assistant. I'm questioning my judgment."

"I've done a terrible thing," Sister admitted.

"You certainly have. You've broken the rules of the convent and, by remaining silent, you lied. You should hope that God will forgive you. As well as William Maloney."

THIRTY-NINE

THE THOUGHT THAT the police would ever consider Mrs. Peabody a suspect in Andrew's disappearance was ludicrous. Like she would steal a child. Like she would know what to do with a child. She could barely feed herself and Oliver.

She wondered if they were still thinking that she might have something to do with Rita Eastman's death. Well, that was crazy as well. As though she, a frail, older woman, could possibly strangle a lady Rita's size, a lady in her thirties, healthy and fit.

The police were just trying to scare her.

They knew perfectly well that Bill Maloney was responsible for the deaths of both Violet Rose and Rita Eastman. He had killed Violet Rose because she walked in as he was stealing the comic books. And he murdered Rita because she was pregnant, with no idea of who the father was and no way to find out. That could have grave repercussions. An affair was one thing, but an illegitimate child was quite another. For eighteen years Bill may have to pay child support, while the entire town talked about the sins the couple committed and the poor child suffered.

Why were they bothering her?

The phone rang—one ring for Connie. She didn't hesitate to pick it up. If they were going to accuse her of murder, she needed as much information as possible to fight back.

"You heard the news?" Bill asked.

"No. Not yet but..."

"Some homeless lady and some nun saw me leaving the library."

"That's not good."

"No actually it is. It was five in the morning and the cleaning lady wasn't killed until after seven. So you see, I didn't kill her."

"Was this the same nun that was hit with a rock?" Bill didn't answer Connie's question, for what Mrs. Peabody thought was an obvious reason. So instead she asked, "What about Rita?"

"I didn't kill her either! Don't you think that maybe the two murders are related?"

"I don't know. But something terrible has happened."

"What could be more terrible than me in the slammer?"

"Andrew is missing."

"Missing how?"

"He didn't show up for school. Sister Hilda Anthony called and said he missed."

"So he missed school. He probably didn't feel like going, kids probably bullying him about me being arrested. Can't say I blame him. Course the kid has no balls."

"It's four o'clock and it's getting dark. Where is he now? A murderer is running around."

"What does a killer want with a kid, and a not very smart kid either?"

"Maybe Andrew saw something he shouldn't have seen. Or maybe the men after you took him."

"Did you tell the police?"

"Of course."

"You didn't say anything about my gambling, did you?"

"Well, no but…"

"Like a bad penny, he'll come back."

"Bill, I'm scared."

"So what the hell am I supposed to do about it? I can't go looking for the kid. I'm locked up in a 9x12 cell for most of the day. Yeah, yeah, I'm going, I'm going. Gotta hang up. There's a line to use the phone. Just be careful of that dumpy little witch that lives at 15 Lily Lane."

The connection was broken.

The dumpy little witch who lived at 15 Lily Lane. That was Mrs. Peabody. Connie should be careful of her?

She should be careful of her husband.

Mrs. Peabody didn't feel like eating the honey turkey with the fresh roll and the potato salad she had bought at the deli. Her head was aching and her heart was twanging. A cup of tea, perhaps?

The doorbell rang.

The police again? Telling her that they had found Andrew?

Maybe they had come to apologize.

Not too likely.

She opened the door a crack.

Mrs. Vogt stood there, carrying a Tupperware bowl, covered with a dish towel. "I'm sorry that I told the police I saw you talking to Andrew. I honestly didn't mean any harm. I just thought he might have said something to you."

"Well, he didn't."

"I made a batch of blueberry muffins and I know you have a sweet tooth. So I brought you over a half a dozen. May I come in?"

Mrs. Peabody opened the door wider.

"Thank you." Mrs. Peabody took the container from Mrs. Vogt's hand before she could change her mind. "I think I know what this is about. And it's not about Andrew being missing. It's about the vote on the *Finster Mansion*."

"It's my husband's job."

"And Joanne Kennedy's as well."

"And a number of others'."

"Nevertheless, as I told Joanne, this issue is bigger than just a few jobs."

"The mansion provides an opportunity for our town to honor the arts. Speakers..."

"I know. Joanne told me about that. And I'm taking all of that in consideration."

"So you're going to veto the bill," Mrs. Vogt asked hopefully.

"I don't know what I'm going to do." Mrs. Peabody was not in the mood for an argument. "What I have to keep in mind is I'm taking the place of Rita Eastman and she was going to vote..."

"In favor of the demolition. She wants a playground because she had a son. But that's a selfish reason also. I don't like to speak ill of the dead, but we all know that she had some problems of her own, sticky fingers and there is some talk that she was stepping out on Lawrence. But again..."

"All of this is irrelevant," Mrs. Peabody said. Yes, Rita had turned up murdered and suddenly it occurred to Mrs. Peabody that maybe with Rita's sticky fingers, she picked up something that could tie someone to the death of Violet Rose.

"I know which way the mayor is going to vote, because he's dishonest. And, of course, Kate will vote to keep the building standing, because of her loyalty to me. So…"

"So it all comes down to me," Mrs. Peabody finished the sentence. "I'm going to give this all a great deal of thought." Mrs. Peabody opened the front door. "And thank you again for the muffins."

She wanted Mrs. Vogt out of the house. She wanted things to go back the way they were, before the murders, when Honeyspoon was a quiet little town and the gossip was harmless. When cleaning ladies could vacuum the library in peace and a woman could steal a spool of thread or step out on their husbands without being murdered.

And when the town could possibly have both a playground and an art center.

Mrs. Peabody decided to skip supper entirely and instead make herself a cup of tea and enjoy one of the blueberry muffins.

Then she would take to her bed.

FORTY

ONCE ANDREW HAD seen Mrs. Peabody, he realized that he had no plans at all. So he walked around and sat in the park, wishing that he had money to go to the Suffolk Theater and catch a movie. He tried to sneak in to watch *The Beast From the Haunted Cave*, but the back door was locked.

It was getting dark and a cold rain was falling. He was hungry but he didn't want to go home quite yet. He wasn't sure what he had accomplished by skipping school, except that there was one less day that he'd have to face Terrence, one less day that the other kids in the class wouldn't go near him in the recess yard, or sit with him in the cafeteria, like being the son of a murderer made him contagious—not that they liked him before, but this was so much worse.

He had walked so long, he could feel blisters forming on his ankles and his plump thighs were rubbing against his wool trousers, creating a nasty rash. The library loomed in front of him. Maybe it was still open. He could stay there.

The side door was ajar but, instead of going up the stairs to the main library where he might be questioned, he decided to hang out in the children's library.

The door was shut but not locked.

No wonder his father had been able to break in so easily.

The room was quiet, almost spooky. He jumped when suddenly the two parakeets started to chirp and fly around, shaking their cage. Above him he could feel the comfort of heavy footsteps. He stood on the threshold, examining the space. So this was the place where that cleaning lady had gotten herself killed. The news said she had been strangled. Probably didn't leave blood.

Still he didn't want to hang around here.

He should have brought his BB gun.

He walked into the library and then made a left down a narrow hall. On the right was a small room with a table, three chairs and a little icebox. Someone had left four blueberry muffins on a plate in the middle of the table and nearby a percolator sizzled.

Andrew grabbed a muffin and decided to help himself to some coffee. He never tasted coffee and now was as good a time as any to start. He took one of the mugs he found on top of the icebox and poured himself a little.

Yuck.

He found some sugar cubes and plunked in three. Didn't make it much better.

He opened the ice box and found a half of baloney sandwich, an apple and a *Baby Ruth* candy bar. He took the candy bar and bit into the blueberry muffin, spilling crumbs all over the floor. He was tempted to just leave them but maybe he should try to clean up, in case he needed to come back.

He left the room and discovered another door. He had to pull on the knob and the thought crossed his mind. What if there was another body buried in there?

The door burst open and he saw that it was like a janitor's closet, or in this case, it probably belonged to the cleaning lady. There was a broom, a dustpan, a bucket, a container of bleach, some *Bon Ami*, a feathered duster, and some beeswax.

The dead lady was probably the last person to open this door and just thinking about that gave him the willies.

Forget trying to clean up. He was going home.

He reached out to close the door. The broom dropped, but not before it toppled everything off the shelf, the *Bon Ami*, the beeswax and the bottle of bleach, which had cracked open and was now spilling all over the wooden floor.

There was no question of him trying to clean that mess up. Best he just leave. But then he noticed a small little panel in the wall, which had been hidden by the cleaning supplies.

He slid it open and saw that an envelope had been crammed inside. His heart started to beat and sweat poured down his forehead. Money, it could be hidden money. He could give it to his mother and that would make everything all right.

He grabbed the envelope and then knew instantly that it wasn't money at all. He saw a small piece of green paper had been folded and stuck inside. He grabbed it and read the typed words—*I saw what you did.*

None of it made sense.

Andrew didn't know what it all meant but somehow it might be important.

Maybe his father wasn't lying. Maybe his father didn't kill anyone at all.

He stuffed the note in his pocket, grabbed another blueberry muffin and quickly left the children's library.

FORTY-ONE

MRS. PEABODY FELL soundly asleep by eleven o'clock and was soundly awake at two thirty.

Her bed sheets were covered in sweat, her stomach on fire. If she didn't dash, she wouldn't make it to the bathroom in time.

Leaning over the toilet bowl, she threw up violently, chills running down her spine. When she finished, she stayed stationary, unable to move, afraid to move, afraid she'd throw up again.

Vomiting was an unusual occurrence for Mrs. Peabody. She often bragged that she had a stomach made of steel, flat and strong. She could eat anything she desired.

Not tonight.

Had she caught some horrible virus—maybe at the counter in *Neisers* or on the shopping cart at the grocery store? Maybe even by touching the newspapers in the library.

She didn't wash her hands enough. Everyone knew that scrubbing germs off your hand made it unlikely that you would catch some sort of contagious disease.

She took a deep breath and smelled vomit. Leaning over the toilet to flush, she almost threw up again.

Until she saw a single blueberry, which had risen to the top.

Then Mrs. Peabody knew without any doubt whatsoever that she had been poisoned.

Mrs. Peabody limped back to bed and wrapped herself in her quilt. Oliver, asleep at the bottom of the bed, hadn't stirred once. At least Mrs. Peabody hadn't fed him any blueberry muffins.

Why had Mrs. Vogt decided to poison her?

Did it have anything to do with the demolition vote? If so, and Mrs. Vogt was afraid that she was the deciding vote, then why hadn't Mrs. Vogt poisoned Kate as well? Was it because she was in favor of keeping the mansion standing? Would Mrs. Vogt be poisoning the mayor?

Maybe Mrs. Vogt had killed Rita because, by Mrs. Vogt's own admission, Rita was going to vote in favor of the playground. But what had that to do with the murder of Violet Rose?

Perhaps it had nothing to do with the *Finster Mansion*. Maybe Mrs. Vogt thought that Mrs. Peabody knew something that she didn't know, something that Mrs. Vogt believed Mrs. Peabody had heard, or had seen. But what could that be?

Maybe Nellie was right. Maybe they were all Communists.

Then just like that it came to her. Why hadn't she thought of it sooner?

The letter that she had received by accident, the letter—or note because it was too short to be called an actual letter—addressed to Violet Rose.

But how would Mrs. Vogt even know about the letter?

Unless she was the one who had broken into Mrs. Peabody's house.

Maybe Rita was blackmailing Violet Rose and that would explain why Violet Rose received a letter in the mail.

Except that Rita was dead also.

Maybe Rita had an accomplice and as the saying goes, there is no honor among thieves. And maybe that accomplice was Mrs. Vogt.

Was it possible that there were two killers running around the sleepy little town of Honeyspoon? With two entirely different motives?

Yes, of course, it was possible. One thing Mrs. Peabody had learned from living so long was that anything was possible. But she also knew it was too complicated for her to figure out. Besides it wasn't her job. Dump it into the hands of the police, who probably had more evidence that they were withholding from the public.

Tomorrow she'd bring the letter to the police. She'd tell them about the blueberry muffins.

Her stomach was aching but she managed to fall asleep for a few hours.

She rose after seven, skipped her usual breakfast of tea and dry white toast with a poached egg, and instead drank a cup of warm water with a squeeze of lemon.

Then she went to search for Violet Rose's letter.

It was gone.

IN SPITE OF the fact that she no longer had the letter, Mrs. Peabody decided to pay a visit to the police station. It was obvious that the letter had been stolen when her house was broken into, which would give her credence to her story of the robbery. She took one of the muffins and wrapped it in wax paper and put it in a brown paper bag before she placed it into her pocketbook.

She threw the rest of the blueberry muffins in the garbage and secured the lid tightly in case Oliver decided to hunt for food.

ETHEL THOMPSON, the secretary to the police—known for her gray tightly permed hair, her old clothing which had turned gray with age, and her gray eyes with gray glasses and her gray personality—looked at Mrs. Peabody with annoyance.

"What can I do for you?" she asked, as though Mrs. Peabody had interrupted her from doing something important—Mrs. Peabody could plainly see that she was reading a *Woman's Day Magazine*.

"I obviously want to talk to the police," Mrs. Peabody said, tight-lipped.

Ethel drew a long sigh and escorted Mrs. Peabody into a small room.

She had been in the room before and, as she sat down, she was hopeful that Wayne would soon come in. After another fifteen minutes, she wasn't quite as hopeful.

Maybe they were watching her on the other side of the mirror. She had seen that once on a crime show. Maybe they were wishing she would start to talk to herself and confess. Not too likely.

Instead she sat up straight and tall, the way the nuns had taught her many years ago, when she attended Catholic school at the orphanage. It was a school for all girls, which Mrs. Peabody was most proud of, none of the mixes of the sexes. Instead she was taught how to be lady, how to walk, how to sit, how to mind her table manners, how to use a handkerchief. All of this was lost on the young ladies of today.

She waited for another five minutes and then rose. It was obvious that they weren't going to take her seriously. Or maybe they were taking her seriously and trying to break her.

Well, they broke her patience.

Her hand on the door, it suddenly burst open and Gary entered. Seeing the deputy sheriff told her all she needed to know.

They weren't going to pay much attention to her.

"What can I do for you, Mrs. Peabody?" Gary asked in an exasperated tone.

"It's more of what I can do for you," Mrs. Peabody answered in an equally curt voice. "I can shed some light on what's been happening."

"Oh, can you now?"

"Mrs. Vogt tried to poison me."

"What?" Mrs. Peabody could see the disbelief in Gary's expression. "Who?"

"Estelle Vogt."

Gary shook his head, as though he wasn't sure who she was.

"Her husband is in charge of the *Finster Mansion*. I think she tried to kill me so I wouldn't vote for the demolition of the building."

"That's kind of extreme, isn't it?"

"These are times of extremes." She rummaged around in her pocketbook and took out the brown paper bag. She unwrapped the blueberry muffin and stuck it into Gary's startled face. "Here. You can test it for poison."

Gary stared at the muffin for a moment, as though he was contemplating what to say next. "We don't have that kind of capability here in Honeyspoon."

Mrs. Peabody dropped the muffin on the table, and several crumbs broke free. "Well, then send it out."

"I don't think the chief will approve of that expenditure. I mean, it's not like you're dead."

"No, I am not dead. Not yet. But two women are."

"They weren't poisoned. They were strangled. I'm sorry." Gary didn't seem the least bit sorry. "There's not much else we could do."

"There's something else. About a week ago, I received a letter that should have gone to Violet Rose. The mailman, Steven, I think his name is, as usual, messed up. Before I realized the mistake, I had torn it open." It was a lie and Gary didn't look as though he believed it either. "There was no return address. Inside was a single piece of green paper which was typed. *I saw what you did.*"

"And that's important why?"

"I think it would be obvious to someone, even someone like yourself. If Bill Maloney didn't kill Violet Rose, then someone else did. You have to find a motive. You have to look at what she was doing with her life."

Gary stuck his hand out.

"I don't have the letter. Remember when you came because I told you that someone had broken into my house. Well, that's when they stole the letter."

"You didn't report anything missing."

"I didn't know until this morning."

"How did this robber even know you had such a letter? Unless you're accusing the mailman." He snorted in disgust.

"I'm trying to help an incompetent police force,

but I can see I'm just wasting my time." Mrs. Peabody grabbed her tote bag, but left the muffin. "Just in case," she said. "I turn up dead."

FORTY-TWO

MARGARET WAS OPENING the library so Kate had the luxury of coming in a bit later. When she arrived, Margaret was nowhere to be found, so Kate assumed she was downstairs.

And then she heard the most awful blood curdling scream.

Obviously Margaret—who had gone below to the staff room—had stumbled on something. Kate could only hope that it wasn't another dead body. Rather than race down to help her co-worker and confront the horror, Kate stood paralyzed, her heart pounding.

At the very least, she should try to make her way to the front desk and call the police. Whatever caused that horrific roar was clearly a matter of life and death.

Before Kate could decide on a course of action, Margaret waddled, huffing and puffing, up the stairs, and hurried to the threshold where Kate stood, still holding a group of romance novels in her hands. "Call the police," Margaret said wildly, waving her lit cigarette—and missing Kate's teased and lacquered hair by inches—would it have caught on fire? "We've been robbed."

"Again?" Kate asked.

"In the staff room!"

Kate couldn't imagine what could possibly have been robbed in the staff room. Their own pocketbooks were always kept close by, upstairs, in the shelves, under the main desk.

"Don't stand there like a ninny! Call the police!" Margaret shrieked.

Why Margaret couldn't call the police herself was a mystery to Kate, but one she thought it best not to pursue. She stumbled out to the desk, picked up the phone and demanded to be connected to the police. Margaret, gasping in the background, caused the operator to connect Kate instantly and maybe caused the operator to listen in to the call.

"This is Kate Tringali. I'm calling from the *Honeyspoon Library*. There has been a robbery."

"We're on it," Wayne said and he was. Within minutes the police cruiser came speeding down the street, as a small knot of people from Maple Avenue, left their homes and stood in the park, surrounding the library.

Kate and Margaret were on the steps, listening to the chatter.

"Another body, I suppose?"

"Must be a patron? Wrong place at the wrong time."

"The library is always the wrong place."

"Won't be going there no more. I'll order my books by mail."

By the time Wayne and Gary were climbing up the library stairs, Kate's heartbeat had returned to normal. She followed them into the library, down the stairs, and into the hall, leading to the staff room. Margaret, reluctantly, trailed behind.

Kate could smell the bleach before she saw it. When she looked down, the wood floors were stained with white patches. She peeked into the staff room and saw her mug half filled with coffee and blueberry muffin crumbs on the floor.

A mouse darted under the table and Margaret yelled again.

"What was taken?" Wayne reached into his pocket and took out a small pad. Kate could tell by his expression, he had already lost interest.

"Well," Margaret hesitated and looked at Kate, "I couldn't really say."

"Is there anything in here worth stealing?" Wayne asked.

"Blueberry muffins," Kate said quickly. "Mrs. Vogt gave me a half a dozen. I had one for breakfast, and I brought in five. Margaret had one for lunch"

"Not enough sugar." Margaret frowned.

"But now there is only two left," Kate concluded.

"So what we have here," Wayne put his pad away, "someone stole two blueberry muffins?"

"No," Margaret insisted. "What we have here is a break-in at the same place where someone was brutally murdered a few weeks ago. The killer could have come back!"

Kate turned around, noticing the janitor closet. Careful not to slip on the puddle of bleach or the wad of *Bon Ami*, she said, "The robber obviously searched through Violet Rose's cleaning supplies. Maybe he was looking for something." She noticed a small panel which she bent over and slid open. It was empty.

"You know what I think?" Wayne said. "We got a report on a missing kid, didn't attend school. Andrew Maloney."

"Probably couldn't face the other kids," Gary guessed. "With a father locked up."

"I think he hid out here," Wayne said. "Gary, why don't you pay a visit to the Maloney house and question the kid? Solve the mystery for these two ladies."

"By the way," Gary said, "those blueberry muffins on the table—did Mrs. Vogt give them to you?"

"Yes," Kate said. "Why do you ask?"

Gary shrugged. "Just wondering," he said.

The two policemen turned to walk away as Margaret shouted after them. "And just who is going to clean up this mess?"

"Hire another cleaning lady," Gary chuckled.

"Yeah, they are lining up the block to work here," Kate mumbled.

USUALLY KATE DIDN'T mind the job of returning the books to their proper places. It was quiet in the stacks and people, who asked for help finding a book, were respectful and grateful.

But today she resented everything about the job, including Margaret, who made her clean the staff room. Shouldn't the police have ordered Andrew to do the job, to clean up the mess he had created? She had a good mind to say she was sick, but she knew that Margaret wouldn't believe her and would torture her the next day.

She was in the stacks and had just finished filing the *Betty Crocker Cookbook*—which wasn't supposed to be checked out. She jumped when she heard someone tiptoe behind her. She whirled around to face Mrs. Peabody.

Her first thought was that Mrs. Peabody wasn't well. A gray tinge appeared on her face. Her lipstick had been carelessly applied and migrated near her nose. Maybe she was having some sort of attack and, before Kate could ask her if she should sit down and rest awhile, Mrs. Peabody asked her if she had eaten any blueberry muffins lately.

Now this was an odd question and instantly Kate thought of what Gary had asked her. "Yes, as matter of fact, I had one for breakfast. Why?"

"Did Mrs. Vogt bake them for you?"

"She did."

"In an attempt to persuade you to vote against the demolition?"

"I didn't think about it that way. I thought she was just being nice."

"You're a young woman and you want to think the best of everyone. But I'm an old woman and I know how treacherous people can be."

Kate had no reply. She grabbed several books.

"She baked me a batch too and I got deadly ill."

"I'm sorry to hear that." Kate moved the cart one stack forward. "Perhaps you're allergic to blueberries."

"I think she put something in it, an attempt to poison me."

"Well, I'm still standing." Kate laughed.

Mrs. Peabody glared at her and Kate moved forward another inch.

"The police didn't believe me either," Mrs. Peabody said. "Even when I told them I had a letter addressed to Violet Rose. It said *I know what you did.*"

"I don't understand what you're trying to say." Kate realized that she had to finish placing the books and start on the overdue notices.

"Violet Rose could have been blackmailed. And when she couldn't come up with the money..."

"Did you tell the police any of this?" Although Kate

found the information interesting, she wasn't about to engage in a lengthy conversation with Mrs. Peabody, going over various theories, when she was supposed to be working.

"Someone stole the letter, probably when my house was broken into. They didn't take me seriously. Another thing, that boyfriend who Joanne is running around with, I just don't trust him."

"Well, you don't have to trust him." Kate gave a gentle push to Mrs. Peabody, in order to gather more books. "You're not the one, who is dating him. Look, what you're saying doesn't make any sense. If Violet Rose was being blackmailed, it certainly couldn't have been by Malcolm. For one thing, he didn't come to town from Ohio until after she was killed."

"No, that's not correct." Mrs. Peabody clamped her thin lips together.

Kate couldn't resist asking, "What do you mean?"

"He was here a week before Violet Rose was murdered. Nellie's friend, Clara, is a receptionist at the *Roger Roberts Hotel*. He is registered there."

Kate was trying hard not to let the surprise show on her face. "I still don't see what that has to do with the death of Violet Rose."

"All I know," Mrs. Peabody said as she followed Kate down another aisle, "is that Honeyspoon used to be a peaceful town and then all these strangers came in." There was no doubt in Kate's mind that Mrs. Peabody wasn't just referring to Malcolm but Stanley as well. "One thing is for sure. There is danger all around us and I'm just trying to stay safe."

"Well, let me just give you a piece of advice," Kate

said. "Be very careful about what you say or to whom. You don't want to end up as the next victim."

Mrs. Peabody's eyes widened and Kate realized that what she had just said sounded very much like a threat. Before she could amend the statement, Margaret came marching down the aisle. "What's going on here?" she asked in a hoarse, bossy voice.

"We're just chatting," Mrs. Peabody answered.

"Well, Kate is working. She doesn't have time for chatting." Margaret turned toward Kate. "I'm trying to put in an order for more Agatha Christie books. For some reason everyone wants to read about murder." She glared at Mrs. Peabody. "In the meantime, the checkout line is almost at the door."

"Yes, I'm coming," Kate said as she scooted the cart to the corner of the hall. She managed to flash a smile at Mrs. Peabody, who didn't smile back. She felt guilty about how abrupt she had been. Maybe she could find a way to make it up to her.

KATE DECIDED ON the way home to stop by the *Finster Mansion* and talk to Joanne. She'd apologize for the misunderstanding and wouldn't mention Malcolm. At least not directly.

Joanne wasn't in her office but coming from the ladies' room. She seemed surprised when Kate apologized. "I guess that's all right. I'm sorry also. I overreacted."

"Yes, I know. I have a question for you about Violet Rose."

"Violet Rose?"

"The cleaning lady. How well did you know her?"

"What are you saying? You're not accusing me..."

"Of course not. Mrs. Peabody came to the library this morning."

"That trouble maker."

"She seems to think that Violet Rose might have been blackmailed."

"That's crazy. First of all, why would she be blackmailed? I didn't know Violet Rose that well. Sometimes she'd come in after the office closed and I'd still be here. We'd talk a little. She was a quiet, unassuming lady. Why don't you ask Father Preston about her? She cleaned the rectory. Mrs. Vogt would know her better than me, after all, she was the housekeeper there. But I hardly think Violet Rose would be the type to do anything bad enough for someone to blackmail her."

"I don't know," Kate admitted.

"Just because Bill has been cleared of the murder of Violet Rose doesn't mean that he didn't murder Rita Eastman. I've been hearing all kinds of stories…"

"Yes, I've heard them also," Kate admitted.

"What's happening to this sweet town? Look, I might as well tell you, I haven't heard from Malcolm for a few days. He told me that he might be away for a little while. Maybe he has another girlfriend stashed away."

Kate couldn't help but wonder—was that other girlfriend, Connie? And if Malcolm had come to town for a specific purpose, would he be leaving now because he had done, what he was supposed to do? Whatever that was.

Kate looked down at a stack of letters, tied with a blue ribbon. She saw the return address—a PO Box in Madison, Ohio.

"I've been reading over his letters," Joanne said stiffly. "I know it's silly." She scooped up the letters and threw them in her purse. "Come on, we'll take the bus home together." She shut off the light. "Maybe he was running away from me."

Or running away from something, Kate thought.

FORTY-THREE

Mrs. Peabody could not believe that Kate had spoken to her in such a tone. Why she almost threatened her! This was not how it was supposed to be. People were supposed to like and respect her now that she had been asked to join the board. She had a good mind to just quit, to tell the mayor it was all too much for her.

She got the bus home, still not feeling well enough for the long walk, when she heard someone calling to her. She turned around and Connie was standing behind her.

Connie looked horrible. Everyone knew that she had once been a popular, pretty girl with her dark hair, her bright blue eyes, her satiny complexion. But little by little her petite frame had given away to added pounds, particularly in the stomach. Her complexion was dotted with acne, and her black hair resembled shoe polish. Since Bill's arrest, her downward physical spiral had grown worse.

"It's been horrible. Andrew running away and then the police calling, saying he was responsible for vandalism in the library. At least he finally came home. But I want to go visit Bill. You know he's been cleared of the murder of Violet Rose, but they're still holding him for the killing of Rita and for the robbery and hurting that nun." She shook her head. "Do you think you could stay with Arthur? Adam and Andrew are at school."

"All right. Give me fifteen minutes. I need to walk Oliver."

"I don't care what people say about you, Mrs. Peabody. I think you're a saint."

Mrs. Peabody managed to smile at the crooked compliment. She knew exactly what people said about her.

Well, at least they couldn't prove that she was a murderer.

Mrs. Peabody did not mind babysitting for Arthur. Of the three boys, he was by far the easiest. A quiet child, he didn't mind playing by himself.

He was upstairs in his room when she arrived, which gave Mrs. Peabody a chance to raid the cupboards. But alas, since Bill's arrest, Connie had definitely fallen on hard times. Her cabinets, which usually had been crammed with all sorts of goodies, chips and sweets, now only held a single bag of oatmeal raisin cookies. Not Mrs. Peabody's favorite, especially since her stomach was still iffy.

She took two for later on, wrapping them in the foil that she had brought in her pocket book. Maybe she should offer one to Arthur, just in case Connie found them missing. Mrs. Peabody could honestly say that Arthur had eaten them.

She climbed the stairs with the bag in hand, and found Arthur on the floor, making odd noises, as he played jacks.

The room was a mess, toys abandoned all over, unmade bunk beds, leftover pizza crusts on the bureaus, silly putty stuck with grape juice on the threadbare rug.

Connie's housekeeping skills had also taken a turn for the worse.

"Arthur, would you like some cookies and milk?"

Arthur looked up and shook his head.

"Oatmeal Raisin."

"I don't like them."

"Why don't you and I surprise your mother and clean this room?"

Arthur shook his head again and kept on playing, as though bouncing that ball was the most important thing in the world.

Well, she didn't have much else to do. She started with the toys, the Chinese checkers, the slinkies, the *Mr. Potato Head*, one *Lionel train*, throwing them all in the toy chest. Someone else could put the pieces of the games, *Operation* and *Risk*, in the proper boxes, but she doubted that would ever be done. She threw the pizza crusts in the bathroom pail, which was overflowing with stained toilet paper and an empty pill bottles. She spotted an apple core under the one single bed stuck in a *Mickey Mouse* ear, and, when she reached for it, she noticed something else.

A plain white envelope, with blue stains on it.

Blueberry stains.

She grabbed the envelope. Arthur was still in his own world, not even looking up at her. Her heart pounding she opened the envelope. Its flap was torn and dirty. A single piece of green paper emerged, folded hastily—which read—*I saw what you did.*

Mrs. Peabody stared at it for several minutes, trying to catch her breath.

"Arthur," she sat down on the floor, wanting to be on his level, "do you know anything about this?"

"What?"

"Is this letter yours?"

"No."

"Does it belong to one of your brothers?"

"Don't know."

And he didn't know, that was the thing.

Then Mrs. Peabody began to wonder. She hadn't thought so at the time, but suddenly, staring at the paper, she remembered a white envelope, addressed to Connie and postmarked from Ohio. Ohio. That's where Kate said Malcolm was from. Was it possible that Malcolm knew Connie and he came to Honeyspoon with a specific purpose and now Connie was helping him?

Maybe the police had the wrong Maloney?

She tried to rise from the floor, but her knees buckled and she fell, rolling towards the bunk beds. Arthur started to roar with laughter, the only time he had showed any expression since she came.

The cuckoo clock chimed the hour, and she wondered if Connie would be home before the boys. She needed to question Andrew, since she found this envelope in his room. Had he taken it out of his mother's mail? Cramming the note in her pocketbook, an idea occurred to her.

"Arthur, how would you like to take Oliver for a walk? I'd let you hold the leash, while we wait for your brothers at the bus stop."

"Okay." He grinned.

Mrs. Peabody left a note for Connie, in case she did come home and wondered if Mrs. Peabody had kidnapped Arthur, the way she had been accused of kidnapping Andrew. She carefully locked the door behind her, which minutes later, she realized was a mistake. If Connie hadn't come home, they'd be locked out. She'd have to take the boys to her own house, something she didn't relish.

Why was everything such a battle?

It was cold and a wet, early snow began to fall. She hadn't dressed Arthur properly and he was whining. "I want to go home. I'm going to catch a cold and I already have tonsillitis."

"We have to wait until Oliver does his business."

"What does that mean?"

While she tried to figure out the best way to explain, she saw the yellow bus coming up the street. "Look, your brothers are coming."

Arthur didn't care about his brothers, nor did he care whether or not Oliver did his business. He was just insistent about going home.

When the boys clambered off the bus, Mrs. Peabody asked if Adam wanted to walk Oliver.

"Why can't I walk Oliver?" Andrew said. "I'm older."

"You can in a bit. But there's something I have to ask you first."

Andrew looked suspicious but, even more so, when she pulled the envelope from her pocketbook.

"I need to know where you got this and where you got the blueberry muffin."

Andrew grabbed the envelope. "That's none of your beeswax."

"It doesn't belong to you, Andrew."

"Well, it doesn't belong to you either." Andrew started to walk away.

"It could be evidence in a homicide."

Andrew stopped and his face crunched up. "What?"

"It could prove who killed Violet Rose."

Andrew dropped the letter, which meant that Mrs. Peabody had to bend down to it. Her knee hurt, her back hurt, her stomach hurt.

"You're not in any trouble." She had to hurry to catch up to the three boys and to Oliver who was pulling on his leash, necessitating Adam to practically run. "And I won't tell anyone where you got the letter. I promise." A promise she would probably break. "Where did you find this?"

"Only if I can walk the dog."

"You can walk the dog."

"I hardly had a turn."

"Andrew, as soon as you tell me where you got the letter…"

"I found it, all right. I was hiding in the library, downstairs, near the children's part. It was in a closet with a broom and some bleach."

So this letter didn't have anything to do with Connie. But her original suspicions were true. Violet Rose was probably being blackmailed and the blackmailer killed her. And maybe Rita was being blackmailed as well, because goodness knows, she had done a lot of sketchy things.

"Adam, let Andrew have a turn."

"I want to go home!" Arthur wailed.

"Fine!" Adam released the leash and Oliver went running.

"Oliver, you come back here!" Mrs. Peabody shouted. "Right now!"

But Oliver had already disappeared from view.

FORTY-FOUR

ONCE IT HIT the papers, everyone knew. Everyone knew that she was a coward.

Even her students.

She felt it the moment she walked into her room. Managing the classroom had never been her strong point, but now it was worse than ever. It wasn't that the students were boisterous, that she would expect. Instead they were irreverent, quiet, suspicious, whispering among themselves. When Andrew's name card came up to read in religion, he refused to say a word. Not much she could do about it. Or about the pupils who, when she gave them instructions, to take out books, or copy from the board, to say the noon time prayers, *stand, turn and kneel*, they took their sweet old time. Some of them didn't follow the orders at all. Sister could hardly go to Sister Hilda Anthony, the principal, and complain.

Not the way the nuns in the convent felt about her.

They were clearly avoiding her. They sat and stood around in small groups, talking in low voices, stopping when she approached. When they passed her in the hall, they didn't look at her, but kept their eyes downcast, careful not to rub against her, as though her cowardice was contagious.

At first Sister was hurt by this behavior, which she understood, because she was deeply ashamed. Her actions were despicable. She had disobeyed the rules of the convent. She hadn't come forward when a man was accused of a murder, which he couldn't have committed. And it appeared that she had no intention of doing so, until Thelma Lou contacted the police.

Yes, it didn't look good.

But really when Sister thought about it, she realized that her sins were not as evil as everyone was making them out to be. She had gotten in trouble by doing a good deed, feeding the homeless. And she knew in her heart that she had every intention of telling Mother Superior on the very night that the police had come calling. It was hardly her fault if she wasn't given a choice.

So her hurt and shame soon gave way to irritation and then to anger.

And the source of her anger was directed at Mother Superior.

Mother Superior set the tone of the convent. If she showed that she forgave Sister, then the other nuns would soon follow. The very least she could do is speak to the nuns about the way they were treating Sister.

After all, wasn't forgiveness part of their religion as well?

After almost a week of being treated like a pariah, Sister decided to do one brave thing.

And that was to speak to Mother Superior.

SHE WAITED UNTIL after a silent dinner, when the nuns all gathered in the community room to watch television, the news—they were still talking about the double murder and whether or not they were related—and then the game show, *Truth or Consequences*. Mother Superior never joined them. She retreated to her office, to do paper work, pay bills, plan agendas, make schedules.

Sister knocked and Mother looked up, not surprised to see her.

"How can I help you?" Her voice was clipped and cold.

"May I sit down?"

Mother nodded.

"I am so sorry for what happened."

"I'm sure you are." Mother was looking at a bank statement.

"But I think I've been tortured enough."

Mother looked up, raising her white eyebrow. "Pardon?"

"I've suffered enough," Sister said, her resolve weakening.

"I don't understand. You're talking about torture and suffering. Do you really have any concept about what that means? Surely you know about the saints. Every morning we read about one of their extraordinary lives. These saints were tortured, endured terrible suffering, physical and mental. They never complained, even when they were burned alive. Always offering up their pain for the souls in purgatory. Do you dare to compare yourself to one of them?"

"Of course not. It's just that none of the nuns are talking to me..."

"Please, stop whining. And the sisters will get over it. They were just caught off guard, as I too, was."

"My students don't respect me."

"Well, that's your own doing. I don't know what you expect me to do. Your actions had consequences. I'm sorry if you're unhappy with those repercussions." Mother grabbed a red pen and started to circle something on the bank statement.

"I just want you to forgive me."

"Of course, I forgive you." But even as she said it, Mother didn't look up.

So Sister said something she couldn't even remember thinking. "I might need some time by myself."

Now Mother did look up, with widening eyes. "What are you saying?"

"I don't know." A lump was growing in Sister's throat. "I let everyone down."

"So now you're thinking of abandoning your vows, vows you took in front of the community, your parents, the bishop, and God."

"No." It was too late to hold back the tears. Her eyes watered. "That's not what I mean."

"What did you mean?"

Sister didn't know what she meant. She reached under her bib, inside her pocket and took out a crumpled handkerchief, blowing her nose and wiping her eyes.

"Well, I'll tell you what we're going to do." Mother's tone softened. "It's obvious that you're in no position to continue with your duties. I'm going to send you away to Mount St. Agnes. You can accompany Sister Louis Michael when she goes. You can help to nurse the infirm nuns."

That was the last thing that Sister wanted to do. She hated being around strange, sick people, even more than she hated teaching. As she sat there she knew that she didn't want to be in a classroom, or a hospital room with a bunch of elderly nuns.

"That will give you some time to pull yourself together, to think about your vows, to put them in their proper perspective and to do some meditating. I will tell the other sisters that you had a mild nervous breakdown, which is hardly a lie. I think the change will be good for you. Those ailing sisters need a loving hand. Making a difference in their lives will help you to feel better about your own life and boost your self-esteem. What do you say?"

As though Sister was in a position to say anything. So instead she rose and mumbled "thank you" because she knew that was expected.

"You may go now. Down in the cellar you will find some valises. Pack only what you think you might need."

That probably could fit in my pockets, Sister thought as she left Mother's office.

This was what her life had been reduced to.

FORTY-FIVE

Mrs. Peabody spotted Connie coming up the walk. She seemed slightly puzzled seeing Mrs. Peabody out with the three boys but Mrs. Peabody didn't have the time or the inclination for an explanation.

"My dog has run away." Mrs. Peabody grabbed the cash from Connie and tucked it into her pocketbook. "I have to find him."

"I wish my problems were that small," Connie said sadly.

Mrs. Peabody didn't bother to respond and say what she was thinking. To her this was hardly a small problem. In the short time since she had Oliver, he had become her whole life.

She wasn't dressed to go hunting but she hunted, nevertheless. She searched the neighborhood and the back of the units, and even near the woods where Rita's body had been discovered. She called Oliver's name so loudly and so often that several neighbors came out on their stoops to ask what the problem was.

They all shook their heads and said no, they hadn't seen any dog wandering. And then they closed their doors.

After searching for almost a half an hour, Mrs. Peabody went home, with the hope that Oliver would be waiting on the doorstep.

He wasn't there.

She checked the back porch.

He wasn't there either.

Just then a thought occurred to Mrs. Peabody. Oliver had come to her door nearly a month ago, but before then, he obviously had a home. What if...what if... Oliver suddenly remembered where that home was, and he returned, and now her little dog was lost to her forever.

She'd find him.

And she'd offer to buy him back from the old owners.

And then another idea crossed her mind and this one filled her with terror. What if Oliver had been kidnapped by the person who had already killed two people? They would hardly hesitate to slaughter a dog.

It was growing dark.

Oliver did not like the dark.

She thought about the neighbors, who had come to their doors. Kate was there with Joanne, Mrs. Notewire, Mrs. Kitchenmaster, even Mr. Eastman. But not Mrs. Vogt. She hadn't bothered. Maybe she knew exactly where Oliver was.

Mrs. Peabody reached for her winter coat, put her key in her pocket and headed for the door. Whatever Mrs. Vogt wanted, she could have as long as she returned Oliver. Honeyspoon was a small town, but never in her wildest imagination could Mrs. Peabody have guessed that the citizens were capable of such extreme actions.

Fear flooding her, she marched up to the Vogt door and rang the bell.

Mr. Vogt answered. He was dressed in an ill fitted three piece suit. The vest was tight, exposing a layer of fat around his belly—which the radio had announced just this morning that fat in that spot was not good for your heart. He was holding a drink in one spidery hand—it looked like whiskey—and a lit cigar in the other—she noticed sharp and dirty fingernails.

"Mrs. Peabody." Strangely, he didn't seem surprised to see her. "What can I do for you?"

"My dog is missing."

"Oh. I didn't know you had a dog." He was slurring his words. Was he drunk?

"I think someone might have taken him."

"I don't like dogs."

"Your wife?"

"She doesn't like dogs either."

"I know. And that's what worries me."

"Huh?"

Mrs. Peabody thought this was no time to mince words. "I think your wife might have taken my dog."

"You mean because the poisoned blueberry muffins didn't work so good?" Mr. Vogt had an awful laugh, more like a cackle.

"Is she here? Your wife?"

"Nope, she's visiting her sister in Chicopee."

A dead end.

"How bout you come in and have a drink with me?"

That was the very last thing that Mrs. Peabody wanted to do. For one thing, except for an occasional shot of sherry when her nerves acted up, she didn't drink at all. But maybe she should go in, if for nothing else to see if there was any sign of Oliver.

"We could talk about the vote coming up for the city council." He winked at her. "And how you're going to vote."

"No, thank you," she said curtly.

"Why don't you just get another dog?" He yelled at her as she walked away.

"Why don't you just get yourself another wife?" she yelled back. She knew that it was a stupid remark but then again it was stupid of people to think you could replace one dog for another.

She turned around when he slammed the door and she looked up.

Someone was watching her from the upstairs window.

Mrs. Peabody trudged back to her own empty house, aware that tears were leaking from her eyes.

Where was Oliver? Was he lost? Confused? Hungry? Wondering where she was? She couldn't bear to think of it.

She sank down on the sofa and removed her purse, which was still partially open. She had just thrown in the money Connie gave her. A two dollar bill. She could use the cash but what did it matter, with Oliver gone. A wave of hopelessness washed over her.

Then she saw it.

The piece of paper she had taken from Andrew. A piece of paper which would prove that Violet Rose was not the sweet, unobtrusive cleaning lady which everyone had believed. Somehow she had done something horrible that could have gotten her killed. Although how that figured into Rita's death, Mrs. Peabody had no idea.

Well, who cared? Without Oliver, it didn't matter to her. No, she didn't care, but the police might. And if she showed them the letter, maybe they would help her find Oliver.

She reached for the phone.

She told Gary that she had some information about the death of Violet Rose. He perked up, but then perked down, when she told him that she wouldn't share that information unless Wayne came to her home.

"Wayne is very busy. We don't have time for this nonsense."

"I can assure you that this is not nonsense."

Finally he relented and said Wayne would be over, but not too soon. And he didn't arrive for another forty-five minutes.

The moment he walked in the door, Mrs. Peabody told him that someone had kidnapped Oliver.

At first Wayne looked startled, but a moment later, he eyed her angrily.

"What does that have to do with the murder of Violet Rose?"

"It does, kind of. That's why I really called you. I'll help you, if you help me."

"What makes you think that someone took her?"

"Him. Oliver wouldn't just take off. He likes to stay close to home."

"And how did you find this," Wayne hesitated, "this dog?"

"He showed up at my doorstep on Halloween Eve. He helped me," Mrs. Peabody stopped, knowing exactly what it sounded like.

"So you see, your little dog likes to wander. And maybe he wandered back to where he came from, his real home."

"This is his real home," Mrs. Peabody said with more conviction, than she felt.

"Well, maybe the pound picked up the dog and they're holding him there."

A flash of hope passed through her. "Could you call?"

"They're closed."

"But you're the police. They would have to open for you."

"Mrs. Peabody." Wayne drew a deep, exasperated breath. "What do you have to tell me about the murder?"

Mrs. Peabody knew that Wayne wasn't going to help her, at least not until the morning. She reached in her pocket and pulled out the envelope, she had taken from Andrew's room. "Andrew found this in the library, in the janitor's closet, where Violet Rose kept her supplies." She watched Wayne's face as he read the note. "You can see that it's identical to the piece of mail I opened by accident."

"Which we never saw. Well, we must have missed this, when we examined the crime scene."

"Why doesn't that surprise me?"

"I would appreciate it if you didn't mention this to anyone."

"I would appreciate if you would help me to find my dog."

"We'll talk about it in the morning."

Mrs. Peabody had no choice as she watched him leave.

SHE BOLTED THE doors but decided that she was going to sleep in the living room. Her bedroom was far away and in case Oliver came home and was barking outside on the stoop, she would not here him.

She knew she wouldn't sleep a wink so she turned the television low, just to hear voices.

She was dozing when she heard the front doorbell

ring. She jumped up. At first she thought it was Oliver, that he had come home. But no, that was crazy. Obviously, a dog couldn't ring a bell. Well, maybe someone had found him. But what if it wasn't about Oliver at all? What if it was the kidnapper or the murderer?

"Who is there?" she asked in a frightened voice.

There was no answer. She wanted to look out the front window, but it was pitch black and she couldn't see anything. And she didn't want the person on the other side of the door to see her.

All of a sudden something came flying through the mail slot. Mrs. Peabody released a scream, thinking at first, it was some sort of rodent.

When she saw what had come tumbling in, she wished that it had been.

It was Oliver's collar with a printed note attached. *Resign from the city council.*

FORTY-SIX

ANDREW OPENED HIS EYES, feeling slightly sick. His head was pounding and he thought he might throw up. He didn't want to go to school. He couldn't go to school.

Oh yes, wait, he didn't have to go to school. Some sort of a teacher conference. No need to get out of bed and rush to dress and run to the bus and be bullied all day.

He was heading for the bathroom, when he heard his mother on the phone. Evidently, she was talking to his grandma, and his mother was crying.

"I don't know what I'm going to do, Mama. Bill has been cleared of the murder of that cleaning lady, but they still suspect him of killing Rita... All kinds of nasty rumors are going around. People say that Bill and Rita were having an affair, which, of course, he's denying... It doesn't matter. They're holding him on a robbery charge, for some stupid comic books and hurting a nun... No, Mama, no one is listening in. Meanwhile the funeral parlor won't pay him for his last week of work because they claim he's a criminal and he already has borrowed off his paychecks...a lawyer? I can't afford a lawyer for Bill, let alone a lawyer to sue... I know I've borrowed money before. But this is an emergency. I can't feed my boys. They're going to turn off my electricity."

Andrew dressed quietly and quickly, not listening to

the rest of the conversation. This was worse than school. Parents were supposed to protect you, give you a safe place to live, and feed you meals and stand up for you in school when the other kids were mean.

They weren't supposed to go to jail or cry to their mothers that they didn't have any money and they didn't know what they were going to do.

He was at the front door when his mother put the phone down and called to him, "Where are you going?"

"Just outside to play."

"You stay away from that library."

Yeah, like he was planning to go back there again.

"And stay away from Terrence Eastman."

"Don't worry. He doesn't want to play with the kid whose father murdered his mother."

Before his own mother could respond, Andrew was out the door, although he did hear his mother complain that he was getting fresher every day. Only at home.

He was heading for the wooded area, not the one by the Eastmans, that was too creepy. Instead he walked to Mulberry Circle, a little up the hill. There was a place, a fallen log, where he used to plop to think things through.

He shuffled on miserably and then he saw Oliver in the distance. The dog was just standing there, looking lost and confused. Andrew was about to call to him—maybe Mrs. Peabody would give him a reward—when he heard the rustling of leaves and he saw a man approach.

He had an odd looking pointed beard, and he was dressed fancy, shiny brown shoes, and a red bow tie, which was visible because of his unbuttoned beige coat.

The man halted, as though he was waiting for someone. And then to Andrew's shock and utter surprise, his mother approached. It wasn't an accident, she went right to him.

What on earth was his mother doing?

Andrew stood rooted to the spot, behind the tree.

"You heard anything at all?" his mother asked.

"Nothing," the bow tied man answered. "I don't know what to do. I tried every trick in the book. I could use force but I hardly think that would work. We need a plan."

"I'm sorry about all of this. But I have my own problems with Bill and all."

"Well, I told you I would give you money for helping me."

"I don't feel right…"

And just like that, Oliver saw Andrew. And, as though, Andrew was a life-long friend, Oliver ran over, jumped on Andrew, knocking him down, right in front of his startled mother.

His mother's eyes widened. Then the man with the bow tie, approached Andrew, his eyes blazing.

"What are you doing here? Spying on us?"

"He's my son," his mother spoke quickly. "Andrew, were you following me?"

"No." And then Andrew said the only thing he could think of. "I was looking for Mrs. Peabody's dog."

"Yeah, well, you found him." The man turned towards his mother. "You better make sure he doesn't tell anyone about this."

"I won't," Andrew promised. And then he began to run, but his heavy little legs caused him to stumble. He tripped several times and he thought he heard his mother calling to him. But he didn't want to answer.

Now he was really scared. What was his mother doing in the woods with a strange man? Did that have anything to do with his father being in jail?

When Andrew was safely out of the woods, he heard the pitter patter of footsteps.

Then he did turn around and was relieved to see that Oliver had followed him.

FORTY-SEVEN

Mrs. Peabody was just leaving to go to the police station, the note and the collar tucked safely in her purse, when she saw Andrew and Oliver, running behind him.

Before Mrs. Peabody could utter a word, Oliver raced to her, his tail wagging, barking and jumping, and nearly knocking her down. She wanted to scold him but her heart was soaring.

"You, you," she finally said to Andrew, "you took my dog?"

"No, I found him in the woods."

"Thank you so much! I could give you a reward but..." She stopped talking suddenly when she noticed that Andrew had been crying.

"What's wrong?" She held the door open because, without a collar and a leash, Oliver might take off again. "Why don't you come inside?"

Mrs. Peabody had a good idea why Andrew had been weeping because she had overheard the conversation between Connie and her mother. Things looked awfully dismal for the Maloney family and Andrew was rightfully worried. She wanted to give him something to eat, but she didn't have candy, or chips, or soda pop, and she only had one shortbread cookie left.

"Do you want some hot tea?" she asked as she closed the front door.

Andrew shook his head, standing by the door.

"Are you worried about your family?" Mrs. Peabody pressed on.

He shook his head glumly. "I'm worried about Mommy."

"She's going to be all right," Mrs. Peabody lied.

"I don't think so. She was with a bad man in the woods."

Mrs. Peabody held her breath. "What did you say?"

"I saw my mother in the woods by Mulberry Circle. She went in there to meet a man, a man that wasn't my father."

"Here, sit down." She practically pushed Andrew into the arm chair. "Why don't you tell me what happened?"

"I can't. I'm too afraid he might hurt me."

"Well, he won't know. Not if I don't tell anyone."

Andrew seemed to be considering this argument.

"What did the man look like? Was it fat? Skinny? Did he have a beard?"

"Yes, a pointy one. He was medium like. He wore a red bow tie. I saw it because his coat was open."

Joanne's beau. "Did he say that he going to do something bad?"

Andrew hesitated. "No, not exactly, but he talked with my mother, about needing a plan."

"What sort of plan?"

Andrew shrugged. "That's all I remember. I ran away."

Mrs. Peabody rummaged through her pocket book for a crumpled dollar bill. "This is the reward for finding Oliver." Andrew looked at it for a few moments and then stuffed it into his blue jeans.

"Do you think that man kidnapped Oliver?" Mrs. Peabody asked.

"No." Andrew was emphatic.

"Why not?"

"Because he didn't seem to care about him, when Oliver took off with me. He didn't chase him or nothing."

"Okay." Mrs. Peabody held open the front door. "Thank you, Andrew. Don't worry about your mother. It's going to turn out all right."

"You won't tell no one. Right?"

"Not a soul," she lied.

MRS. PEABODY THOUGHT about whether or not to tell the police. After mulling it over for several minutes, she decided that they should know. After all, there was a child involved, three children actually and if Connie was planning something with Joanne's beau, something illegal, well, that would hardly be fair to her sons.

Not to speak of the fact that someone had taken Oliver, although, except for being hungry, he didn't seem worse for the wear.

Mrs. Peabody bundled herself up in her old gray coat and her worn out saddle shoes, and trudged to the bus stop.

"I NEED TO speak to Wayne," Mrs. Peabody, thoroughly exhausted from being up the night before, told a disinterested Ethel.

"He's not here," she answered pompously. "He's out on a case."

"What about Gary?"

"He's on the phone. I'll let you know when he's off."

Mrs. Peabody sat herself down on the hard bench

and waited. She thought it wouldn't be anytime soon and she was right. Twenty minutes. She asked Ethel several times if Gary was ready but Ethel just shook her gray curls.

"All right, you can go in." Ethel finally relented and held the door open, not to the tiny room where Mrs. Peabody had been before, but to what looked like Gary's office. Gary was sitting behind a desk, stacked with papers, empty coffee cups and a half eaten Swanson TV dinner.

There was no second chair.

Mrs. Peabody reached inside her pocketbook and threw down Oliver's collar and the note, which had been attached. Gary stared, indifferent. "What the hell is this?"

It occurred to her then that Wayne had never mentioned what happened, obviously not thinking it was of any importance. "My dog was kidnapped. I called last night and Wayne came over. I told him so and he didn't believe me. But here is the proof."

"Is the dog still missing?"

"No, Andrew Maloney found him in the woods." Mrs. Peabody thought about asking if there was a spare chair somewhere, so she could sit. Her back was bothering her. Maybe they didn't want you to sit. Maybe that was the whole point. "Andrew also saw his mother, talking to a man, a stranger that Joanne is dating, the fellow she found in the *Lonely Hearts Club*. They are planning something."

"Planning what?"

"He didn't hear that part."

"You mean, like planning to run away together?

Well, you can hardly blame Connie, can you? After what Bill has put her through?"

Suddenly Mrs. Peabody felt foolish.

"I don't know what you expect me to do with this information. Connie hasn't done anything wrong that we know of. And if she is stepping out on Bill, then it's a good thing that Bill is locked up. Because, if he hasn't committed a murder, he just might. Besides, I think we all know what sort of kid Andrew is, breaking into the library for instance. He's a kid, who is craving attention and who can blame him? So he makes up a story."

"He told me not to tell anyone. And he seemed genuinely frightened."

Gary waved his hand, as though he was swatting a pesky fly.

"What about my dog?"

"You found him, didn't you?"

"I did not find him. He was with that strange man. Read the note. It's apparent that someone does not want me on the city council."

"And why would that be?" Gary had stopped paying attention. Instead he was staring down at some papers on his desk.

"I'm not sure. Maybe it has something to do with the *Finster Mansion* being torn down." Mrs. Peabody hesitated. "Rita Eastman was the deciding vote. Maybe that's why she was killed. And now," Mrs. Peabody swallowed, "it's on me."

"And the cleaning lady? She was voting too?"

Mrs. Peabody didn't answer.

Suddenly Gary's eyes narrowed, as he gave her a sharp, sideways glance. "So how are you going to vote?" he asked, almost nonchalantly.

"I haven't made up my mind."

Gary shrugged again and looked down at his papers.

Mrs. Peabody grabbed the note and Oliver's collar. "Thank you," she said. "As usual you've been no help at all."

It was as she was leaving that Mrs. Peabody realized why Gary had pretended to take little interest in what she was saying.

Because he already knew.

Because he had something to do with the murders.

MRS. PEABODY HEADED for the mayor's office. She hadn't told Gary about her decision because she thought it was none of his business. She was going to resign from the city council. It had all gotten too complicated. What did she care if the old *Finster Mansion* stood for a hundred more years? If people liked listening to concerts, and hearing boring people speak, or examining local art, that was fine with her. On the other hand, if they wanted their children to have access to seesaws, sandboxes, swings and slides, while the mothers sat around smoking and drinking coffee and complaining about being overwhelmed by motherhood, so be it.

None of it was worth a hair on Oliver's head.

Mayor Poduck saw her right away and, unlike Gary, he took her concerns very seriously.

"Looks like someone doesn't want you to vote," he said heavily.

"That's putting it mildly. I have to be honest with you. I don't care about the *Finster Mansion*. Why should I? It has nothing to do with me."

"Did you ever think that maybe it's not about the mansion at all? Maybe it's the new sidewalks on High

Street or whether we should plant a vegetable garden down by the railroad tracks."

"I suppose that's possible, but no one is bringing me muffins or paying for my coffee so they can plant cucumbers in the flats. I want to resign."

"Resign?" The mayor's brown eyes bulged. "The vote is Wednesday, four days away. At this time, it would be impossible for anyone to take your place. I don't think you're being fair to the community."

"I'm just trying to be fair to myself and my dog."

The Mayor studied Mrs. Peabody for a few long minutes, making her feel very uncomfortable. "Do you know why I asked you to be on the city council, Mrs. Peabody?"

"You couldn't find anyone else?"

The Mayor laughed. "You know, I used to play cards with your husband, Louie, down at the Elks. They were good times. And your Louie, he wasn't much of a talker. But when he did talk, it was all about you."

"Me?"

"How much he admired you, how he thought you were such a strong person, how you never backed down. He said when you made up your mind, that was it. You stood your ground. It used to drive him crazy, on one hand, but on the other, he respected you."

Mrs. Peabody was skeptical. If Louie had admired her, he never left a clue. Still she wanted to believe it. She needed to believe it.

"So I'm asking you to reconsider."

"Maybe. I'll let you know."

"At least until Wednesday. Then it won't matter as much."

"No," Mrs. Peabody headed for the door, "I don't suppose it will."

"And Mrs. Peabody," the mayor called after her. "I know that you will do what your conscience dictates."

MRS. PEABODY DECIDED to stop at *Neisers*. She hadn't been there for a while and she was craving a piece of blueberry pie—although she doubted that Nellie would give her even a broken piece for free.

The counter was crowded and maybe it was Mrs. Peabody's imagination but people seemed to be staring at her, when she sat down.

"Well, here she comes," Nellie said, the coffee pot in one hand, a cup in the other, "Miss City Council. So how have you been?" she asked as she poured.

"I've been fine," Mrs. Peabody said. "In spite of the fact, that I've been bullied and threatened."

"Bullied and threatened?" Nellie repeated, her eyes widening.

Suddenly the babbling from the city hall secretaries, and the *Dorothy Dodds* salesclerks, and the traveling salesmen lowered.

"My dog was kidnapped. I was given an ultimatum to resign from the city council or else. Well, I don't know how I'm going to vote on the *Finster Mansion* but I do know that I can't be bought. Now I'll have a piece of blueberry pie and I'll pay for it myself."

As she dipped her fork into the crust—which tasted slightly sour—Mrs. Peabody wondered if she had just signed her death certificate.

FORTY-EIGHT

"Hi, doll face."

Kate hated it when Stanley called her doll face. In fact, she hated Stanley. If she knew it was he on the other end of the telephone, she would have never picked up. She wished there was a way you could tell who was calling you, but no one had invented such a thing, and she doubted if it was even possible.

"What do you want, Stanley?" She could not keep the resentment out of her voice.

"I want to see you, maybe go out to dinner."

"I can't afford it."

"We could go to a cheap place."

"I'm tired, Stanley. It was a long day."

Stanley's tone changed. "You know I'm getting sick and tired of your attitude, Kate. I came here, hoping we could have a fresh start, that we could pick up where we left off in New York."

"That was a long time ago. And I'm a different person now."

"You don't have to tell me about a long time," Stanley said bitterly. "Fifteen years I sat in a jail cell, just because I had a little too much to drink, and that damn homeless guy walked out in front of me. You know when you offered to drive, I should have let you. But you were more smashed than me, so I did a good deed and took the wheel. But, if it had been the other way around, you'd be the one with a prison record. And this is the thanks I get? It don't seem fair."

Kate thought it best not to answer.

"I wonder what your librarian friends would think of your past."

"I won't be blackmailed."

"Oh really? That sounds a little like the conversation I had with Malcolm. He accused me of practically the same thing because I know something about him, why he came to Honeyspoon. And trust me, it has nothing to do with that blonde floozy friend of yours."

Kate heard the sound of breathing at the other end of the phone—short, little gasps. She knew who was listening. "You can hang up now, Mrs. Peabody," Kate said, as she clanged down the phone.

Kate had a good mind to go to the telephone company and ask for a single line. But she couldn't afford it. Maybe she could get two other people, though. The Maloneys were all right, but Kate was sick and tired of her nosy neighbor.

And she was tired of being intimidated. She wanted to be free. She'd tell Stanley to leave her alone and, if he wanted to tell the world about her getting drunk one night in New York City, then let him.

But not yet. Not until she learned what Stanley knew about Malcolm. And no, she wasn't being a nosy parker herself, but, if he had a tainted past, he might be dangerous. And Joanne needed to know that.

She lifted the phone again and then put it down. If all of a sudden she changed her tune with Stanley, he might think she was giving into the blackmail. And he might refuse to tell her anything about Malcolm. But why even involve Stanley? Why not go straight to the source and simply ask Malcolm. She knew where he was staying.

She better hurry. The last bus downtown was leaving in fifteen minutes.

KATE HAD NEVER been inside the *Roger Roberts Hotel* before. On the outside, it looked luxurious and stately, but once in the lobby, it was entirely a different story. The red Oriental Carpet was worn and darkly stained, faded on the edges as though moths had been enjoying a tasty meal. The red and white wallpaper was peeling, the few gray chairs sagged and the coffee table was littered with months old, *Popular Mechanics* and *US News and World Report* magazines. A single bowl held a few apple cores. The lobby had an unpleasant odor, musty, tobacco, garlic and a strong smell of gas.

"Can I help you?" An overweight woman, speaking in an English accent, with a nose like a paddle, was dipping French Fries in ketchup.

"You must be Clara," Kate said. "I'm a friend of Nellie."

"What do you want?" Clara brought a French fry to her mouth. A red blob dripped on her pointed chin.

"I'm looking for Malcolm Harris."

"Mr. Harris has gone out for the evening."

"Oh. Do you know where he might be?"

"Maybe."

"Well, where is he?"

Clara held out her plump, red stained palm.

Kate took the hint. She opened her pocketbook and reached inside her wallet for two one dollar bills. Careful not to touch Clara's sticky hand, she placed the money on the counter.

Clara dipped another fry into the ketchup.

Kate took out another two dollars and placed it on top of the other money.

"He's at the *Victory Theater* next door."

Kate didn't bother to say thank you but she was grateful that the movie theater was close by. She really didn't want to see *The Day the Earth Stood Still* and she didn't feel like paying for a ticket.

It turned out that she didn't have to. The man in the ticket booth told her that since it already started, he wouldn't charge her. She couldn't see much as she peered around in the gloomy darkness, but it looked as if the theater was pretty much deserted. A handful of people sat downstairs, mostly teenagers, who were necking. Malcolm was nowhere in sight.

Kate walked up to the balcony.

A couple was kissing and an old man was snoring. She spotted a single man, sitting by himself in the middle of a row. She stumbled over a bucket of popcorn and a spilled soda to get to him.

He was facing the screen and didn't acknowledge her. Maybe he couldn't see her in the dark.

"Malcolm, it's Kate," she said in a wheezy whisper. "Joanne's friend. Why don't we go somewhere and talk?"

Still he stared straight ahead.

"I really need to talk to you. I know you have a reason to be in Honeyspoon but with all the murders going on...well, you being here doesn't look good. I also would like to know your connection with Connie. I saw you together in the park."

Nothing.

And then Kate noticed something rather unusual. It

wasn't only that he wouldn't speak but to her horror he wasn't moving. Not one inch.

Gently she touched his arm and he toppled to the floor.

Malcolm was dead.

And she couldn't stop screaming.

FORTY-NINE

Mrs. Peabody was sound asleep when she was woken by the loud and unpleasant wail of the telephone bell. Of course, the ring wasn't for her and, looking at the clock, she saw that it was four-twenty in the morning.

Someone was calling Kate at four twenty and, at that hour, it had to be important.

Not bothering with her robe and her slippers, she jumped out of bed. The wood floor felt like ice cubes on her feet, as she raced into the living room and picked up the phone.

"Hello."

She had answered the phone before Kate.

Another click. "Hello," Kate said in a hesitant voice.

"Is this Kate Tringali?"

"Yes. What is this about?"

"This is Detective Shea from the Boston Police Department."

"Boston? What do you want with me?"

"It's about the murder of Malcolm Harris."

Mrs. Peabody had to bite her lip to stop herself from gasping.

"Just so you know," Kate didn't sound so sleepy now. "I was down at the Honeyspoon Police Station for most of the night talking to our local police. I don't know what more I can tell you or why you'd even be interested."

"There have been three murders in a matter of weeks in your small town. It's the opinion of the state that your local police, as well meaning as they are, could use a little help."

"All right." Kate sounded angry and Mrs. Peabody could only hope that she didn't hang up the phone before satisfying Mrs. Peabody's curiosity. "So I'll say it again. I went to the movie theater to find Malcolm. What I found was that he was sitting in the seat, dead. I don't know if it was a suspicious death. The man could have had a heart attack…"

"The coroner said that Malcolm was strangled."

At a movie theater? What was the world coming to?

"I don't understand," Kate said.

"Neither do we. What did you want with Malcolm?"

"If you're a detective then you know that he was dating a friend of mine. I thought perhaps he was just using her. I wanted to tell him to stop seeing her."

"And this was your business?"

"Joanne is my best friend. I would hate to see her hurt. That's all I know."

"Well, here's the thing, Miss Tringali. You may know more than you think you know. And that knowledge might put you in danger."

No one spoke for several seconds and Mrs. Peabody could only hope that they didn't hear her breathing.

"Listen," Kate finally said. "What I do know is that I don't know you. I don't know if you're a real detective, or just a reporter, looking for a scoop. Or maybe someone connected with all three killings." God, Kate was smart. "If you have any more questions for me, then you can meet me down at our local police station, when Wayne and Gary are present. I have nothing more to say to you, Mr. Shea, or you either, Mrs. Peabody."

Clang.

Kate knew that she had been listening and before the detective could ask her any questions, Mrs. Peabody hung up the phone. She padded back to her own bed, but she doubted that she could sleep.

Evidently Malcolm had been strangled while watching a movie and Kate had found him. Mrs. Peabody wasn't born yesterday. She knew that Kate had a very good reason to question Malcolm. Hadn't she told Kate herself that Malcolm was in town before the first murder was committed?

A chill ran down Mrs. Peabody's chest as she tightened her blanket around her. She remembered another phone call, which she had heard hours ago. Stanley threatening Kate. Not only Kate but Malcolm as well.

And what about the fact that Connie had been seen with him?

That was something the police should know.

But first, maybe she should talk to Connie. She owed her that much.

Mrs. Peabody couldn't go back to sleep. She was too anxious to talk to Connie.

She was up at six—not wanting to wake Oliver because she wasn't about to walk him at this ungodly hour. She went into the kitchen, put on the broken percolator, grabbed two slices of raisin toast from the bread box and put it in the toaster.

After pouring herself a cup of coffee, and heavily buttering her toast, and then heaping on some marmalade, she took herself to the front window, opened the curtains, hoping to see Connie come out.

At six fifteen, she saw the milk truck pull into the small cul-de-sac. Mr. Wiggins emerged, dressed in his usual white uniform, and he appeared to be whistling. He went to the back of the truck and emerged carrying his stainless steel rack, containing several quart bottles of milk, hunks of cheese, dozens of eggs. He started with the Maloneys, and then to her surprise Connie answered the door.

Mrs. Peabody waited until he left, then she opened the door, tightened her robe around her, and knocked on Connie's door.

Connie, who was wearing a pair of oversized pajamas—probably Bill's—opened her mouth in surprise.

"Mrs. Peabody. Is everything all right? Aren't you feeling good?"

"I feel fine." That was a lie, although Connie herself looked tired and rather ill. "Did you hear the news?"

Connie's blank expression told Mrs. Peabody that she hadn't.

"Malcolm Harris is dead. He was strangled at the movie theater."

"Oh my God!" Connie put her hands over her face.

"I know you and Malcolm were friends."

"No, not really. I was helping him, giving him leads on antiques. I never saw him before he came to Honeyspoon, honestly."

Mrs. Peabody didn't believe her and the doubt must have showed on her face. "Don't you think that the police should know about your connection? I mean, if they should find out themselves, with all that has happened…"

"No! Please!" Connie begged. "I didn't have anything to do with his death. And I can't become involved. My boys, they already have a father in prison. If the police start to question me, if they make more of this." Tears welled in her eyes. "I swear to you…"

"But maybe Malcolm has something to do with the murders."

"That's not possible. He couldn't have. Not with these murders. I mean, how could he? Wasn't he murdered himself?"

Mrs. Peabody could hardly deny that.

"Please, don't go to the police. I am begging you."

"I won't." Mrs. Peabody decided then and there that it wouldn't be prudent to get herself involved. "I promise."

A light snow had become to fall, so early in the season, which forecasted a long, cold winter.

She trudged back into the house, her mind whirling as she repeated what Connie had said to her. *"Malcolm had nothing to do with the murders, or at least those murders."*

Which meant he had something to do with another murder.

And suddenly just like that, all the pieces fell into place.

FIFTY

Sister Regina Rachel did not want to go to the Mother House. She didn't want to take care of aging, sick nuns. She didn't want that to be her life.

But what could she do? Leave the order? Where would she go? How would she survive without a job, a home?

She had just finished packing a few things in her suitcase—a very few things, since there wasn't much to take. Nuns weren't allowed personal property. She packed her extra habit, four sets of underpants, one black sweater, three pairs of extra hose, a sleeping shirt, four hair nets and on the bottom, she stashed a bar of lavender soap, which she had received as a Christmas gift two years ago. At least her drab belongings would smell sweet.

She slammed shut the cardboard suitcase and looked around at the small cell like room, which had been her home for eight years. There was nothing about it she would miss, but who knew what she was going to.

She was headed for the door, when she heard a rap.

Time to go to a new life—not necessarily a better one.

She opened the door to Mother Superior.

"The van is here?" Sister asked.

Mother Superior shook her head.

"I'm sorry to tell you this, Sister. But your father has

taken a turn for the worse. The car has been fixed so I'll be able to drive you to the hospital."

WHILE MOTHER SUPERIOR DROVE, Sister sat in the front seat of the station wagon, silent and stunned. Finally, holding back tears, she said, "I can't believe that this is happening. It's all my fault. I disappointed my father and now he's suffering."

"Don't make this about you," Mother Superior said sharply. "Your father was an elderly man with a medical condition. If God wants him, God will take him. God doesn't need your permission."

That wasn't what Sister had meant at all, but she thought it best not to comment or argue.

They didn't speak again until they reached the doors of the hospital. "I'll park the car," Mother Superior said. "And you go up to the room. I don't want to intrude, so I'll stay in the chapel, praying that God's will be done."

Sister left the car, hurried inside the revolving doors, and waited forever for the elevator. Her heart heavy with dread, she walked down the long, narrow corridor to her father's room.

Nora was there, sitting by his bedside. "He has pneumonia."

Sister asked the question she had been dreading. "Is he going to make it?"

"Who knows? He doesn't think that he is, that's for sure. He keeps rambling on about all the things he's ever done wrong, the sins he's committed. The time he took beer without paying from *Pat's Grocery Store*, or sneaked into the *Suffolk Movie Theater*, or kissed Mrs. Ross at the Christmas Party."

"If that's all he has to confess…"

Suddenly Sister's father began to groan and Sister rushed to his side.

"We're here, Daddy," she said.

"You're going to be all right," Nora said in a tone that was far from reassuring.

"Daddy, I'm sorry," Sister said suddenly.

"You shouldn't be sorry, Roselyn. I'm the one who should be sorry. I forced you to join the convent because I wanted one of my daughters to be a nun. It wasn't fair to you. And I took money when I shouldn't have."

"You took money from the diocese?" Nora asked, sounding slightly alarmed.

"No, from a worker."

"Why would a worker pay you money?"

"To delay the renovation on that mansion. So we wouldn't come in on time, when we promised. I think maybe," he gasped, "something needed to be hidden."

Nora and Sister looked at each other. No doubt it was puzzling but right now Sister didn't care. She felt as if a tremendous burden had been lifted from her. Her father was not disappointed in her. He understood. He blamed himself.

"It was a long time ago," Nora said. "None of that matters now."

Suddenly a buzzer went off. The shriek bought a gaggle of nurses into the room, pushing Sister and Nora out of the way.

"Is he going to die?" Nora screamed.

The question wasn't asked to anyone in particular and no one in particular answered. The door was closed. Sister and Nora stood in the hall. Nora shook her head, "This is horrible," was all she managed to say.

"I wonder what he meant by that," Sister said.

"How can that matter now?" Nora approached the door, as though she was trying to listen to what might be happening inside.

"Well, it wouldn't," Sister said. "If people weren't getting murdered left and right."

"What are you talking about?" Nora asked, almost in an angry tone.

Sister didn't answer, because she didn't know. Suddenly the door opened and a nurse came out.

"Is he going to be all right?" Nora questioned anxiously.

"For now. But your father is a very sick man."

Sister drew a deep breath. In spite of it all, she was grateful that her father had given her permission for her to do what?

FIFTY-ONE

As she sat down with a cup of coffee and her last shortbread cookie, Mrs. Peabody tried to think of ways that she could prove her theory. There wasn't anyone to ask, except maybe Connie. But if what Mrs. Peabody thought was correct, then Connie had lied to her and what would prevent Connie from lying to her again?

Somewhere buried in her brain was the answer but it was as if a fog was hovering over her head and she couldn't remember. She turned on the television in the living room.

The newscaster—a big, burly man with red hair and a ruddy complexion—was talking delightfully about Malcolm's murder. The police—which really consisted of Wayne and Gary—could find no connection between Malcolm's killing and the murders of Violet Rose or Rita Eastman. Which made Mrs. Peabody think that they were lying or they were just stupid.

He went on to say that a shocked community compelled the state to bring in the Boston police to help—which meant the person who called Kate was legitimate. A notice of the upcoming Community Board Meeting, which would be voting on several items—whether the *Finster Mansion* should continue to stand or whether it should be torn down to make room for a children's playground; whether or not the city should spend money on new sidewalks for High Street; whether guard rails should be installed on Riverdale Road, which was known as *Suicide Highway* and whether or not the city should expand the library to include a record room.

"As much as we'd like to, we are unable to do all of these things." The major was standing on the stone steps of the city hall. "We simply don't have the money. We have to choose. And those choices will be up to the current council members."

The mayor went on to say that "the committee will be happy to listen to suggestions but the time is running out for the fiscal year and all matters will be decided on Wednesday evening."

Mrs. Peabody half-listened to the political news from the capital. She could barely do anything about what was happening in Honeyspoon, never mind Washington. Then the picture flashed to an old woman who just had a hundredth birthday party at the Holiday Inn. The toothless lady was grinning ear to ear—Mrs. Peabody doubted very much that she would live that long—as everyone, happy as larks, danced around her.

Suddenly just like that Mrs. Peabody remembered something, another party and another photograph, taken long ago, which just might prove what she suspected.

THE FIRST THING that she had to do was take herself to the library to learn whether what she suspected was even possible.

She walked and fed Oliver and, once she was assured that he was safely tucked inside, she got the early bus downtown.

On route to the library, she checked the phone booth on the corner. Pulling out the coin return, she was delighted to find 15 cents. She could use it to buy herself a cup of coffee.

That dour woman again, standing in that black coat, ringing the bell, begging for money for the *March of Dimes*. As Mrs. Peabody got closer, she realized that the woman was elderly, even older than herself. Standing in the cold, not even for something she could personally benefit from, made Mrs. Peabody feel somewhat guilty.

She threw the 15 cents in the bucket. The woman rewarded her with a grin.

Mrs. Peabody waited, shivering, at the entrance to the library. At first Kate seemed surprised to see her, and then her mood changed to one of annoyance. "Obviously, I haven't had a chance to even get the newspapers, let alone ready them for viewing."

"I'm not here to read the newspaper, at least not the current ones. I need to look at some microfilms."

Kate frowned. Mrs. Peabody knew that Kate hated that chore. It wasn't easy to set up and no matter how many times Kate explained to her, Mrs. Peabody always needed help.

"What is it that you're looking for?" Kate slid the door of the library open.

"I'm looking for a two copies of the *Honeyspoon Herald*. One from four weeks ago today and one from nine years ago. Halloween Evening, October 31, 1948."

Kate stopped on the stairs and gazed open mouth at Mrs. Peabody. "Can I ask you why you need these particular papers?"

"I'd rather not say until I'm sure."

Kate drew a deep breath. "Well, it's going to take me a few minutes. I have to set up for the opening. In the meantime, you can wait in the reading room."

"I'll wait. Actually," Mrs. Peabody could hardly avoid the subject, "I'm surprised you're here. You had a horrible shock."

"I'd rather not talk about it."

"Do you know why I think Malcolm was killed?"

"I can't imagine what you're thinking." Kate headed for the front desk.

"I think he knew something about the murders."

Kate turned around and stared at Mrs. Peabody. "You think he was one of the murderers?"

"No. Malcolm was no killer."

"Mrs. Peabody, really. You should let the police handle this. You should mind your own business."

"Well, the police have been doing a really good job so far," Mrs. Peabody said sarcastically. "There have already been three killings."

"And you don't want to be the fourth."

The way Kate uttered that sentence made Mrs. Peabody doubt what she had just been so certain of.

It was cold in the library and Mrs. Peabody shivered. Perhaps no one had yet to put on the heat. She watched as Kate grabbed a raspberry pink cardigan from the back of her chair.

"Please wait in the reading room."

Mrs. Peabody waited, which seemed to be a long time, amusing herself with a copy of *Ladies' Home Journal*. Lots of advice for housewives with busy husbands and noisy children. She wondered how different her life would have been if she and Louie had had children.

"Okay," Kate walked into the room, carrying the film. "I got the one from Halloween and the paper from four weeks ago today. And I'll thread them both for you. But as soon as Margaret comes in, I have to go downstairs to the children's library. It's Saturday and it's story time. So if you have any other problems, you'll have to ask Margaret."

Mrs. Peabody didn't want to ask Margaret. She didn't like Margaret and she had a feeling that Margaret didn't like her.

"I'll be fine," Mrs. Peabody said, although lately she wasn't feeling too fine. Her legs always ached, they were stiff and, at times, unmovable. Her dizzy spells were getting worse.

Kate set it up for her without saying a word and then left. Mrs. Peabody took a long, deep breath and then got to work.

First she looked at the paper, which covered in depth the death of Chester Benteen, the man who had leaped to his death from the *Finster Mansion*'s attic. The police surmised that Chester, new to the area, had been smoking marijuana. He had recently graduated from the *University of Massachusetts* with a degree in architecture. Chester was using the writing room to author a book about landmark buildings and he was intrigued with the *Finster Mansion* and its structure. His battered body was sent to his parents in Minnesota.

Then Mrs. Peabody turned her attention to the earlier paper. She remembered a picture of the Halloween Party, taken that evening but she knew it wouldn't be on page one. The headlines brought a smile on her face. The war had been over for several years but the country was still elated and feeling optimistic about the future. Prices were soaring—which compared to prices seven years later was really a joke—and families were buying little houses on little streets.

Mrs. Peabody turned several pages before she found what she was looking for.

A photograph taken on a block party. She remembered it as if it was yesterday. A beautiful October evening, rather warm for that time of year, but no one was complaining. Most of the neighbors had come dressed up, but not Mrs. Peabody. She was wearing a pretty green dress which was trimmed in lavender. She loved that dress and would have kept it forever if the moths hadn't eaten through the cotton fabric.

Louie hadn't gone. He wasn't a people person.

Yes, Mrs. Peabody remembered the evening but not everyone who attended.

Kate Tringali had just returned from New York. She wasn't in costume either, but in a pretty, frilly, red polka dot dress with ruffles and puff sleeves. She looked very stylish, very New York. But in the nine years that had passed, Kate had already grown wary and matronly. Bill Maloney was dressed as The Grim Reaper and even in black and white, his eyes looked cold and hostile. Connie was wearing the costume of a flapper, a woman in the 1920s. She was thin as a reed, before her other two pregnancies. Rita was dressed as a school girl, with a plaid skirt and a white blouse. Larry Eastman hadn't dressed, nor had Mr. Kitchenmaster—his wife looked like an overweight ballerina. Mr. Wiggins came dressed—as a milkman. And Mrs. Notewire was dressed as one of her cats.

There were several others in the background, long gone from the neighborhood but in the corner someone lurked in a clown costume. Mrs. Peabody would not have recognized him if she had not remembered what he wore on that sultry October evening and beside him, someone else looking confused and just a tad bit frightened.

The question which was nagging on her mind was what had become of them?

FIFTY-TWO

ANDREW WAS FEELING sick to his stomach. Not so much a physical sickness, when he had to take to his bed, it was the scariness of the situation, which made his stomach lurch with nerves, as though there was a big, fat hole in his abdomen.

His mother had tried to explain about the man in the woods. She said he was a friend, who was going to try and help his father. But even as she said it, Andrew suspected his mother was lying.

It was an awful thing when you couldn't trust either of your parents.

But when all was said and done Andrew himself was the blame. If he hadn't told the police about his father stealing the comic books, his father would be home right now since he heard his mother tell his grandmother that the police no longer suspected his father of murder. His mother was crying night and day but last night was the worst. The doorbell rang and a scary man—dressed all in black—barged into the living room, thrusting a piece of paper into his mother's hands.

Andrew looked over his mother's shoulder and saw one word in large print—EVICTION.

"This is ridiculous," his mother had argued. "You can't kick us out of our home, where we've been for seven years, where we have children, just because we missed one month of rent."

"One month?" The man repeated. "Lady, we haven't seen one dime of rent from you in seven months."

Seven months?! From his mother's expression, Andrew knew that she was as astonished as he. His father had always paid the bills, well, obviously, not all the bills. Andrew also knew that his father was a gambler and that's where the rent money had gone. But if his father had been at home, he would have fixed the situation. He wouldn't let anyone throw the family out in the street. As much as Andrew hated his father sometimes, it was obvious now that his mother was paralyzed without him.

It was Saturday, a day Andrew usually looked forward to. But what was there to do? Where was there to go? But he couldn't stay in the house, that was for sure. Only this time, he was going to be smart. He wasn't going anywhere without his *Red Ryder BB Gun*, the one he had traded from Terrence. The one that caused all the trouble.

He hid it under his coat and as he was leaving, his mother called out, rather sadly, "Have fun playing with your friends."

Like he had friends.

He walked aimlessly. It was colder out than he thought and he wished he had taken his gloves and his scarf. But he didn't know where they were. Usually his mother made certain that he was dressed for the weather, but now she didn't seem to care about that.

He needed someplace warm just to sit and think for a while. He thought about going to the library but that was several streets away and he was tired. Besides, he might not be welcome after the last visit. Huffing and puffing, he saw the *Finster Mansion* up ahead.

The iron gate was open and he spotted a bench which was perfect for sitting. He collapsed there, hoping to catch his breath before he moved on.

He sat there for a few moments, looking at the bare trees, his legs circling the dead leaves at his feet. He had the distinct impression that someone was watching him, someone in the bushes. Out of the corner of his eye, he saw a swish of black. If his father wasn't a murderer, then someone else was, and that someone else was still running around. Which meant that he wasn't safe.

He rose quickly. He couldn't leave—at least not the same way he had entered, not when someone dangerous was out there, just steps away.

He walked further inside, the dying leaves sounding ominous as they crunched below him. He spotted an open window, close to the ground.

Andrew knelt down and saw a cellar. He could hide there for a while, just until the man left. Well, maybe not. Maybe it wasn't any safer down in a basement than outside. Besides, he probably couldn't even fit inside the window.

Maybe he could. So using all of his strength, he pushed the window open a bit more. Now he could see that it was just a basement with a lot of boxes and paintings, and some file cabinets. And a stone staircase.

He could enter through the window, climb the staircase and just walk out the back door.

It was a daring move, but lately Andrew was doing lots of daring things. The problem was that no one knew how brave he had become. Well, maybe he wasn't brave at all. Maybe he was just dumb.

First he threw down the BB gun. It landed with a loud

crash. He could only hope that he hadn't broken it. Then he had to squeeze his body through the small gap—because there was no way he was going to abandon the gun. So he hurled into space and landed flat on the stone floor on his behind. There was plenty of fat there to protect him, but still he felt sore and was sure he had cut himself. He was also laden with dust and debris. And if his mother should ask him, what happened? What would he say? Maybe she wouldn't notice. She was busy with so many other things. Andrew was the least of her problems.

He rose slowly and looked around, shocked at his sudden landing. The cellar was being used as a storage space, probably lots of valuable things inside, but what did he know? Anyway, he wasn't a thief like his father.

He picked up his gun, feeling slightly protected.

Out of the corner of his eye, he saw something dash by him. At first he thought it was a mouse—he was used to mice, the project was loaded with them—but as the creature ran behind a box, he saw a long, black tail, and knew that what he had been looking at was a beastly rat.

Rats bite, they gave you rabies, they killed you. He thought about killing one of them first with his BB gun, but then reconsidered. For one thing, it might create a noise, and if anyone else was in the mansion, it would alert them of his presence.

And besides, it might be messy.

Andrew hurried to the stairs and, slowly tiptoed up, holding the BB gun with one hand, and the crumbling railing with the other.

And then he heard something else.
A cough.
He wasn't alone.

FIFTY-THREE

MRS. PEABODY ROSE with shaking legs. She went to the front desk, where Kate was stamping some books for a nurse, who was standing beside an elderly man in a wheelchair. Mrs. Peabody couldn't help but think how nice it must be to have someone care for you. Perhaps this nurse would read to him from the poetry books Kate was stamping.

Mrs. Peabody could never remember anyone taking care of her, even as a child. She wondered if she herself had children, if they would have done so. Her husband—Louie? No—the only person he cared for was himself.

"Are you finished?" Kate asked.

Mrs. Peabody nodded. "I'm sorry. I don't know how to disconnect it."

"Why don't you come with me, so next time you do know."

"I would. But I can't. I have to get to the *Finster Mansion*."

"It's closed on Saturdays."

That was what Mrs. Peabody feared.

Suddenly Kate jumped up when she saw a group of rambunctious children head for the staircase leading to the children's library. "Excuse me," she shouted after them. "But the children's library doesn't open until eleven."

At that precise moment, as though it was meant to be, Mrs. Peabody happened to look down at the dish on the side of the desk, which contained Kate's keys. One of the keys was clearly marked *Finster Mansion*. She remembered suddenly that the Mayor had said that committee members each received a key in case of an emergency meeting. Without hesitating long enough to change her mind, Mrs. Peabody snatched up Kate's keys and put them in her pocket.

"Thanks for your help," she called to Kate as she left through the front door.

IT WAS THE wrong thing to do and Mrs. Peabody knew it. Later she would return to the library and drop the keys, hoping that Kate would think she herself had misplaced them.

She didn't have a choice, not really. There was something much more at stake here. At least that's what she told herself as she walked slowly to the *Finster Mansion*. She knew exactly what she was looking for but not so certain about what she would do once she found it.

She walked through the iron gate, which was already open, and then to the front door. She had to struggle with the key. It seemed to stick. And when the door was finally open, it was heavy and unyielding.

Finally in the front hall, she stopped to look around. Of course, she had been at the mansion many times before but this time it was different, deserted, eerie. She stood in the hall for a few minutes, looking up at the twenty foot ceilings. The doors on either side were closed tightly and she wondered if someone was hiding in there.

Not just someone.

The murderer.

Again, without thinking, because if she thought too much, she would not walk further into the hall.

She approached the carpeted staircase and slowly, holding on to the rail, her head swerving behind her—in case someone should come up and give her a good hard push—she climbed. Her footsteps not making a sound.

She reached the second floor and walked along the large corridor, decorated with oil paintings on either side. She thought about what the mansion might have been like when Mr. Finster lived here with all of his pets. The mansion had been the site of many balls, and annual games, children parties and fairs. It was a time of bubbling excitement and the small events that were co-hosted here now paled in comparison.

She couldn't resist peeking into one of the rooms and was surprised to see that it was still a bedroom. A canopy bed lay in the middle of the room with a spread that had once been white but now had turned gray with dust and debris. There was a pretty bureau and a make-up table, covered with a dirty silver cloth and assorted perfume bottles. She wondered why these rooms weren't put to better use and thought that maybe she should raise that question in front of the city council before they voted.

She smelled the unmistakable odor of cats—and carnations.

Well, she wasn't here to explore. She knew she was just putting off the inevitable. So instead she turned around and saw the narrow staircase, leading to what was probably the servant quarters. These stone stairs were not carpeted. Her footsteps echoed in the house and if anyone else was present, then they would surely hear her.

The stairs were steep and they were circular and her heart was hammering by the time she reached the top. She could only hope that the servants had been in better shape than her.

She arrived at the top and took a deep, hard breath. A number of little rooms veered off to the side. She peeked into one and saw a stack of boxes, paintings against the wall, books piled up almost to the ceiling. One room had one typewriter—was this the reason for the renovation? Where were the rest of the writing rooms?

Mrs. Peabody walked further down, ducking so her head wouldn't hit the ceiling. Yes, this was the larger room, the one that had been renovated. A huge window overlooked the yard. Mrs. Peabody stood by it for a moment and thought that years ago, that plot of land might have been a pretty rose garden.

The room was painted in a cheery ocean blue, but something was wrong. For some reason she felt that the room was enclosing on her.

She left and went next door, a room full of newspapers and piles of old, moth ridden clothes. Hurrying back to the blue room, she knocked on the wall and it didn't seem solid. Also the paint on this wall was slightly uneven.

Could her suspicions be right?

And how would she prove it?

She was about to go back down the stairs when she heard a door slam.

FIFTY-FOUR

"THERE'S A CARTON of Mary Rinehart books which arrived yesterday," Margaret said the moment she walked into the library. "They need to be unpacked and entered into the system. I noticed that you didn't put the morning papers out yet. People are waiting in the reading room. Also, there are magazines that are piling up, *Good Housekeeping*, *Family Circle*, *Saturday Evening Post*..."

"It's been a busy morning," Kate muttered.

Margaret peeked into the small room. "Who was using the microfilm?"

"Mrs. Peabody."

"So early in the morning?"

"Yes, it was early. Barely ten o'clock."

"First things first. Put the newspapers out so Mr. Stringer and Mrs. Vogt would stop looking impatient in the reading room." No doubt they couldn't wait to read the latest about the murders.

Mrs. Vogt pounced on her the moment Kate entered the room. What was it like to find a dead body? Did you faint? Did you scream? How long was it before the police arrived? Kate just shrugged her shoulders and walked away.

The truth was that she was feeling perturbed by Mrs. Peabody's conversation.

Of course, Mrs. Peabody hadn't bothered to disconnect the microfilm. Probably because she didn't know how. Kate scanned the headlines of the recent paper, which was open to the page about the death of Chester Benteen.

So what?

It was the picture of the Halloween picture, taken so long ago, that gave her pause. Everyone dressed in costumes, looking so young and gay.

She had come back from New York and, although Kate was smiling, she remembered feeling depressed. Her dream had died and she wasn't sure what she was going to do.

So here she was.

Kate studied the picture and then saw the clown, whose eyes looked unusually dark. Well, maybe it was just a trick of the newspaper, a smudge on the film. But what was it about the picture that made Mrs. Peabody bolt out the door after asking about the *Finster Mansion*? Obviously, she had seen something, but what was it?

Whatever it was, Kate was at a loss. She disconnected the machine and walked by the front desk. Looking down at the little ceramic bowl, she noticed that her keys were missing.

Maybe she had never put them there. With Mrs. Peabody at her feet, it was possible that Kate just shoved the keys back into her pocketbook. So she dragged out her purse from underneath the counter and searched, moving aside her wallet, and used tissues, and cough drops sticky with tissues and her Revlon *Cherries in the Snow* lipstick—No keys.

With her stomach sinking, Kate realized what must

have happened. Mrs. Peabody had taken her keys because she wanted to gain entrance to the *Finster Mansion.*

Margaret was helping an elderly gentlemen find books on the Civil War, so even though Margaret frowned upon using the library phone for personal use, Kate quickly dialed, keeping her voice low.

"Yeah?" Joanne answered in a sleepy voice.

"It's me. Kate. I have a question for you."

"It's Saturday morning, barely eleven o'clock. I like to sleep in. And the police were here last night. Asking me all kinds of questions about Malcolm. All I can say, if he was involved in something dangerous, then I'm a very lucky woman I wasn't with him when he was murdered."

"You have a good point. The *Finster Mansion*, it's not open today?"

"I just told you it's Saturday morning and I sleep in. I know the committee is thinking about keeping it open six days a week, but, if that happens, then they're going to have to pay me time and a half. And give me Monday off. As it is…"

"Mrs. Peabody was here."

"Why should I care?"

"She asked me to set up the microfilm equipment for her. She wanted to look at a picture of the Halloween Block Party nine years ago. She also wanted the newspaper from four weeks ago. She was reading about Chester Benteen's death. Then she was in a rush to get out of here and go to the mansion. What's this all about, Joanne?"

"How should I know?" Suddenly Joanne sounded more alert, as though she had bolted upright. "The woman is crazy, she has bats in her belfry."

"None of it makes sense. Why that party, why so long ago?"

"I remember that party well. It was the last time I saw my husband and that whore."

Kate knew that she had hit a nerve. "But I don't understand the connection between Chester and that party."

"Neither do I. But if Miss Busybody is headed for the mansion, she's out of luck," Joanne said. "Because that place is locked up tighter than a drum."

"Well," Kate hesitated. "I think she might be able to get in." She could hear Margaret's footsteps. "She might have stolen my keys."

"Your keys?"

"The members of the city council were all given keys to the mansion in case of emergency meetings. I guess Mrs. Peabody didn't get hers because no one turned in Rita's."

"Why are you calling?" Joanne sounded hostile. "What makes you think that any of this has something to do with me?"

"Kate," Margaret's shrill voice rang out. "It's time to go downstairs to the Children's Library for story time."

"I have to go." Kate quickly hung up the phone.

"There are plenty of things to do here," Margaret said, as she grabbed a cigarette. "So there is really no time for chit chat. And don't forget to feed the birds and clean their cage."

"Sorry." Kate was tempted to say that the phone call was an emergency but she didn't want to go into detail. But before she went downstairs, there was one other thing she had to do.

She reached inside her cardigan sweater and pulled

out the piece of paper she had buried into her pocket a few days ago. It had Chester Benteen's name on it and a call number for a book.

Quickly, Kate went over to the file cards and looked up the number.

She held her breath as she read the title of the publication.

It was the blueprints for the *Finster Mansion*.

FIFTY-FIVE

Mrs. Peabody stood shock still. She knew that she should move, she should run, but where to? Instead she was fighting the urge to sag to the floor.

Maybe it wasn't the murderer. Maybe it was Mr. Vogt, wondering who had come into the mansion on a Saturday. Mrs. Peabody wondered if she should tell him the truth, if she should call the police, if Wayne would even believe her.

The footsteps were light—not a man's.

Joanne Kennedy.

"What are you doing here?" she asked.

Mrs. Peabody thought fast. "I'm on the committee."

Joanne stopped her. "Obviously, we all know that."

"Well, before I voted, I thought that I should look around here. See what I'm actually voting for. See what my vote will save. I have never been to the top floor and since this was the room that was renovated..."

"So you actually stole Kate's keys just to look around?"

Mrs. Peabody's mind was racing as an icy chill ran though her.

"Are you going to deny that you stole her keys?"

Mrs. Peabody did not want to be accused of stealing. "Actually, I planned on returning them to her. It's more like I just borrowed them. And really, I should have had my own key but the mayor..."

"After you insisted on looking at that Halloween picture."

Mrs. Peabody thought the less she said, the better.

"I want to know why you were looking at that picture."

Mrs. Peabody didn't answer the question. Instead, she said, "I'd like to leave."

Joanne was blocking the door, with no intention of moving. "Not until I know what you hoped to find looking at that picture."

Mrs. Peabody decided to tell her a half truth.

"I knew that Malcolm looked familiar. I just didn't know how. But then I saw the picture of Helen..."

"That slut."

"I saw the resemblance. I knew that they had to be related."

"So what?"

"Maybe he came here looking for his sister."

"After all these years?" Joanne released a rough, hoarse laugh.

"Well, maybe," Mrs. Peabody paused. "He didn't know quite how to go about it and then you posted that ad in the *Lonely Hearts Club*, and he saw an opportunity."

"What does that prove?"

"Nothing. Nothing at all."

"Except you think I did something to Malcolm? Is that it?"

"I don't know." Even to Mrs. Peabody her denial sounded weak.

"And it doesn't explain what you're doing here."

"I thought I explained."

"Like I'm going to believe you."

Mrs. Peabody's eyes darted around. She was looking for a way out. Could she push past Joanne? She might, if Joanne wasn't holding a letter holder in her hand.

"You know." It wasn't a question.

Then Mrs. Peabody decided. She wasn't going to die a coward. "All right. I thought you might have killed Helen and Bruce and buried them somewhere in the house. Because that would explain why you didn't want this building torn down. And somehow poor Chester must have been asking questions about the structure. Maybe he suspected that there was a gap in the wall. So you pushed him out of the window. And maybe you were blackmailing Violet Rose, because you knew she had done something horrible…"

"Me blackmail Violet Rose? I was afraid that she might blackmail me. I thought that she might have seen me push Chester out the window. And she was acting very strange. I couldn't trust her. So I followed her into the library and I strangled her. And then I ransacked the place, hoping people would think that there was a robbery there." She laughed which was more like a cackle. "I had no idea that Bill Maloney had actually robbed the library earlier. And then Rita, well, Rita was the swing vote and nothing I said or did would change her mind. The fact that Bill was involved with her, too…that's what you would call fortuitous, as though God was on my side." Another empty laugh. "Or maybe the devil. And you? Well, I didn't want to draw attention to you by committing another murder. But I could make you look as if you were a dotty old lady."

"So you kidnapped Oliver and stole my letter."

"I didn't mean to steal anything, just move things around so you would start to doubt yourself. But I stumbled on the letter that was addressed to Violet Rose, and I knew if I took it and you mentioned it and you had no proof, people would start to doubt everything you said."

"But you are a blackmailer, Joanne."

"Blackmail? No way."

"You did guess who Malcolm was."

"He was smart. He began to figure out why I was so insistent that the mansion be kept standing. And I should have killed that troublesome Connie and blamed it on Bill as well. She was Helen's friend, had introduced them. She was helping Malcolm. Still you have absolutely no proof. And did it ever occur to you, that it wouldn't be easy for me just to bury two bodies during the renovation? How could I do that?" Suddenly Joanne started to yell. "How could I do that? How could I do that?"

Joanne stopped yelling when she heard footsteps on the stairs.

"I think I can prove it," a quiet voice said.

FIFTY-SIX

SISTER DIDN'T KNOW what she was thinking—or maybe she did. Maybe all of it, all the doubts, all the questions, were leading up to this moment.

After she left her father and Nora—who was still at her father's side—Sister was supposed to go to the chapel and meet Mother Superior. Her suitcase was in the back of that old station wagon, so she was going to be driving her straight to the Mother House, where Sister would be shown to another cell like room, where she would be given a handwritten schedule, up for early Mass, breakfast, nursing duties, lunch, nursing duties, dinner and then an hour of free time, which might include watching television—programs which would be monitored—or playing a game of *Scrabble* or Checkers or Chess—at the convent someone had donated the game Clue but Mother Superior thought that that any board game that involved murder was unsuitable—or maybe Careers—as though the nuns ever had a choice of interesting jobs—back to the chapel for evening novena and then to bed. One day after another, with no variation, and no hope while everyone waited for the day when their humdrum lives would be over and then they would be scooted straight to heaven, where they would sit beside Our Lord and the Blessed Virgin because of their years of service.

But Sister did not want to wait that long for peace.

So instead of heading left to the chapel, Sister walked out the front door, as though she was not a nun, who had taken vows of obedience and chastity and poverty, but as though she was just another person, free as a bird.

She had gone several blocks before reality set in. What was she doing? Where was she going? She should turn around right now, go back into the hospital, into the chapel. Mother Superior might never need to know that she had taken a brief detour, that for a few glorious moments, she felt liberated.

But she didn't turn around, just kept going, further and further away, as a chilly wind whipped her veil.

Until she was in front of the *Finster Mansion*. She was aware that the wrought iron gate was open wide, and as she stood, deciding what to do, she saw Andrew Maloney walking swiftly into the front yard.

Something about the way Andrew was moving seemed to Sister, as furtive, not quite right, as though Andrew was running away from something. Concealing herself behind an oak tree, Sister watched, expecting Andrew to walk through the front door.

Instead she saw the most incredible sight. His eyes darting, almost as though Andrew knew that someone was watching him, he made his way toward a basement window, where he stood for several minutes, before cranking it open wide, dropping a BB gun inside—where it made a deafening crash—and disappearing inside the mansion.

Why was Andrew carrying a BB gun? Was he planning to hurt someone?

Why would he climb in a cellar window, Sister wondered, *when he could just walk through the front door? Was he intending to stay hidden in the basement?*

And really what business was it of hers?

Sister reached underneath her starched bib, into her deep black pocket and pulled out her pocket watch. It was almost eleven thirty. Too late to return without giving an explanation.

Somehow the thought of confessing to Mother Superior that she had broken the vow of obedience again was enough for her to head to the front door of the mansion. She was surprised that it, also, was wide open. Was there some sort of concert or play going on?

When she stepped inside, the house was quiet, creepy. And then she saw the sign on the door, which she hadn't noticed before indicating that on Saturdays the mansion was closed.

And yet—an open gate, an open window, and now an open door.

Her instinct told her that it was time to flee. Until she heard screaming above.

"There is no way you can prove that I buried something doing the renovation."

At first Sister thought she might be hearing things. Hadn't her father just mentioned the renovation?

"No one can prove that. No one."

If Sister found out what was going on, then she might have an excuse for why she left the hospital, a half-baked one, but an excuse, nevertheless.

"How on earth do you think that I could have buried someone without anyone seeing?"

Sister took a deep breath and tromped up the first staircase.

"You can't prove a thing. And no one is going to listen to you. That's, of course, if you even have a chance to say what you want to say."

The second staircase, where the voice was louder. "You can't prove anything."

SISTER REACHED THE top of the staircase and saw a little, elderly woman standing in the corner, with frightened eyes and a younger woman, grasping a letter holder.

Before Sister could think, she quickly said, "I think I can prove it."

FIFTY-SEVEN

When Mrs. Peabody saw a nun enter the room, she thought that surely she was hallucinating. Maybe it was still Halloween Evening and this was all a dream. There had been no murders, and even Oliver, the dog she had so learned to love, was a figment of her imagination.

Maybe she was dead. Maybe Bill Maloney had killed her and now she was in some sort of purgatory for her sin.

Joanne's angry question, "Who the hell are you?" snapped Mrs. Peabody out of her stupor.

"I'm Sister Regina Rachel."

"What are you doing here?"

Sister seemed to be contemplating answering the question, but instead she said, "It may surprise you to know that I have a different name. Roselyn Randazzo."

Mrs. Peabody saw Joanne pale.

"I thought you'd recognize the name," Sister said. "My father was in charge of the renovation here. A little while ago, he thought that he was dying, so he had a confession to make. Someone paid him money to stall the renovation, because this someone had something to do. He always thought it was suspicious, like maybe someone was hiding something. But he took the money. My father didn't die. With God's help, he'll live a while longer. And then he can identify you."

"So you see, Joanne," Mrs. Peabody said. "It's all over."

"Not quite."

One moment Joanne was standing in front of Mrs. Peabody, with her back to the door, the next moment Mrs. Peabody was lifted off the floor, a strong arm around her torso, and a sharp object against her neck.

"You move, Sister, or Roselyn, or whatever your name is, and this old lady is dead."

"I'm not going anywhere," Sister said calmly, "but surely you can't kill us both."

"Oh, you would be surprised with what I can do." And what she could do was pull the letter opener closer to Mrs. Peabody's neck. Mrs. Peabody felt a prick and her own warm blood creeping down her neck and staining her cardigan sweater. "I've already killed five people, starting with the shooting of Bruce and Helen, which, by the way, they deserved. So two more doesn't faze me."

"Five people?" Sister seemed aghast.

If there wasn't a letter opener cutting into her throat, Mrs. Peabody would have counted them for her. Helen and Bruce, Violet Rose, Rita and Malcolm. But she couldn't talk. She couldn't say a word.

She saw Sister's eyes widen as she turned around and looked at the door, as though she had heard something. But all Mrs. Peabody could hear was her own terrifying heartbeat, as she stood frozen with fear. Sister glanced away quickly, but not quickly enough. Joanne was a cunning monster and she noticed. She whipped around, loosening her grip on Mrs. Peabody just a bit. Mrs. Peabody tried to wriggle away and then she heard a huge pop as a pellet flew into the air, hitting Joanne in the leg.

Joanne fell to the floor, splattering more blood on Mrs. Peabody,

At the door stood Andrew, holding his *Red Ryder BB Gun*.

FIFTY-EIGHT

THE ONLY WAY that Kate could possibly leave the library after story time was to feign illness, except she wasn't really pretending. As she was reading *The Cat in the Hat*, she began to feel ill. She grew cold every time she thought of that Halloween picture.

It had been taken the night before Bruce and Helen disappeared, never to be heard from again. Where had they gone? Why hadn't someone been looking for them? Why Joanne didn't even have the opportunity to get a divorce—what if she wanted to get married again? Wouldn't she want to find Bruce just for that purpose alone? Why hadn't she searched?

Because maybe—just maybe Joanne knew where the couple was. And maybe Chester suspected something also—which was why he had been searching for the blueprints to the mansion. If there had been bodies buried somewhere then that would explain why Joanne was so eager not to have the mansion torn down.

What was Kate thinking? Joanne was her friend. No one had friends who were murderers, at least not real people.

Yet something wasn't right. Mrs. Peabody might be a busybody and a snoop, but her curiosity had probably given her some clues. Kate had made a bad mistake, telling Joanne about what Mrs. Peabody had discovered and by admitting that Mrs. Peabody was headed for the *Finster Mansion*.

Kate might have put Mrs. Peabody in danger.

One thing was for sure. Whatever was happening was happening at the *Finster Mansion*.

Kate told Margaret, she just needed some air, so her time was limited as she hurried down the streets. She wasn't sure what she was going to do once she got there but never in her wildest imagination did she think she would be greeted with such a scene. Two ambulances were parked outside the mansion. In one, Mrs. Peabody was lying down covered with a bloody sheet and a heavily bandaged throat. On the other stretcher, Joanne lay down, also covered with a blood stained sheet. A nun was speaking to Wayne and Gary and Andrew Maloney, holding a bb gun, stood by the nun.

Kate raced to Joanne, but before she could ask Joanne a question, Joanne was whisked into the ambulance, the doors were shut and the car sped off.

Mrs. Peabody did not look as though she wanted to speak.

Kate decided to shimmy over to the two policemen, who were busy writing in their little pads. "What happened?" she asked, as she skidded towards the group.

Wayne glanced at her, and glanced away. But Andrew was full of conversation.

"The lady in the ambulance was trying to kill Mrs. Peabody. She had a letter opener at her neck. But I shot my bb gun, and I aimed for her leg and then she fell down."

So it was true all of it. Joanne, her friend, was a murderer. How could Kate have missed it all?

Andrew turned towards Wayne. "Does that make me a hero?"

"Yes, you're a hero," Wayne agreed. "And just think about how proud all your friends will be when they read about you in the paper. Although," he paused, "maybe you should hand over that bb gun. We might have to keep it for evidence."

Andrew frowned. "But it's a good thing I had it, right? I don't know why she would want to hurt Mrs. Peabody. Mrs. Peabody is a nice lady."

"Yes, she's that," Kate agreed.

She was a nice lady and Kate knew then what she would have to do. And that was to go to the hospital and visit with Mrs. Peabody. To apologize and to find out what the heck had happened.

She didn't doubt for a moment that Mrs. Peabody would be eager to fill in the gaps.

FIFTY-NINE

Mrs. Peabody sat up in bed and looked in disinterest at her dinner tray. Some sort of mystery meat, fatty and gray, overdone roasted potatoes, hard as stone, little peas covered in sour cream, and a wilted salad of lettuce and soggy cucumbers. Dessert was white custard with a yellow scum on top.

It didn't matter. Mrs. Peabody couldn't eat anyway. It hurt her too much to swallow.

The young doctor on duty told her that she was very lucky, that God was looking out for her today. An inch more and the letter opener would have severed the main artery and she would have bled out.

Well, Mrs. Peabody guessed, that's what happened when you exposed yourself to a serial killer.

She pushed the tray away and saw Wayne, standing by the threshold. Certainly he could not be there to yell at her again. He wasn't.

"I'm here to apologize and to congratulate you. You unmasked a killer."

It even hurt to smile.

"Well, here's the thing, Mrs. Peabody." Mrs. Peabody did not like the words...*here's the thing*. The phrase always preceded bad news. "Malcolm offered an reward for any information leading to the location of his sister. $5,000, which, to be honest, I think that Connie was counting on receiving. But, of course, you're the one who solved the mystery, so technically the money belongs to you."

Mrs. Peabody felt her stomach jump and then sink again at the word "technically."

"We're wondering if maybe you would be willing to spilt the money with Andrew Maloney. Connie could use the cash, with Bill being in prison and all. He did save your life. Without Andrew, well, I don't have to tell you what might have happened."

Mrs. Peabody whispered, "It's fine." And it was fine. $2500 would be enough...maybe she and Oliver could take a little trip on one of those new locomotive trains, after she bought that color TV and a brand new percolator. "But," she said, each word was like a dagger in her throat. "I need someone to take care of Oliver right now. My poor little dog! He's alone in my house. Don't let him escape!"

"Don't worry about Oliver," Wayne said. "I'll go get him myself and keep him down at the police station. He can be our mascot for a couple of days. I hear they're going to keep you here for observation." He winked at her. "Stay out of trouble."

And then he was gone. Well, at least Mrs. Peabody didn't have to talk. Something was heavy on her mind. Joanne had admitted to the killings, all five of them. She admitted to breaking into Mrs. Peabody's house, to stealing Violet Rose's letter and to kidnapping Oliver, and then writing the note. But she denied having anything to do with the blackmail, the blackmail letters that Violet Rose received. And what about Rita? Was she being blackmailed also? And by whom?

Even in Mrs. Peabody's bewildered state, none of it made sense.

Well, none of it was her business.

She reached for the buzzer. What she wouldn't give for a glass of Mountain Dew.

But before she could ring, Kate walked in. "I've come to find out how you're doing," she said. "And to apologize."

Another apology.

"I should never have doubted you. And I never should have told Joanne where you were. I can't believe everything that happened, which I heard on the news. And I can't believe who Joanne turned out to be. I've known her for years!"

Mrs. Peabody couldn't say what she wanted to. That it didn't matter, because when you looked into someone's past, everyone had something they wanted to hide, something that they hoped no one would find out.

"All of this made me think about myself, about my situation. I would love to live in a bigger city. Maybe not New York, maybe Boston. What do you think?"

"Life is short," Mrs. Peabody whispered. "You have to do what makes you happy."

"I talked to the mayor. We're going to put off voting about tearing down the mansion for a couple of weeks, although I can't imagine why anyone would want to keep it standing, after everything that's happened."

Neither could Mrs. Peabody.

"Can I get you anything?"

"Mountain Dew."

And just as Kate was about to leave, she bumped into another woman, whom Mrs. Peabody had never seen before.

"I'm Nora Randazzo, Sister Regina Rachel's sister."

Mrs. Peabody nodded, noticing how Kate stood at the door, listening.

"We were all wondering what my sister was doing at the mansion. One moment we were visiting my father, the next moment she left. We all thought she was going to the chapel to meet Mother Superior and then she shows up blocks away."

Mrs. Peabody heard the nun tell the police that she had followed Andrew there, although that didn't explain why she had left the hospital. It wasn't up to Mrs. Peabody to say anything, even if she could talk. With all that had happened, that was a lesson she had learned.

"Anyway, I was just talking to my father's doctor. This hospital took very good care of him. Now he's going to be released, but he'll need someone to stay with him for a while." Nora frowned. "Mother Superior came into my father's room very upset," Nora continued. "My sister is being transferred to the Mother House to care for the elderly nuns and they were running late. Do you happen to know where my sister is now?" she asked Mrs. Peabody.

"Police Station," Mrs. Peabody said, in a hoarse, hurtful voice.

"I'll get you that soda," Kate offered and then suddenly they both left the room, for which Mrs. Peabody was grateful. She was very tired. And very happy.

Thanks to the turn of events, she was no longer just the neighborhood busybody. She was an amateur detective, just like Jane Marple, in the Agatha Christie books.

She would be respected now and even consulted,

when the police had a difficult case. Even Wayne had treated her nicely.

Mrs. Peabody closed her eyes and drifted off to the best sleep she had had in a long time.

SIXTY

SISTER REGINA RACHEL was just finishing giving her report to the police, when she saw Mother Superior crash through the precinct door.

"My Lord!" she said. "Where have you been? I went to your father's room to ask your sister where you were and she said that you left a while ago. Somehow you ended up at the police station. You were supposed to go right to the chapel. I really would like to know how this happened."

Sister decided to keep it simple. "I took a walk to clear my head."

"If you wanted to take a walk, you could have had the courtesy to tell me and I would have gone with you. Nuns shouldn't be out in public alone. You know better than that. Besides, I was worried sick with all these murders. I was frightened that you might be the next victim."

"They caught the murderer," Wayne said suddenly. "So you needn't worry."

Mother Superior glared at both policemen. "That's not the point. Sister was due at the Mother House hours ago and I have to drive her. They're waiting for her." She turned towards Sister. "I'm not even going to ask you how you got mixed up in this sordid situation. You can tell me in the car. But really, I think a change of scenery will do you a world of good."

Sister felt her face redden as Wayne looked away. A moment ago he was praising her and saying how brave and how noble she had been. And here Mother Superior was giving her a dressing down in front of everyone.

"Well, come along, please." Mother Superior gave her a slight push.

"I'm sorry," Sister said. "But I can't go."

Mother Superior looked as though she had been slapped. "Are you ill?"

"No."

"What seems to be the problem?"

"I just can't go with you."

The two detectives were silent, their eyes wandering from one nun to the other. Sister knew that this wasn't the place to have the conversation, but she was backed into a corner.

"You have taken a vow of obedience."

"I know that," she admitted miserably.

"And what you're telling me now is that you're breaking that vow?"

Sister could only nod.

"And what are you going to do? I have already assigned your class to another sister."

"I understand. And you're absolutely right, Mother. A change of scenery will do me good. So I'd like go home and take care of my father. Just for a while, to think things through."

"You were a novice for seven years. You had ample opportunity to think things through. If you walk out of the convent now and return to secular life, you can't come back. Is this truly what you want?"

Although she wasn't sure, Sister managed to nod again.

"Have you thought about what people are going to say?"

Sister knew that Mother Superior really didn't care what people said about Sister. What she did care about was that it wouldn't look good for Mother Superior to have someone leave her convent. And perhaps she was afraid that Sister's bold act would inspire other nuns to do the same.

"Just because somehow you're involved in a capturing a murderer doesn't make you a detective."

Sister shook her head. "This is not a decision I've made lightly, Mother. It's something I've been thinking about for a long time. I'm sorry. I'm really sorry. I know I've disgraced the entire order."

"It's not for me to judge you. That's God job." Mother Superior shook her head, swishing her black veil and then she turned around and walked out of the police station.

Sister waited several minutes, careful not to look at the detectives. Then she walked out of the door herself.

She would be of service to people in her own small way. She would take care of her father. And she would see that Thelma Lou was helped.

She took a deep breath into the crisp, autumn air.

And freedom.

SIXTY-ONE

THE NEXT DAY they let Mrs. Peabody return home and she was happy to be there. Her throat was healing—she had Oliver by her side—she had a little money so she could buy a few treats and according to the *Honeyspoon Herald*, she was a hero.

Mrs. Peabody had overheard someone say at the hospital that the nun, who had helped to save Mrs. Peabody's life, was now planning to leave the convent. Well, an experience like that would make one question everything, and maybe yearn for something completely different. Although most people went the opposite way and suddenly found God.

In fact Mrs. Peabody was so grateful that she resolved to go to Mass on Sunday and even put a dollar in the collection basket. After all she would soon have 2,500 of them.

Connie had stopped by and thanked her for sharing the money. Well, it was the right thing to do. And Mrs. Peabody wanted to do the right thing.

Kate had called and invited her to a spaghetti dinner. She said her boyfriend was leaving town and, with Joanne in prison, Mrs. Peabody was guessing that maybe Kate needed another friend.

Yes, things were looking mighty glorious for Mrs. Peabody, who had a lot to be grateful for.

She prepared a nice dinner for herself—the pork

chops she had saved in the freezer—one for her and one for Oliver—frozen French fries, corn niblets. She even helped herself to a can of *Dr. Pepper*. For dessert she had two shortbread cookies—no need to scrimp, she would be buying more.

She had just finished a cup of tea, when the phone rang. She was surprised that it rang three times, sharp and insistent. That meant it for her. Well, maybe so. Maybe the newspaper wanted to interview her or maybe Wayne needed help on a difficult case.

She picked it up and heard a click. Someone was listening on the other line—Kate, Connie, maybe even Andrew.

"Hello," she asked in a perky tone.

"Mrs. Peabody?" A voice she did not recognize, hoarse and muffled.

"Yes."

"I saw what you did."

"Pardon me."

"I know what happened that day at *Bear Paw Amusement Park*."

Mrs. Peabody sank on the little chair by the phone.

"What are you talking about?" Her voice croaking ever so slightly.

"I know what happened to Louie on that roller coaster was no accident. I have no doubt that you will give me whatever I want."

And then a click—and another click.

Mrs. Peabody stared at the phone for a long time before putting it back in the cradle.

She looked down at her little dog. "I think we're in trouble, Oliver," she said.

* * * * *

ABOUT THE AUTHOR

MARIANNA HEUSLER is the author of eight novels including three prior St. Polycarp mysteries, *Murder at St. Polycarp, Cappuccino at the Crypt, No End to Trouble* and *Trouble Purse Sued.* She authored a historical fiction novel in 2018—*One Stone Left Unturned* is a mystery that has references to the past—the fate of the Russian Romanov Family in 1918. *Mrs. Peabody's Party Line* is the first book in her new Honeyspoon Murder Mystery series.

She is also the author of hundreds of published short stories and her mini mysteries have frequently been featured in *Woman's World*.

A retired teacher, she has taught at all grade levels in Catholic Schools and also taught third grade in a private all girls' school on the Upper East Side of Manhattan.

Marianna lives in New York City with her husband, Joel, her son, Maximilian, and her little dog, Dolce. She spends her free time, writing, working out, and volunteering for the WomenHeart.

You can learn more about Marianna by clicking onto www.mariannamystery.com

Or by following her fashion blog at mariannaheusler.typepad.com

1x   15.00
5x4   20.00
        30 00
10x3   ────
        6 8
5x20   100
        ────
        165

165